The Golden Touch

An Appleton, WO Romantic Mystery

Carole Brown

Story and Logic Media Group
New Carlisle, OH
Printed in the USA
... For the discriminating reader
...because we believe story *needs* logic.

The Golden Touch: © 2021 by Carole Brown
An Appleton, WV Romantic Mystery

 **Published by STORY AND LOGIC Media Group, New Carlisle, OH**
For the discriminating reader ... Because we believe story *needs* logic.

Cover Design by SAL media
Published in New Carlisle, OH
Printed in the USA

ISBN 13: 978-1-941622-66-7
ISBN 10: 1-941622-66-6

Library of Congress Cataloging-in-Publication Data
Brown, Carole
The Golden Touch /Carole Brown
ISBN   978-1-941622-66-7 (pbk)

1. Series fiction 2. Cozy Mystery 3. Romance
4. Inspirational fiction

I. *The Golden Touch.* Library of Congress Control Number:
2021936820

Praise for award winning author
Carole Brown

Carole Brown has the ability to transport us to the wonderful town of Appleton, WV. and to make its citizens come to life in our imaginations. What could be better than that?

--Larry Vaughn, author of *A Crash Course in the Bible.*

"I was as delighted with meeting the unique array of characters as I was watching the mystery unfold."

--Cheryl Colwell, suspense author

Carole Brown is a prolific writer who captures the hearts of her readers. Whether she's writing fiction, non-fiction or children's books, you can expect a blessing.

The latest book in the Appleton, WV Romantic Mystery series is a page-turner you can't put down. If you are gifted with that "unique investigative gene" you will be trying to solve the mystery from the first chapter to the last, but you'll never find the answer until Carole reveals it in the last few pages of the book. Sweet romance and intrigue will keep you reading until the mystery is solved.

--Ann Knowles, author, editor, and owner of Write Pathway Editorial Services

Carole Brown writes with a touch of humor, just enough mystery-suspense to keep the reader turning the pages to see what happens next, and a nice mixture of sigh-worthy romance. Looking forward to the next book in the series.

Carol Ann Erhardt,
Christian Romantic Suspense author of
Joshua's Hope and the Havens Creek Series

Carole Brown does a wonderful job of balancing romance and mystery, keeping her readers engaged while at the same time entertained. This series is a good read for anyone who loves curling up with a good book, one that will cement your faith in happy endings.
--Barbara Derksen, author of the
Wilton/Strait and
Finder Keepers Mystery series

Carole Brown is one of those refreshing authors who writes novels that keep you up at night. Whether you are reading one of her mysteries, historical suspense or romantic suspense novels, you won't be able to sleep until you find out what happens.
--Tamera Lynn Kraft,
Author of "A Christmas Promise" and
Resurrection of Hope"

Carole Brown has the literary ability to ferry you into the heart of each story, depicting each setting in exquisite detail, allowing you to follow along with the characters as they think, feel and discover. Though each novel is a masterpiece in its own right, Carole's distinguishable writing carries throughout everything she writes. One of the best up and coming suspense writers of our time.
--Jamin Baldwin,
Author and Freelance editor

In Memory of:

Ashley Brown

and

Barbara Williams
who first encouraged me to
never give up!

Dedication to:

All the young children
who have been
trafficked

Acknowledgments:

Danny,
My best encourager,
My best editor,
My best plotter
I love you!
Thanks for all you do!

And to my CHAMPIONS!
You know who you are.

Carole Brown

An Appleton, WV Romantic Mystery

Strange screams and threats
are only the beginning of troubles
at Ryle's newest venture

The Golden Touch

A Few Irish Words:

Daft cow: crazy woman

Feek: Gorgeous girl

Gowl: an annoying person

Pure: really/very

Sham: a friend

Chapter One

Ryle Sadler stared at the unkempt bed and breakfast in front of him. The urge to buy this place was stronger than ever, and he couldn't understand it. He'd never bought or invested in anything on an urge. He'd prayed about this crazy urge for sure. Many times. No answer came back from God. Only this confusing push to buy it. Now.

He hadn't amassed his wealth by going on urges. No sirree. Coming from the poor side of town had taught him plenty, and two of those things were listening and learning. Those had gotten him where he was now.

The Golden Touch. That's what the investors in the world called it, and that's what he had. Or so they said. It scared him, truth be told, that everything he touched turned to gold. Didn't matter whether it was stocks or an act of generosity in helping a struggling business person. Every time—so far—had been successful.

But this, this business that Maisie, the owner, cared little about, was neither of those things. If he bought it, would it change his touch? Would it be the knife to cut the string of wins he'd experienced so far? Would it be his first failure? After all, what did he know about bed and breakfasts?

Nothing.

A young woman exited the place, her purple hair a distraction from her beautiful features. She didn't know her own beauty or worth. Toby and Amy Sanderson, Jazzi Sanderson's sister and brother-in-law, had confided that she'd taken a room there to be on her own—in spite of the inn's rundown condition.

He'd had little to do with women. Too little time, and, frankly, no one so far, who'd, garnered his attention long enough.

But this woman. Ryle's heart gave an unusual ping forcing a frown on his face.

She saw him then, and gave a shy, little wave—a complete contradiction to her reputation— the smile on her face as bright as the sunshine from the heavens.

And then he heard the voice.

Invite Jazmine Ashley Sanderson to help you at the bed and breakfast.

No. That was crazy. What was wrong with him? He'd never done such a thing. Invested in businesses by using his money, yes, to do what he felt was his calling. But asking a woman he barely knew to help him get this place up and running? Would she laugh at him? Would the whole town of Appleton consider him the biggest fool ever to cross their path? Her sister, Amy, had been upset with her when Jazmine had refused the offer of staying with her. Why had she insisted on renting a room here, of all places?

She did have a reputation. And not such a good one.

What if she accepted, thinking it was a lark, an easy way to get some money, with no improvement in her personality? Or worse, be irresponsible? Could he trust her to have the same vision as he?

No, it wasn't his responsibility what she did. But then, he didn't think helping someone continue on the broken path they were on was beneficial either. Still, his calling was to help. What they did afterwards was their responsibility.

So, what's it to be? Will you obey my direction on this?

The dark cloud suddenly covering the sun seemed to be frowning at him.

"I always have." Ryle couldn't even hear his own whisper as he mouthed the words.

And as suddenly, as it had been covered seconds ago, the sun popped from behind the cloud, sending its golden beams straight down to shine on the bed and breakfast.

Ryle gave up the struggle. It might be interesting— and a learning process for him—if this adventure was a failure. Time would tell.

The groan that escaped his lips assured him he wasn't looking forward to it.

Chapter Two

"**I**'m going to ask you one more time to move into our apartment above Undiscovered Treasures. At least you'll have furniture. You'll be closer to the eating establishments, and I won't have to worry about you stuck out here alone at night, or listen to Amy's worried comments about Jazzi. Come on. Jazzi can stay with us. You'll have the apartment to yourself." Toby's friendly gaze picked up the coaxing where his words left off.

He was a good friend, and Ryle Sadler enjoyed being with him now and then, but it made no sense to move into town when Toni Deluca-Douglas's Construction business would be finished in a few more days. He didn't mind roughing it, and obviously Jazzi didn't either.

"Again, no. Thanks though, I appreciate the offer. But I like my privacy, and I like it here. As for Jazzi, that's up to her. Besides the place is close to being fully remodeled and updated. Why move now?"

Toby wasn't ready to give up yet. He turned to Toni. "You agree with me, don't you, Toni?"

"The structure is in great shape. No problem there." Toni Deluca-Douglas's dark eyes sparkled as she assured Ryle Sadler. "We've finished the interior and will continue with the plumbing repairs in the basement and the repairs for the porch this week."

Ryle slid an I-told-you-so glance at Toby Gibson. The frown on his friend's face was as plain as plain could be. Toby wasn't ready to give up yet.

"You're about the stubbornness man I've ever met." His growl was more disappointment than anger.

"But, I didn't say it was the best idea." Toni grinned at the two men beside her. "The water will probably need turned off for a few hours. The gas lines are already finished and inspected so they should be fine. I don't foresee any major problems in the basement, but who knows? I'm not taking sides, but Toby's offer is pretty generous."

"Really?" Ryle tossed at her as he walked away. "Thanks, but it's settled, Tobe. I don't mind the hindrances so stop fretting like an old woman."

Truth be told, he was anxious to get the last repairs on the building finished, the landscaping and the furnishings in place. And he wanted to be *here* where he could keep an eye on everything. He'd never enjoyed a lot of society, although he could handle it as well as most, if he had to, so solitude—or almost solitude—was right up his alley.

He hadn't earned his reputation by sitting on the sidelines. He'd traveled some for business, but he'd based himself mostly in New York City. There, he'd been able to amass the fortune that had made him a multi-millionaire. Few people knew that, and it was just the way he liked it.

When he'd settled in Appleton, it'd been happenstance, but the longer he lived here, the more he'd grown to love the place.

Ryle wandered down the hallways of his new acquisition, room to room checking the improvements made to it. The furnishings would be delivered soon. Bloomin' Life—Amy Sanderson Gibson's flower and landscaping business—would begin the landscaping on Thursday, and the plan was to finish it next week. After that—well, after that, if no unexpected hindrances popped up, they should be just about ready to go. Once the hiring of a few more employees was done and making sure all the outside equipment was here, then he and Jazzi would open this business. They had the private dinner and showing for their special friends and a few select people he knew, then the open house for the community to get through. And by the response from the ads Jazzi had placed in various magazines and newspapers, they were booked through Christmas.

Things were looking good.

But truth be told, this place had grown on him by leaps and bounds, as if it was trying to tell him something. That was his imagination, he knew. Still, the more time he spent here, the more it seemed like—well, home.

He'd never had that strange feeling before.

Ever.

He caught a glimpse of the purple-haired young lady—Jazzi Sanderson—moving through what was to be the kitchen, a notebook in her hand, a serious expression across her fair complexion. He couldn't stop the smile that tugged at his lips, nor did he want to. She'd been a good investment. Smart, cute, and once she realized he was serious about hiring her, a good worker. It was early yet, but he didn't foresee any problems with her. All business, she seemed to be.

He stopped strolling through his prospective bed-and-breakfast to stare out a front window. A big, black SUV drove slowly up the long, curving driveway. Could be an inspector coming to check that all was in order. He headed toward the front door.

Jazzi and Toni came toward him, deep in conversation. Both women nodded and kept walking, but he stopped them.

"Either one of you know who is coming up the drive in the SUV?"

Jazzi shook her head, but Toni moved closer to the window. "That looks like..."

Ryle cast her a quick glance. "Like who, Toni?"

She returned his glance. "Months ago, before Caroline was married to Andy, this guy was really interested in her."

"You think this is him? Why would he be here?"

The vehicle pulled up in front of the door, and seconds later, the driver's door opened. A tall, black-haired man stepped out and appeared to be studying the surrounding property before turning toward the door.

"That's Linc."

"Linc?"

"Lincoln Tillis, the man who was interested in Caroline. We haven't seen him around forever."

"I know him." Jazzi's words were softly spoken and hesitant.

"You know him, Jazzi?"

"I know of him." The frown on her face didn't bode well for any good social interactions between the two. "He came by asking a lot of questions from some of my friends several months ago. That was back in New York, of course."

"Why?" Ryle heard the knock on the door, but ignored it.

"Why what?" She switched her gaze from the window to him.

"Why was he questioning your friends?"

"I don't know. Had enough sense to stay out of it, for once."

Ryle straightened. "Well, let's find out what Mr. Lincoln Tillis wants here in Appleton, and specifically this place."

~*~

Jazzi's insides felt like they were dissolving into mush. Not only from fear of what this guy—this Lincoln Tillis—wanted from her, but also from keeping back some of the truth from Ryle. She hadn't lied. No. But she'd conveniently neglected to tell him her whole history. But then, she really preferred Ryle never learned about her past contacts. Her admiration, as she preferred to call it, for him was growing faster than Jack's beanstalk.

She'd vowed to her sister, Amy Sanderson, now married to Tony Gibson, that she'd changed. She really wanted to, but was she strong enough? The Lord knew—if there really was a god—she'd failed plenty of times.

It'd been few and far between—her visits back to Appleton—since the first time she'd left. She'd shaken the dust of the place from her feet despite her parents begging her not to go.

But this time? This time had been different. And she was pretty sure it hadn't been the community that had changed.

Ryle, who'd stepped in to escort her when Toby and Amy had begged her to attend events with them, had treated her as if she was special. Not forward or casual like so many of her boyfriends had shown toward her, but as if she was worthy of being escorted like a lady.

Her? Who'd seldom acted like a lady. More like a wild, undisciplined child.

The sigh that escaped her lips exhaled in a rush, but she had no more time to ruminate on her past failures or even Ryle. Voices in the entryway alerted her to the fact that unless she hightailed it out of the room pronto, she would be dragged into a questioning session with this man she feared more than a lot of others.

Because she knew who he was, what he did for a living.

With a last glance at the doorway, Jazzi hurried toward a second doorway that led to the library. There she could find her way to a section of the inn where Tillis couldn't find her.

Yet.

~*~

"Come on in. We're in the final remodeling session, but let me see if Jazzi minds making us some tea. Or would you prefer coffee?" Ryle ushered the man in the dark suit, Toni following both of them, into a room where three or four folding chairs were spaced out for the workers when they took a break. He lifted a walkie-talkie from his belt and spoke into it, but Jazzi didn't answer. Replacing it, he shook his head ever so slightly.

"Coffee, if you don't mind." Lincoln sat and crossed his legs, seemingly relaxed and at ease with himself and the people around him. "How are you, Toni?"

"All's well in my life. What about you? We haven't seen you for awhile. Keeping busy, I imagine."

"Life never gets any slower."

His chuckle was quiet but effective in assuring Ryle that he was serious.

Toni turned to Ryle. "Let me go get the coffee. It'll take just a minute, and I don't mind."

Ryle nodded. "Thanks, Toni. I'm afraid we haven't met. Tillis, is it? Toni mentioned she met you awhile back."

"Yes, I met her and several of her friends some time ago. It's a great town. People are friendly, and everyone keeps the streets and shops clean and attractive." Lincoln paused a moment, studying Ryle. "But that's not the reason I'm here. It's more work related. I have business in town. Been talking with several in the community and hoped you might shed some light on certain things."

"Don't know about that. I'm fairly new and have been busy with overseeing the repairs. Besides, I know little about what goes on in town."

"You never know. Wondered if you'd seen anyone new around? Any odd things that's caught your attention. You haven't had any trouble here, have you?"

"Not really, and no, I haven't noticed anything unusual."

"Well, I wish your answer was different, but then, I'm glad you haven't had any trouble." Tillis recrossed his legs. "Wondered. The kids and I have decided to move to a smaller town, and since Appleton is familiar and an all-around nice place, we thought we'd rent a couple rooms till we can locate a house we like."

"You're in a hurry?"

"A little. I'll be around for awhile, checking things out both for business and for a house."

"We're not quite ready for renters yet, and we're pretty well booked for the remainder of this year."

"I see. Well, I'm sure we can always rent hotel rooms at the next town over."

Toni walked in with the coffee. "Ryle, you take

yours with cream, right? Linc?"

"Black, please. Thanks."

"Tillis is looking for some rooms to rent till he can find the house he wants. He and his kids are moving to Appleton."

"Really, Linc?" Toni's face lit with genuine pleasure. "That would be great to have you and the kids a part of Appleton."

"We won't be moving till we have, at least, a temporary place."

"Wish we could offer you rooms, but unless someone cancels, we have nothing available."

"No problem." Linc nodded and set his coffee cup on a coaster.

"Here's my card. You're welcome to check back, just in case something does come open..." Ryle handed him a business card.

"I'll do that." Linc stood and started toward the doorway before turning back. "Did I hear you talking about someone named Jazzi?"

"You did. She's my manager, and a fine one." Ryle studied the other man. How did the man know Jazzi? She'd not been here—if he'd heard right—until months after the man had been around.

Toni seemed to genuinely like the man, but there was a vibe about him that set Ryle on edge. There was more to him than seen on the surface.

Ryle led the way to the front door, but it was a good thing he was in front of the man because the frown he felt plastering his face would have raised questions. He seemed sincere and pleasant enough. Toni obviously liked him, so why suspect there was more to the visit than needing rooms? Or a few questions that went nowhere.

Though Jazzi had insisted she didn't need a small suite, he'd been just as adamant that she did need one and had assigned to her one in the private section that was large enough for three suites. Not only would Jazzi have one, but he would, and an extra one between them that would be kept for special friends and relatives, if needed. The chef would have his own quarters near the kitchen area, along with the two housemaids and an assistant manager.

But what if this Tillis wasn't all he seemed? What if there was an ulterior motive behind his supposed moved to Appleton? Something involving Jazzi? Or one of his other new friends? How well did anyone in Appleton really know this man?

He'd dealt with plenty of bad men in his short life span. It wasn't as if he'd be taken by surprise, not with his radar quivering into life.

Lincoln Tillis had better watch his step. Ryle's antenna of distrust was seldom wrong.

And he wouldn't stand for Jazzi being harassed.

~*~

Jazzi had overheard the entire conversation between Lincoln Tillis, Ryle and Toni, and never had her hastily heated canned soup sat so unpleasantly on her stomach before. She felt almost sick as she hurried to her own suite. Or was it fear?

If he was in town for business, then how would she ever keep clear of the man?

She wouldn't.

Plopping herself down upon the luxurious bed—that Ryle had insisted be bought and installed right away for her while he still slept on the floor in his rooms—and rested her head on her palm. What a mess. Why did everything she attempt turn into drama?

But then, the man hadn't said a word why he

was really here. Other than searching for rooms and asking vague questions.

Could it have something to do with her past life? The life she'd fled and hoped to forget?

Or was Ryle in trouble?

No. Not him. He was so upstanding. A real gentleman.

Granted, she could tell there were hidden depths to him. Maybe some things no one knew about, that he kept to himself. But whatever they were, they weren't bad things.

She knew it, and no one or nothing would cause her to doubt that.

~*~

Ryle carried his Dagwood-styled sandwich in one hand, a banana and several fresh strawberries in the other, an unopened bottle of water under his arm, as he headed to his room that night.

What a day. Toni's work crew had made real progress. That new man, Lincoln Tillis had taken off right after their conversation—which if he'd admit it—was perfectly fine with him. What had prompted him—always on the alert and careful about his business dealings—to be so lavish with an invitation for him to possibly stay *here* if things worked out?

But he did plan on it being the best bed and breakfast in West Virginia. So why wouldn't someone ask to stay here, maybe thinking they'd get a room before they were all rented? Ryle shook his head.

And why was the man here? Why was he in such a hurry to move here he was willing to stay in an expensive bed and breakfast? Maybe he'd better ask a few more questions about the man before allowing him to get too close.

Always paid to know your enemy.

Enemy? He didn't know the man. Not a thing. Could be he was who he seemed with no ulterior motive.

He'd make sure of that.

Strange how Jazzi had disappeared. But the girl had a right to a break now and then. She could have thought there was no need of her presence. Since he'd hired her, she'd been diligent and on top of everything. She and Toni Deluca had seemed to bond well, but she shied away from too many people. If all went well, perhaps she would eventually blend right into Toni's group of friends.

Ryle shut the door to his room and stood silent a moment reflecting on the progress done today. Just a few more days—weeks—and they could hang out the big sign Andy Carrington had painted for him. It felt strange to feel a pang of excitement. That hadn't ever happened before. Not with any of his other rescued business dealings.

But this...this almost—he hated to admit it— felt like...a dream come true.

His home. A business, yes, but home.

How long that lasted was yet to be seen.

Ryle swallowed the last bite of his sandwich, swallowed the last bit of water in the bottle, crushed the plastic and stood. He stretched, flicked off the lamp nearby then moseyed over to a window and stared out, allowing his eyes to adjust to the darkness.

His spirit quieted from all the questions circling in his brain, his body relaxing as it had done since he'd moved into this unfurnished room.

...and felt his heart jolt as his eyes caught a movement. What was that? A deer and her fawn?

A large dog lost? A homeless person looking for a place to rest his head tonight? Hoping this place was deserted?

Or someone scoping out the place, hoping to find something to hock for money?

The slapping of feet on the hallway wood floor came through his door loud enough.

Jazzi.

Chapter Three

Jazzi's eyes slid open, instantly alert, her breathing rapid, fear like red ants skittering over her body. It'd been a sound that had awakened her. An unusual sound. She knew because the silence and peace emanating from the place had been a balm to her soul from the minute she'd first seen it. That—and the fact that Ryle had asked her to work here—had been the force that had encouraged her to give him a happy 'yes' answer when he'd offered a manager's job.

Now?

Jazzi threw back the covers. She needed a spot of fresh air.

Sliding her feet into her bedroom scruffs, she wrapped her housecoat around her and headed for the front door. Easing it open, she left it ajar and walked out onto the veranda.

It was a large wraparound porch, and would be perfectly divine once repaired. She could imagine sitting out here in the evenings staring out at the stars, people quietly talking, and at times only the night sounds crowding out the daytime cares and thoughts.

Jazzi stretched then paused as a sound interrupted her. Lowering her arms, she turned slowly and stared out into the night. The security lights hadn't been installed yet, but the moon shed a bit of light over the grounds. Leaning forward, she studied the area, first the veranda where she now stood, then the yard beyond.

Nothing.

She was about to turn away when a figure walked slowly into view directly in line with her sight. He faced her, although she couldn't make out his features, but the fact that he appeared to stare directly at her energized those red ants to expand into scorpion-sized creatures.

She couldn't move, couldn't scream, held by that dark figure twenty feet from her, all the more threatening because of the intense silence.

Blinking, she hoped in that micro-second that she'd dreamed the figure, but no such luck for her, and she swallowed, wishing she had the nerve to run out there, screaming at the unknown figure, attacking him, scaring him like he was her...or something.

But the image of her past friends, her past life was too vivid, too real to do such a foolhardy action. If this person was real, if he really knew her, and if she was the reason he was here, then God help her.

She was doomed.

She sucked in two long breaths. Should she scream for Ryle? He was big and strong.

No. Before she could even imagine anymore, the vivid images of what she'd always suspected her past friends could and had done in the past, swept through her mind. She was frozen in time...

One step back, then two, and the figure moved. Quickly. Out of sight, but certainly not out of mind.

Leaning against the wall for a second or two, Jazzi heaved in several quick breaths before running, her feet slapping lightly on the wooden floor, into her rooms. She dived for her bed, jerking the covers around and over her head.

There were no curtains in her room, but she could block out any sight of that figure with her blankets.

Just not the image that shivered right behind her closed eyelids.

~*~

The sunbeams stroked Jazzi's face the next morning. A smile widened her lips before she could even open her eyes.

And then the memory of that figure from the night before smacked her wide awake, and she sat up, sliding a glance toward the window.

Ah, it was daylight. No more scary figures from the night. Nothing to hurt her now. It was sunny and bright.

Her walkie-talkie crackled, and she scrambled to grab it up from the table across her room.

"Hey."

"Hey."

It was Ryle.

"You okay?

Had he seen that figure too?

"Why shouldn't I be?"

"Just thought I'd check. You're usually up way before ten."

"It's ten?"

"Afraid so."

"Give me fifteen minutes."

"No rush. If you want the day off, just let me know. You've been a barrel of energy and efficiency."

"Uh, no, thanks. I'm on my way."

A minute shower and quick dressing should do the trick. She'd grab a bite on her rush through the almost-completed kitchen and be ready to drive the nightmare from her memory.

She hoped.

~*~

Ryle hooked his walkie-talkie to his belt but stood quietly thinking about his manager. Jazzi might be a little rough around the edges, but she was a fast learner and smart. She'd taken right to being his right-hand and worked hard at keeping him happy. Just the type of employee he appreciated.

He settled at his desk. Not much paper work today. He'd taken care of the pressing issues yesterday. If Toni's crew finished the work later this week, or by next week at the latest, it'd be right on time for all the ads he'd paid for weeks ago to get this business booming.

Picking up his cell, he made a couple quick calls, then strolled to the window to stare out it. The pounding in the background from the DeLuca construction company, the muffled sounds of murmurs and an occasional laugh blended into the air. A distinct difference from the night before when he'd spotted—something slithering between the trees. Whatever—whoever—it'd been, the incident had created an uneasy feeling inside him.

He sure didn't want any bumps in the road for this project.

He'd never been much on unusual manifestations of Christianity, but he'd also never been more sure this one was God-blessed.

"What's on the agenda today, Ryle?"

He turned and studied his new partner in this endeavor. She did look a little wan this morning—what was left of it. Perhaps she hadn't slept well.

"Are you sure you feel like working today? There's not much on the agenda..."

"I'm fine. And I'd like to check with Andy

Carrington once more about those paintings we ordered for the main rooms. I'm hoping he's able to have them finished before we open."

"Can you take care of that? I want to run into town to meet with Starli about our opening night menu."

"Sure. We have some chef applicants scheduled this week, and did you decide whether you're sticking with two house cleaners or more?"

"Let's go with two for now. I think two should be enough. But I'd like a general helper who can fill in where needed. You may need someone to help you here or there, our chef may need a little help, and we might need someone to fill in for a maid if one is sick or whatever."

"Right." Jazzi nodded. "Sounds good. Also our first choice for a caretaker decided not to take the job. What shall we do about that?"

"Can you put out another ad? Maybe go broader to see who responds? I'm pretty sure we'll be okay through this fall and winter—although I may have to pitch in quite a bit without a groundskeeper."

"Will do."

"I'm also having lunch with the guys then will head to that equipment place to pick out the yard equipment we looked at last week."

"We've got our day planned."

"We do. Thanks, Jazzi. You're doing a great job."

"I love the job."

The happiness that shone from her eyes made him glad he'd heeded that bit of urging from...God? Yeah, it was. He picked up his cell and started to leave. "See you this evening. Want me to pick up a pizza?"

"You do know I love pizza, don't you?" she

teased.

"I thought you might." He headed out the door.

"Ryle, be careful."

He hesitated a second, but didn't stop. That sounded like a warning to him.

Now why would Jazzi Sanderson be warning him?

~*~

As Ryle drove away from his property, he glanced back at it in the mirror. Looking good, it was. Amy Sanderson Gibson, Toby's wife, would provide the plants for the landscaping, and with the employees who did the landscaping for her, it should be shipshape in no time.

Perfection is what he wanted, and he paid good money to get it.

One more glance back as he turned onto the main road. A frown replaced the pleasure he'd just experienced at how well everything was coming together.

Something was wrong, but he couldn't put a finger on what the trouble was.

He'd find out soon enough. He always did.

~*~

Five men sat around the circular table in a corner of Apple Blossoms, the high class and best restaurant in Appleton, West Virginia, and in his estimation, the whole state.

Three of them were his friends. Toby Gibson, Perrin Douglas, and Joel Peterman-Blair. Normally Andy Carrington would join them today, but he was too busy fulfilling the order for the original paintings he and Jazzi had ordered. The other two men seated there were acquaintances he'd seen around town and knew in passing but they had never joined him and his friends for lunch. At least since he'd formed friendship with the others.

He didn't say anything, only raised an eyebrow at the friends staring up at him.

"There's a problem, Ryle. Sit, and we'll see if we can get it resolved." Perrin explained. "Our good mayor thinks there is trouble with you opening the B and B."

Trouble? No way. He had the best lawyer in the country who handled any problems cropping up in his business. Never failed to head off problems, even minor ones. This was a manufactured one. Had to be.

Ryle sat and turned slowly toward the two men, their faces sober, as if they had earth shattering news to share. He studied their eyes then took in their hands, their poise—or lack of it—and the flush on their face. He hadn't been in business for this long without knowing how to read his opponents.

"This is Melvin Slater. He's our current mayor, and his chief assistant, Lynn Winston. Go ahead, Melvin."

Joel, by including himself and Ryle's other friends, was definitely drawing a line in the sand and letting him know they were on his side.

"I'm sorry, men, but this is a private matter better discussed with only Sadler."

When Ryle didn't speak, Toby spoke up. "Ryle? Would you prefer we leave?"

"Stay." Ryle didn't look at his friends, but kept a steadfast stare at the two newcomers to him.

"We just received a letter requesting a hold on you opening the bed and breakfast."

What? Sounded fishy to him. Why now when the remodeling was almost done?

"Why is that? I paid good money for it, the deed was signed and given to me, and is now secure in my bank. Why wasn't this raised before I bought it? I don't go into business without a lot of research."

Ryle crossed his legs and allowed himself to again briefly study the two men across from him. He could feel the glances of his three friends, the support, and possibly a bit of hesitation, but, as if in unison, they returned their own glances toward the other two.

Mayor Slater lifted a hand. "I understand, but the person asking for this didn't realize what was going on until it was sold. He's saying he was part owner—"

"Only one name was on the deed, and she willingly and happily signed it over to me. Everything was done properly and legally."

"I'm afraid he's saying it wasn't the most updated deed."

Ryle stared at the man. Was he serious? His lawyer didn't make mistakes. Her company did elaborate research on any business they took on, and his was at the top of the list.

"That's hard to believe. It would be on record at the courthouse."

"You're right, of course, but you do know recorders make mistakes. According to this person—"

"Who did you say this person is?" Ryle interrupted him. Seemed odd that the man—or woman—didn't want to be identified.

"I didn't say. He wants to remain anonymous."

The mayor's voice was a little husky. As far as Ryle knew, the man had never given any of his friends' trouble.

Slater started to cross his legs but decided not to. "May I finish?"

Ryle nodded at him.

"According to him, he has proof that the recorder purposely lost the correct deed then vanished. I'm assuming the recorder must have had a grudge against—"

"What kind of grudge, and why would he have one?" Ryle again interrupted the man.

They mayor's face sobered even more if that was possible. "He didn't expand on those details."

"Then I think you need to find out. I can't be bothered with vague and unsubstantiated claims that aren't true. I want the details—sooner rather than later." As a brief bit of anger surged through him, Ryle rose to his feet. "If what this man says is true, and I doubt it, then you can rest assured I will get to the bottom of it, and find out all the details. And if not, if this is nothing, I will hold someone accountable for the waste of time and money on my part."

"Hold on. Mayor Slater, do you know and trust this man? Is he a citizen of Appleton? And why does it have to be a secret if he does have proof of wrongdoing?" As usual, Perrin was the epitome of composure.

"I'm not at liberty to share who is lodging the complaint right now, but rest assured, he had a deed that seemed legit. Of course, he needs to have it verified, but it seems reasonable for you to put a halt to the opening till all is deemed fine."

"That isn't going to happen." Ryle shoved back his chair, stood then paused. "Toni DeLuca assures me her crew will be finished, at least, by next week. You have till then to get to the bottom of this. After that, I'll have my lawyer call you."

As he turned to walk away, he glimpsed his three friends stand and move to follow him. Ryle allowed himself a thin grin. Loyalty. Another thing he loved about this small community.

"Hold on. You know, I can have a temporary stay placed on your property, then no one will go near it until investigators have cleared it."

Ryle didn't bother to look back at Slater. "Try it, and I'll sue the pants off everyone involved. I've dealt with these kinds of things too many times. I'm no novice, so don't try to threaten me. I'll repeat one more time. You have till next week to let me know the evidence of what this accusation's about. Shouldn't be all that hard if he already has this alleged deed in hand."

And Ryle walked out of the restaurant.

"That was impressive." Toby stepped up beside him, the smile on his face as wide as a banana lying sideways. "Do you really have a lawyer on call?"

Ryle returned his friend's grin, but he wasn't about to share his intimate business with even Toby, as much as he liked him. "It'll give the mayor a nudge in the right direction, I'm thinking."

"I'd say." Toby slapped him on the shoulder.

"You know, we're here if you need us." Joel offered.

"Thanks. Appreciate that."

Perrin was rubbing his chin as he shoved open the door of the restaurant. "I've never cared much for our new mayor. The way he got the position didn't seem right or fair. I always suspected foul play there, but never could put a finger on it."

"Probably should have someone look into it." Toby agreed. "You know of any good investigator we can trust to do this on the quiet, Perrin?"

"I might know of a person."

Ryle listened to his friends' discussion and started to object, to let them know he didn't need their help then mentally shrugged. What could it hurt? He had his own trusted investigators that were ready when he called.

Chapter Four

Ryle and his friends stopped in at the Coffee Cafe for a sandwich after leaving Apple Blossoms restaurant. None of the others mentioned what had happened there, and it ended up being a relaxing hour of fellowship for Ryle.

But when he left the place, he headed straight to Toni Deluca-Douglas's work office. She'd told him earlier she wouldn't be by the bed and breakfast till tomorrow, but he didn't want to wait. Fortunately, she was in.

"Ryle. Come in. Is there a problem?" Toni, sitting at her large cherry-wood desk, motioned for him to enter after Roxie, her secretary had intercomed her to let her know he was there.

"Maybe." Ryle settled into one of Toni's two leather chairs positioned in front of her desk. "Just met the guys for lunch, but unfortunately, we were disturbed by your good mayor and his sidekick."

"Melvin and Lynn? What happened?"

Toni's frown wasn't for him, Ryle was sure, but obviously, she had doubts about the two.

"Seems someone has requested a hold on opening the bed and breakfast. Claims the deed we paid for is bogus, and the correct one is in the hands of a person the mayor declined to identify."

"What? How often does that happen?"

"It can happen. I've heard of it, but it's rare." Ryle eyed Toni. "You ever heard of anyone but

Maisie owning this place?"

"No. Well, I never gave it much thought. As far back as I can remember, she's been here. Rod and Roxie claim it used to be in a lot better shape, but she let it go to ruin. I really think she didn't care or have the energy to keep it up."

"Hmmm. I thought she was odd when I bought the place, but honestly I figured she was old and maybe a little senile and wanted out of it all. She was happy enough when I handed her the check."

"It does sound strange. I hope it works out for you. Are you still planning on opening week after next?"

"I am. Unless I get the proof, I will continue as planned. I'm not worried, but I don't like trouble. I have the feeling that there is someone behind this who has something up his sleeve, but right now I have no idea what that could be."

"Right. And if someone had wanted the place, why didn't they put in an offer before? Maisie had it on the market for several years before you bought it. It makes no sense."

"I agree."

"I was going to wait till tomorrow, but I think I'll drop by later and check on the guys to make sure there haven't been any hiccups."

Ryle stood. "Perfect. Thanks, Toni. You've been great to work with."

After Ryle left he headed to the equipment store and picked out two large mowers, a small dozer, and several other pieces of equipment he figured the place would be needing. With that major task off his list, he made a quick stop at the local grocery and picked up food they'd need for the rest of the week. A stop at the pizza shop, and he headed home.

Home. He liked the sound of that. And Jazzi would be waiting...

~*~

Jazzi had gone to Andy Carrington's home and checked out the pictures he had ready. They were just what she'd imagined and hoped for. She assured him she was very pleased and knew Ryle would be too. Andy promised to have them delivered the first of next week, and without a chance to visit with Caroline, she'd headed back home.

Home? Well, it certainly felt like it. Far more so than any other place she'd ever lived in. And that included her childhood home with the Sandersons. From the time she'd learned she was adopted, she'd felt displaced and different. She knew and acknowledged it to herself that her parents had never given her any doubt that she was their daughter as much as Amy, but something inside of her wouldn't accept it. She'd rebelled and rebelled and rebelled, blaming them for her problems when in her heart she knew it wasn't true.

They'd held steady, never accusing, never refusing to help her out when she'd been in trouble, never giving her an inkling of suspicion that they were tired of her troubling ways.

It was only when she'd fled New York, where she'd lived under a false name, straight back to Appleton, that her eyes had been open. Little Amy, as she'd always privately called her sister, had been so helpful and accepting she'd been drawn to stay. And once her parents had returned from their umpteenth cruise, they'd hugged and cried so much at her return, she'd almost felt smothered.

But she'd cautiously accepted their love

offers, and then Ryle had offered her the job. The one thing in her life that really interested her and was a worthy endeavor. Amy had married Toby, her parents had taken off on another trip overseas, and she'd settled into life as manager of Ryle's upcoming remodeled bed and breakfast.

Now, back at the bed and breakfast, she stared out the window again, the final mild sounds from the basement a background noise, and watched as a battered, sixties station wagon drove slowly up the driveway. She almost laughed when the driver turned off the engine, and the vehicle coughed and sputtered as if in protest.

An elderly lady, yellowish-white hair topping her ruddy complexioned-face, waddled up to the porch, dragging an old, worn-out piece of luggage with one wheel missing.

Jazzi knew her instantly, and she still looked as harmless as the last time she'd seen her, so she headed to the front door and opened it.

The woman peered at her with narrowed eyes, her faded blue eyes giving her a worn out look. "Well, are you going to let me in or do I have to stand out here the rest of the day till you make up your mind? If you have one."

Not a very encouraging way to get invited inside, but Jazzi laughed. "Of course. Come in, we've not completed the renovation yet, but..."

The woman waved a hand. "I know that. Just came to get some things."

Jazzi stepped forward to stop her. "Wait a minute. What things are you talking about?"

The woman looked at her as if Jazzi was the one who'd lost her mind. "You should know. I owned this place for nearly fifty years. I reckon I kin git the things that are mine iff'n I want."

She was huffing as if Jazzi had offended her.

Jazzi opened her mouth to answer, when Ryle walked in from the back entrance and down the hallway. "What's going on, Jazzi?"

"Maisie says she's after her belongings, that she left items here and wants to pick them up—"

"He said I could." She sniffed. "Don't young people keep their word nowadays?"

"Maisie? Maisie Hall?"

"That's what I go by." The woman peered at him. "Who are you?"

"I'm the man who bought this place from you. Remember? Ryle Sadler."

She nodded. "I remember. Odd name you have there."

"Maybe." Ryle grinned. "I kind of like it."

She harrumphed at him, but then gave him a smile filled with missing teeth. "Got the best of the bargain, I did. This old place will fall down 'round you one of these days. If it doesn't scare the skin right off'n yer backs."

Ryle winked at Jazzi when the woman wasn't looking. "What do you mean? I don't scare easy."

She gave him a look that said she wondered about his sanity and another harrumph. "Wait till y'all hear the screeching and moaning."

"The place screeching from age?"

"Nope. There's spirits in this place, and they're wanting loose." She shook her head, gripped her luggage and started to move on. "You beware now. I'm warning ya. Ain't my fault if someone finds you white as a ghost and dead as a dormouse."

"Here, let me get that for you." Ryle reached for her luggage.

"Thanks, gits pretty heavy."

"You lead the way, and I'll follow. Jazzi, you wanna come?"

Maisie jerked around. "No. She can't come."

"Why ever not?"

"Cause she has fear in her. It would be too much on her iff'n she hears them cryin' out."

Ryle stared at her for a moment then looked at Jazzi. "Well, then, Jazzi, you stay here and guard the place while I help Maisie collect her things."

Jazzi watched as the two began descending the basement steps.

~*~

Ryle walked slowly down the steps to the basement, half dragging, half carrying the luggage bag. Maisie was on his heels, and he could hear her puffing breaths of air.

He'd agreed to her—demand?—to leave a few items in the basement, but only if she retrieved them before his prospective opening date. And that they'd be placed in a container of some sort. He'd refused to be responsible for her items, so she'd reluctantly signed the exemption paper releasing him of responsibility if something happened to her property. She'd snarled and growled, but he wouldn't give in.

He'd really figured she'd never show up again. What on earth could she have so valuable that she had to leave it for an indefinite period to an unknown person—him?

He wondered about her mentality. That nonsense about noises and whispers was a thing of storybooks and nightmares. Besides, how many nights had he slept here and heard nothing strange or out of order?

Until lately.

He reached the basement floor and settled her luggage a bit away from the stairs then turned to help her the last few steps.

Too late. She was already at one wall, running a hand over the bricks, her murmurs a creepy whisper, but with no understandable words.

Ryle watched as she wandered around the whole room, muttering and ignoring him, almost as if she'd forgotten he was there. But after one circle around the room, she moved back toward him and motioned for him to follow her. Back in a dark corner was a small room, and she drew from her pocket a large key, inserted it, but nothing clicked.

She withdrew the key, held it up to her eyes, nodded a bit and reinserted it.

Nothing. Maisie turned and glared at him. "This key has always opened the door."

"It doesn't now. I had the locks changed."

She opened her mouth, probably to scold him, but he pulled a set of keys from a pocket and held up one of them.

"I had all the locks changed." He inserted his key, twisted, and the door creaked open. "There you go."

She stepped inside, but when he moved to follow, she held up a hand. "No. Stay where you are."

Ryle did as she asked. He heard the rustling sounds coming from inside the room.

Of a sudden, she peeked out of the room. "Come."

And Ryle went.

"Open it."

She was pointing to her luggage, so Ryle leaned down and unstrapped the thing then pushed it closer to her. She gripped it and pulled it even closer. "Turn your back."

Ryle didn't want to. He wasn't sure he could

trust her. "No, I won't, but I'll step outside the room. If you need me to help you, call out."

His curiosity was getting bigger by the minute. He heard more rustlings, another screech, then a loud snap as if the luggage top had been slammed shut. "You kin git it now."

She exited the room, leaving the door open, and headed for the stairs.

She'd left the large chest open, and Ryle cast a glance inside it. Empty. Turning away, he grabbed the luggage bag, hefted it and hurried to follow Maisie.

Up the stairs they went, and Maisie marched straight to the front door. Jazzi opened it, Ryle carried the bag to her station wagon, and the old woman climbed in.

But before she shut the door, she looked at him. "Beware. You've been warned."

The car started—sputtering and creaking—and wove its way down the drive, with Maisie's warning floating in the air around their heads.

"What on earth is she talking about?" Jazzi asked as they stood watching her leave, the woman's gray head just barely visible.

"I have no idea. But I'm thinking we shouldn't ignore her warning."

"Really, Ryle? You believe that nonsense?" Jazzi stared at him in disbelief.

"Really. I have a feeling there's more to her words than she told us."

"What do you mean?"

"I have no idea. But somehow we'll be finding out before much more time passes. You mark my words." Ryle grinned then and walked straight back into the house, wondering if Jazzi was as curious as he was about Maisie's odd warning.

He reckoned he'd find out soon enough.

Chapter Five

Jazzi and Ryle sat in the two lone lawn chairs in what would soon be the entry way eating their warmed up pizza. After Ryle had downed four slices and drank two bottles of water, he sat back. "Now that's what I call a hearty supper."

"It was good." Jazzi had eaten two slices and shook her head no when he urged her to go for a third piece. "I would have thought you'd not be hungry after a lunch with your friends."

"Wasn't much of a lunch. We didn't get to eat at Apple Blossoms."

"Why not? Or is it none of my business?"

"Of course, it's your business if you want to know. The mayor and his right hand man told me he was putting a hold on our opening date. Seems an unknown someone is claiming the sell was illegitimate. That he holds the current deed."

"What? That makes no sense. The mayor had to have gotten false information."

"He was pretty insistent, but I told him he had 'till our opening day to show me something concrete. After that he could talk with my lawyer."

"You have a lawyer on call?" What kind of employer did she have? Was he that rich he could keep a lawyer? Except for her parents, she knew no one else who kept one permanently. Must be nice.

He didn't answer her question. "That's why I plan on getting to the bottom of this."

"I agree. What can I do to help?"

"Right now, just keep on top of everything for me, deal with any minor details. Make sure you're here if any of our workers needs you or has a question. I'm going to take off and be gone for a couple of days, but I trust you. You know the place now as well as I do."

"I can do that. I'm going to call Amy in the morning to make sure the shipment of plants is still on schedule before opening. If so, she and her landscaping crew will be here later this week to begin the work."

"And you're positive she can finish it in a week?"

"All the hard stuff was done earlier. The clearing up of overgrown, unsightly plantings and weeds. The ground has been dug up and fertilized for the plants. She assured me everything's fine, but I'm a little worried about that shipment."

Ryle stood. "Then I'll leave you to it. I should be back in two days, but if I don't make it and you're the least bit afraid here by yourself, feel free to grab a room at Amy's or even a hotel in the next town over."

Jazzi shook her head, forcing the thought of that man at the edge of the woods out of her thoughts. "I'm not the least afraid. This place is peaceful and makes me happy."

"Okay then. I put groceries away when I got back from town so there's plenty of choices if you want a snack later or for breakfast. I'll see you when I get back."

Jazzi watched as her boss walked away. How did he stay so thin the way he ate?

She stood and began gathering their paper plates and the leftover pizza to take to the kitchen area. She just might eat more pizza for a snack after a while. And donning her pajamas and reading a good book just made an evening alone even better.

It took her an hour to go through the inn one more time to make sure all things were in order and she hadn't forgotten anything that would need done before opening day. Pictures for the walls were ordered and readied to be delivered from Andy Carrington, Amy was taking care of the landscaping and indoor plants, furniture would be arriving soon, the kitchen was almost ready once the restaurant-styled stove was installed. The only things not done yet were hiring a cook and the general help Ryle wanted. And the caretaker, of course.

Now to cuddle up in bed with her book...and hope she had no more unwanted people standing outside her window tonight.

She needed a cat for company. Or maybe a big, bad dog would be better.

~*~

Jazzi heard the truck coming up the driveway early the next morning and hurried to see who it was. Right behind the large truck bearing a bed full of plants and trees, came Amy's small car. When they parked, Amy climbed out and waved at Jazzi who'd stepped out on the veranda.

"Hey there, Jazzi, is Ryle around?"

"No, he had some things to take care of, but wanted me here in case you needed anything."

"Great." She looked at Kory, her landscaping supervisor, then spoke to the other crew members, giving them instructions and turned back to Jazzi. "The plants came early, and Kory said they were ready to start when I was. Seemed like we might as well start today as tomorrow."

"Perfect. I'll be out in a few minutes to follow you around like a puppy dog." Jazzi called after them.

Amy grinned at her, but Kory, who'd strolled up, both laughed and teased. "Do that. We love animals, don't we, Amy? Jazzi makes a beautiful one."

"Go along, you two. I won't say what kind of animals you are." She waved a hand at them, and grinned.

They laughed again, claiming her the victor of their back and forth teasing.

Twenty minutes later, Jazzi moseyed outside and circled the building, but she didn't see the two until she reached the back of the structure, close to the kitchen entrance. They were both holding shovels and digging into the ground.

"What's going on?"

"We were hoping to plant that tree there..." Amy tilted her head toward the tree leaning against the steps then wiped the back of her hand across her forehead. "We just found this. There's this concrete something here, and I nor Kory have any idea what it is."

"We're thinking it might be some kind of marker? But there's no writing engraved on it. We need to get this dirt scooped back to make sure." Kory tossed another shovel-full of dirt to the side.

Jazzi plopped down on the grass nearby, careful to stay out of reach of those shovels-full of dirt being tossed aside.

Kory cast her a glance. "It might take us awhile if you have something to do. We can call for you when it's uncovered. Wouldn't want to discover a bag of diamonds in here without you or Ryle present to claim them."

"Ha. Funny. But I can go grab you both a drink."

"Sounds good, Jazzi. Thanks. Give us a few more minutes, if you will, and we should be able to take a break and enjoy it."

"Gotcha." Jazzi retreated inside the kitchen.

Jazzi hurried to her room and grabbed some clothes she'd wanted to wash today then stuffed them into the already-installed, heavy duty washer, and allowed a small amount of detergent and softener into their individual cups. Closing the lid, she returned to the kitchen, poured tall glasses of homemade lemonade. She remembered how to make it from her mother's directions, and the only way she drank it. Store bought was out for her—and set the glasses on a tray along with a small plate filled with four oatmeal, raisin cookies.

She might not be the best person in the world, but she knew how to bake and make lemonade.

When she walked down the four steps of the back porch, Kory hurried over to her. "Let me get that for you."

"I'm good. Do you want to drink this out here on the lawn or on the veranda?"

"Out here's good. The more we scoop out the soil, the more concrete we see." Amy leaned her shovel against the inn's wall. "Hmmm. Those cookies look divine. Oatmeal raisin?"

"I made them. I hope you both like lemonade. It's homemade."

"Who doesn't like homemade lemonade?" Amy bit into one of the cookies. "Wow. You made these? Really? Delish."

"I haven't tasted any this good since my mother passed away."

"Thanks, Kory." She hadn't been around this tall, quiet but likeable man much. Only time she'd seen him was when he came with Amy to figure out what needed done with the landscaping. He'd always been polite to her, but they'd never talked much.

"Amy, I can't believe you're out here shoveling dirt."

"I told her one of the guys could do this, but she wanted to help." Kory shrugged his shoulders.

"Kory doesn't get to tell me what to do even though I've known him since college. I like to dig in the dirt once in awhile. Strengthens my arm muscles."

Jazzi grinned at her sister, but Amy held up a hand.

"When he moved near here, I was looking for a landscaper I could occasionally hire when I needed one. He seemed the perfect choice, although there are times I question my decision." Amy set her almost-empty glass on the tray. "Seriously, I couldn't get along without his crew. Let's check out a few more inches. If we can't tell what it is, we'll have to cover it up again and let someone else figure it out."

"What if it's a casket?" Kory's fake spooky voice had Jazzi and Amy laughing at his suggestion.

When Amy and Kory came up with nothing except more concrete, they gave up, recovered it and moved on to their next planting.

But Jazzi stood still, pondering what a slab was doing under the ground, hidden as it was. She was very much afraid it meant more trouble for Ryle.

~*~

Ryle was in his own small plane headed to

New York City. He wanted to talk with his lawyer in person and see if he could find out who was causing this hitch in his plans to open the bed and breakfast. He grinned to himself. He really was going to have to name the place soon. They couldn't open with just calling it the bed and breakfast. Wouldn't be much of an enticement to potential clients.

He'd run from his previous life. Mother dead, father—who knew where? He hardly remembered him. Ryle had been in some minor trouble as a lad, but one thing he'd done right was get his schooling. His mother had made him promise, and he'd kept that promise. But everything else, the community, the people there and the few rough necks he'd hung with, he'd left them behind.

Thankfully, in college, a young woman his age had befriended him. That friend had gone on to become one of the most respected and successful lawyers in the Big Apple. And when she'd encouraged Ryle to use his gift in marketing and investments, Ryle had followed that advice.

And that young woman was still a close friend who always pushed everything to the side when Ryle needed her.

Ryle figured he'd be there around nine and be at his friend's at nine-thirty, spend a couple hours talking with her, and then make the two stops tomorrow to take care of some business.

Almost four hours later, Ryle was knocking at his friend's door, and when the door opened, the wide smile on Emilia Pavlo's face was a welcome he'd not seen for a long time.

"My friend. You did not tell me you were coming. I would have arranged a party."

"Really? You don't like them anymore than I

do, so I find that hard to believe."

"I would have too. A party for two." She gave him a corner-eyed glance even as she reached to give him a hug.

"You're still as beautiful and rotten as ever."

"That's why we enjoy each other's company so much."

"Right. As long as we don't overdo it."

"Of course. That's a given." She moved to the modern, chrome-filled kitchen. "Something to eat? Drink?"

"I'll take whatever you have to drink. Nothing to eat."

She pouted. "I just made a Caesar—"

"No, thanks. I remember those casseroles you created in college. Not much for them even today." He plopped down on the white sofa. "Now if you cooked like my manager does at the bed and breakfast..."

Emilia didn't say a word, but she stared at him, as if searching a meaning behind his words. "And is that manager something special?"

"Meaning the best manager in the world? Yes, she is. A gem." He'd put a stop to any of her speculations right now. Especially seeing as how he needed her.

"Uh huh." She grinned as she carried his drink to him. "So how's business?"

"That's what I want to talk with you about."

"I take it you can't stay long."

Ryle nodded. "I need to leave in a few hours. Have another stop or two to make before heading back."

"More business?"

"Yeah. Two different businesses asking for help. I'll check them out and see what I think." He crossed his legs. "You know I bought that rundown bed and breakfast. Renovations are almost completed, but yesterday, the mayor of Appleton told me he wanted me to put a hold on the opening. That someone—he wouldn't divulge who—had lodged a complaint that the sale was illegal because there's a lost deed involved. I told him he had till opening day to show me the proof. After that he could talk with my lawyer."

"Good thinking. So what's the problem?"

"I need you to see if you can find out who this person is. My intuition is telling me something's not right. If I could find out the name of that person, and his reasoning, then we can circumvent any trouble he or she is planning to cause."

"I can do that. I'll need the name of the mayor and anything else that possibly can be of use. I'll have my detectives start working on it immediately, and I should have an answer by next week. Hopefully."

"You do know you're the best, don't you?"

"Of course. That's why you use my services. And why I earn every penny you pay me to stay on call."

"Of course." Ryle's answer was a bit sardonic, and he knew it. "Anyhow, I've got to go. Give me some paper and I'll write down what I know."

When Ryle stood minutes later and headed to the door, Emilia followed him.

"If you need anything else, give me a holler."

"A holler? You're turning into a regular hillbilly."

"Yeah, I am, and I kinda like it. You need to come by and check out this town. I'm thinking it's going to be my hometown for a long, long time."

"I never thought I'd see the day."

"I can work there as well—and maybe better—as anywhere. It's much more peaceful and friendly, for sure."

"Then good-bye for now, my friend. I'll let you know as soon as I know anything." She gave him another hug and opened the door for him.

Ryle knew she was watching him as he strolled down the hall. At the elevators, he looked back, and she gave him a little wave and a nod then disappeared back inside her townhouse.

A rich lady, thanks to her family, and dedicated to her work. His best friend.

He'd helped her family out when a supposedly-loyal employee had almost ruined her father. With the wise investments Ryle had advised, and great lawyers, Emilia's father recovered. The family had claimed him as a part of them from then on. He loved them, and although he'd been offered a high-paying job at one of Emilia's father's businesses, he'd declined the offer. He wasn't meant to be tied down to a desk job.

Once again, Ryle took off in his plane, loving the feel of the controls in his hand, but mostly loving the aloneness he felt.

Ryle had never felt freer than when he was flying by himself, and especially at night. The stars and occasionally the lights from ground were far removed from the problems of earth. He felt closer to God, a new thing for him. His mother had left him with one other thing besides urging him to get his schooling: a trust in God. Yeah, he'd abandoned it for awhile, but he'd found his way back. Still felt like a child, but he was gaining ground.

Two hours later, he pulled close to the hangar and walked straight to the cab waiting for him.

Now to get some rest so he could rise early.

~*~

The sun was barely peeking over the horizon the next morning when Ryle met the first businessman. By nine-thirty, he'd finished with the second one and returned to the hangar where his plane—per his instructions last night—was waiting, fueled and ready to go.

Two hours later, he pulled into the driveway of the bed and breakfast. He'd left his plane at the Charleston airport and driven in a steady but slow pace all the way home. The moment he stepped inside the door, he smelled the bacon and sausage coming from the kitchen area. He headed there.

"You know you don't have to cook for me."

"You're home." Jazzi turned from the stove. She'd wrapped herself in a colorful apron and was just pulling biscuits from the oven.

"Hmmm. That smells good. Looks like you've made enough for an army."

She laughed. "Maybe. I figured since I was cooking a late breakfast/early lunch, I might as well make enough for Toni's crew."

"Great. Every one of Toni's workers will get nothing done today. They'll be hanging around the kitchen begging for lunch and supper. And maybe wanting to do some flirting on the side."

"Well, I don't mind the cooking, but it's out for the flirting."

"Why so? You're a beautiful woman, and from what I can see, talented in cooking, decorating and managing."

"Not interested, thank you." She placed two plates on the smaller kitchen table, paper napkins and coffee cups. "I hired two maids while you were gone, and we made a discovery yesterday."

"We?"

"Amy and Kory, her landscaping manager. I don't know what to make of it, but it was surprising."

"Don't tell me there's trouble."

"I don't know the answer to that yet. Amy came early. Said her landscaping crew finished up a different project the day before. They wanted to go ahead and begin, and since the plants had already arrived, she agreed."

"That's a good report. What's the surprise?"

"They found an odd piece of cement under the ground close to the back stairs. They wanted to plant a small tree there, but had to move on when they discovered the concrete."

"Really?" Ryle reached for another biscuit, spooned sausage gravy over it and dug in. "Any idea what it could be?"

"No. They dug wider than they needed trying to figure out how large it was, but it didn't work. Seems it must be pretty big."

"That is odd. Could be a storage tank, maybe?"

"We don't know how long it's been there or when it was placed there."

"Right. I sure would like to know what it is. And they had no idea why a cement slab would be under the ground?"

"None."

"That is a problem. Let me think on it for awhile and see if I can make a reasonable decision of what to do. I just might know the person to help us out here."

Jazzi liked those *help us out here* words. She glanced at the huge wall clock on the wall. "You've got time to rest—"

"No time to rest. I'll grab a quick shower and be ready to check things out." Ryle scooted his chair back. "If you keep coddling me like this, I'm going to have to give you a raise before we even open the place."

Jazzi didn't answer him, only smiled and began gathering the dishes. He strode down the hall, headed to his room. Thank God for small blessings like Jazzi.

~*~

Ryle knew just the person to call to help with the slab of concrete. Athan Meadows was a widower with a four-year-daughter. His Aunt Fay Anna cared for the child while he worked. Athan was a quiet guy, but smart and perceptive.

But before he did that, he'd talk to Toni Deluca-Douglas first.

When she answered her phone, Ryle got right to the heart of his question. "I'm sure you heard about that slab of concrete that Amy and Kory dug into the other day?" At her acquiesce, he continued, "Do you think I should have someone check it out before opening day? I like to stay ahead of any potential problems."

"Hmm. If that slab doesn't seem to be hurting anything right now, I'd think twice about digging up a large area, creating an eyesore or a spot that isn't visually appealing."

"And what if I can have it checked out without creating such a thing?"

"Then by all means, do it. If it was me, I'd rather know what might end up being a problem after opening."

"That's what I was hoping you'd say. By the way, I was really impressed when I drove up to the place. Looks like that million dollars you promised me."

"Glad to hear it. We'll talk later then."

When he hung up, he thought about what

Toni had said. She was right about creating an ugly site so close to opening. And she'd agreed with his plan.

Five minutes later he was on the phone with Athan Meadows.

When Athan answered the phone, his voice wasn't boisterous as some men's might have been, hearing from Ryle—turned friend. Ryle had saved his business after some big-name clients had weaseled out on paying, but his words showed he hadn't forgotten Ryle or what he'd done for him.

"Ryle Sadler."

"It's been awhile, hasn't it? You still living down south?"

"Yeah, but Aunt Fay Anna's wanting to move farther north. Says the hot weather is wearing on her."

Ryle's interest peaked. "So she likes snow? Skiing?"

"Yeah. Anything to do with winter is right up her alley."

"Why not move up here?"

"Where's *up here*?" There was a bit of amusement in Athan's voice.

"You haven't heard of my new adventure?"

"Haven't heard anything from you for quite a few years."

It wasn't an accusation from Athan. Just a declaration.

"I bought a rundown place in the quaintest town ever, called Appleton, here in the good ole mountain state—"

"You've moved from New York?"

This time the man was shocked.

"I sure did, and am happier than I've been for awhile. I'll tell you more when I see you."

"You're coming south?"

"No, you're coming north."

"I'm coming north?"

"You are. I have a new problem here." Ryle went on to explain the concrete slab. "Do you have time to check it out? Our opening is happening in just a few days. I need to find out if this is something serious and whether I need to move the opening date or not. Can you come?"

"We have a new project scheduled, but it's not urgent, so I'm pretty sure I can move it till later in the month. I can be there tomorrow."

"Why not bring your aunt and daughter? Stay for our opening. Maybe you'll decide to move here."

"It's pretty quick notice to drag them away, but I'll talk to Aunt Fay Anna and see what she says."

"Well, then, I'll see you tomorrow. I owe you."

"No," Athan's quiet voice argued. "I owe you. See you."

Good. He could rest a little easier now.

But that thought didn't stop his curiosity—or was it worry?—about that mysterious concrete slab.

Chapter Six

It was midnight, and something had wakened him. Ryle could see his lit clock easily from his bed. Two a.m. He lifted his head, but didn't move otherwise, listening.

He was a light sleeper and had always been able to run on a few hours of sleep. Noises, disturbances and movements all woke him, and this time was no different. But whatever had wakened him...

The sound came again. A low—it sounded like a hurt animal—or was it a person?

Jazzi?

Ryle sprang from his bed, grabbed his pants and slid into them then slid his feet into his bedroom loafers. He hit the hallway running and called out in a loud whisper as he approached Jazzi's room.

"Jazzi. Jazzi, are you okay?"

He needn't have worried. She was standing in her doorway, her brow creased from either irritation at being awakened or confusion. Had she heard the noise too?

"I'm awake, Ryle. I thought—I mean, something woke me. I'm pretty sure it was a moaning as if—"

"...an animal or someone was hurt." Ryle finished her sentence.

"Yeah. That's what it sounded like." Her blue eyes gazed at him. "Were we dreaming?"

"No. We both heard it."

"Then...where did it come from?"

"I don't know." He returned her gaze. "Unless..."

"Unless what?"

"Remember. Maisie said we'd be hearing moans."

"Surely, you don't believe in ghosts."

"No. But something or someone is trying to make us think this place is haunted." Ryle rubbed a hand over his face. "It's such a childish act."

"I don't understand. We've been living here for months and heard nothing. Why all of a sudden do we hear noises?"

"Exactly. Right after the confrontation with the mayor to stop the opening. Right after Maisie visited yesterday. Right after the discovery of the slab of concrete. That's too many incidents happening in a short period of time to be an accident."

Jazzi straightened. "Then what shall we do?"

He stared at her, noticing her deep blue eyes. Again. "First, I think we need to make sure you're safe."

"I'm not afraid."

"But I'm afraid for you. If someone is playing tricks on us to keep this place from opening, it's hard to tell what they might do. I don't want you in harm's way." He started to walk away. "I'll grab a pillow and blanket and sleep outside your door."

"Ryle, you don't have to do that. I'm a big girl and have been in a lot scarier situations than this."

He hesitated. "Are you sure?"

"I am. And what about the two cleaning women?"

"I'll walk by their rooms. If I hear nothing suspicious, I'm pretty sure we can rest assured they're safe."

Jazzi nodded slowly. "I suppose you're right."

"I know I am. We'll talk tomorrow then." Ryle headed toward the employees' rooms in the back of the inn.

One thing about it, he was determined to open this bed and breakfast.

Nothing would stop him.

He hoped.

~*~

Jazzi re-entered her room and walked to the window. She wasn't worried about the sounds so much. She had bigger worries.

With that Lincoln Tillis man hanging around—if he did—she'd be uncomfortable in trying to avoid him so much. Like all the time. She wasn't about to have him questioning her. About anything. So what was she going to do about it?

Ryle was such a good man. With hidden depths, she could tell. But that didn't mean he had a bad background, just that he was very private. And that was something she could sympathize with. She ought to know.

Was that moaning really what had awakened her? It was a crazy idea, but she'd definitely heard what sounded like a moan. And like Ryle had said, it was too much of a coincidence for those things—the mayor trying to stop the inn's opening, Maisie showing up right when she did—to happen one right after the other.

Jazzi sighed. One thing about all of this, she would not let anything stop Ryle from being ready to open this place on the planned date. Not if she had to move heaven and earth.

~*~

"I know what I'm going to do." Ryle blasted into the kitchen the next morning where Jazzi sat at the table eating an egg sandwich. He sidled closer, eyeing her sandwich. "Really? I love egg sandwiches."

"This one is good. Very good. It has thick cheese and thin slices of ham on it, with garden grown tomatoes and leaf lettuce. Hmmm. Delicious. I wish you'd gotten up earlier. I could have made you one."

"It's six-o-one. How much earlier do I have to get up to get fed around here?"

Jazzi grinned. "I was up at five-fifteen. Hence the sandwich."

"You're too cruel."

"I know it." Jazzi stood and opened the microwave. "But not selfish. Here's your sandwich. I heard you up and knew if I didn't make two, you'd be begging for half of mine."

Ryle laughed and sat down at the table. "You're the best, you know."

"If you tell me enough, I might start believing you. Then you'll be in trouble." She sat down a cup of coffee and pushed the hazelnut creamer closer to him. "Enjoy."

"Oh, I will."

"So what were you saying about knowing what you're going to do?"

"I'm going to sleep in the basement tonight."

"What? Ryle."

"Why not? You nor I believe in ghosts. There's a reason for the moaning, like the house creaking or wind blowing. I'm going to find out what it is and laugh so hard that whoever is trying to convince me to leave will end up with mustard on their face."

"You're an awful tease, you know." But what a wonderful man he was. She'd never met any other man who was like him.

And she really wished she didn't like him quite so much.

"One man can't resolve everything, but I'm sure going to try."

He was grinning sheepishly, and Jazzi knew he was thinking otherwise. Her own feelings though insisted he came pretty close to being able to do just that.

"No, he surely can't." Jazzi agreed and watched as he chomped down on the last bite of his sandwich as if he hadn't eaten since last week.

Ryle laid his napkin beside his plate. "That was better than any grandeur dinner I've had in New—in the past. Absolutely delicious. I should just hire you as a chef—but no, I need you too much to be my manager."

"We got a bite yesterday evening from that ad I placed in the Charleston paper yesterday morning. You're to interview him late this afternoon around three thirty."

"That should work." He stood. "In the meantime, I'm going to supervise the delivery of the outdoor equipment this morning then check out the basement. I know it seems as if Toni and her crew should have found something, if there was anything to find, but what if there isn't anything to find?"

"What do you mean?"

"What if there's something there, but not easily discerned? Hidden in such a way that it can't be found easily?"

Jazzi pondered his questions. "Could be, but they did some pretty extensive work there."

"I know, but all their replacements were on the inner side, nothing against the back wall. It could mean something."

"Hmm. You may be right."

"Right or wrong, I mean to get to the bottom of this newest problem. You feeling up to handling all this?"

Jazzi turned from the dishwasher in surprise. "Why would you ask that? Of course, I am. I'm excited to help."

"A good answer. I'll see you later."

~*~

Ryle not only wanted to accomplish the things he'd mentioned to Jazzi, but he planned on taking a stroll around the hundred-some acres. He'd been meaning to forever but just hadn't had the time. Well, now was the time, and he figured he could ramble through a good portion of it before having to interview the possible cook person. It was time to scout his land and see what potential there was to creating some interesting activities for his guests and himself too.

He loved to ski, and although there wasn't always enough snow for that in this area, most winters they could always fall back on artificial snow.

A large swimming pool would be enticing, and whatever else would draw in the people, he was prepared to study on it. But all those plans could come next spring—if the inn showed significant progress.

The shores of the small lake had been cleaned up. Picnic tables, chairs and swings had been situated around it for relaxing. An area for fishing and small boats had been redone.

An hour later, with the delivery truck right on

time with his equipment, Ryle looked over all the items he figured they'd need and was pleased with his purchases.

Now for that stroll.

He hoped by next spring to have hired two full time gardeners to care for the large acre of land he wanted planted with vegetables of all sorts. Corn, green beans, broccoli, and so much more. Closer to the house he planned on an herb garden and smaller veggies such as radishes, lettuce and cabbage. He might even decide to create a garden filled with fruit trees and berries. His cook, he would insist on, would be a person who specialized in healthy meals.

It was at the top of one fairly decent mountain, he stood and enjoyed the scenery around and below him, feeling his problems taking wings. All would be worked out in time. He was sure of it.

Stepping off—roughly measuring—the top of the mountain, he figured they'd need a small building where his clients could rent skiing equipment. One side could handle the equipment business, the other healthy snacks and drinks.

He stared down the mountain and found himself relaxing. He could get used to this atmosphere and place.

It was time to head home. Home. He loved the sound of that, and the thought of Jazzi waiting there didn't hurt anything either.

That was a pleasant thought.

~*~

Patrick—Paddy, as he claimed his Irish friends called him—McKinney was a big man, not fat, but big boned, gruff and good at what he did, or so he claimed. Ryle liked him immediately.

"I like what I'm hearing from you, Paddy. But

I like to prove that I'm right about my intuitions. What say, you look over our supplies in the kitchen and see what you can prepare for our supper tonight? Mind you, I want fairly healthy and out of this world good. Think you can do that?"

Paddy shrugged his big shoulders. "If you have the ingredients, I can cook it."

"Good. I'm looking forward to seeing what you can do."

"You have a room for me? I brought my things with me."

Ryle smiled. The man was confident, that was for sure.

"We do, and we can have it ready for you in a half hour."

Paddy stood. "Then I'll go check out that food stock you have."

Ryle met Jazzi in the hall. "Did you hear?"

"I did, and I like him. Are you hiring him?"

"Probably. Depends on how he cooks. He comes with good recommendations. Can't figure out though why he wants to move here."

"Same reason I moved here, I'd say." Jazzi smiled.

Ryle had no real idea why Jazzi had returned to her home town. According to Toby, Jazzi had always been a bit on the wild side. He didn't really care. He wasn't in the business of judging people. Only what they did with their lives mattered to him.

"I'm going to go gather up things I'll need tonight—"

"Tonight? In the basement by yourself?"

"I don't think I'll be sleeping any, but you never know. That moaning might just put me to sleep."

"Ryle." Jazzi stared at him, another worried frown on her forehead. "I don't think you should be down there by yourself."

"You're worried about me." He was joking but when he saw the look on her face, he knew she was serious. "I'll be fine."

"I think you ought to have someone down there with you."

"Who in their right mind wants to spend a night in a damp, dark hole?"

"Seems you want to."

"I don't want to, I have to. There's the difference."

"Why don't you call Toby and have him come? Amy can come too, and we'll have a girls' night."

"Jazzi, I don't need anyone."

Not even me? The question that shoved its way into her mind was a surprise. Hadn't she learned a lesson not to trust anyone, especially a man? Even Ryle, as good as he was to her, might turn against her any day.

She turned away. "Of course, you're right. You need to do what you think is best."

Ryle touched her arm. "Jazzi, stop. Call Toby and Amy. It'll be fun all of us together. We haven't had much time to socialize lately."

"I'll call them, Ryle. I'm going to go and straighten my room. I haven't had time to do it."

"Well, when we've hired that last person as your assistant, and he or she begins their work, they can do that for you. You'll be too busy, I figure, to worry about cleaning rooms."

"Oh, no, I won't ask someone else to clean up my messes. Besides, like I said, I like my privacy."

"Are you sure? We won't hire anyone we can't trust."

She gave him a smile. "I'm positive. I prefer to have my suite as private as I can."

Ryle watched her walk away. She was tall, but thin, usually shy about expressing her opinion, probably afraid of being rebuffed. Someone had hurt the girl badly, and it wasn't her family.

One thing he liked about Jazzi—along with her ability to manage well and her cooking—was her quietness and gracefulness. She didn't realize how beautiful she was. That purple hair which might seem fun to a lot of people, didn't suit her. He was glad to see her allowing it to return to its original black. He'd never tell her that. It was her business what she did.

~*~

When Ryle heard the ringing bell from the kitchen downstairs while he was upstairs checking each room to see that the furnishings were in place and all was in order, he smiled. Paddy was letting him know all things were ready for his supper. He wasn't sure where Jazzi was but figured she would hear the bell.

They met in the hallway.

"Ready to check out our potential new cook who's already settled in?"

"I'm pretty sure he's determined we'll love his cooking. I hope so. I really like him."

"Me too. Let's go see if his talk matches up to his cooking."

"Let's!"

Even before they'd entered the kitchen where they'd elected to eat till the dining area was furnished, the smell of something divine wafted to them. They both glanced at each other and grinned.

"That smells promising."

"You bet."

When they entered the kitchen, all was in perfect shipshape. No unwashed pots and pans lay strewn about the room. No dirty dishtowels. He stood with arms akimbo, a white, white towel slung over one shoulder, and a smile as big as a twelve inch ruler on his face.

"Welcome. I have tonight prepared for you a Caesar Salad with Raspberry Dressing, my own recipe of Blackened Chicken, Green Beans with Slivered Almonds and Garlic Parmesan Roasted Red Potatoes."

"It smells wonderful, Paddy. Thank you."

The chef nodded his head in acknowledgement of Jazzi's compliment and pulled out her chair. Ryle smiled at the man's manners and lofty manner. He liked this man.

One bite, chewed and swallowed, and Ryle had made his decision. It was only when the man offered a simple cheesecake desert topped with fresh raspberries, and they'd eaten it, that he asked Paddy to join them at the table.

"Paddy, what I want for the bed and breakfast is a man who can cook for several guests, most times only for breakfast and lunch. I want the meals to be topnotch, that will coax our guests to eat all their daytime meals here. I believe, and Jazzi agrees, that you're the man."

"Of course, I am. I had no doubts you would choose me."

"You're settled in?"

"I am. I travel light."

"Good. Do you mind me asking what you mean about traveling light?"

"Not at all. It's better you know ahead of time." The big man settled more comfortably in the chair that seemed to groan a bit. "I'm a traveling man. Not because I've been fired or because I'm a ne'er-do-well, but because I've not yet found the place that feels like home. When I do that, then that's the place that will be my last. It's as simple as that."

Ryle stared at the man, surprised at his answer. "Paddy, I believe I understand you. It's how I felt all my life, and although I've met and kept several good friends, I've never found the place that I could call home."

"You haven't?" Paddy's brows drew together. "You understand what I'm saying? Because when I've explained that ahead of every job I've taken, no one has understood."

"I do. It was only when I chanced upon this little out-of-the-way town—the longer I stayed— the more I knew. And once I bought this place, I was immediately at home."

"That's what I need to feel. I won't leave you stranded if I go sometime in the future. So far, I like you too. The two meals a day is a great idea. I'm assuming you have a reason for no dinner meal?

"I do. One of our best friends has an upscale restaurant in town—Apple Blossoms. We don't want to horn in on her business. Besides it will give our guests the opportunity to visit the town, shop at some of our unique shops and enjoy the best classy meals in West Virginia."

Paddy narrowed his eyes and stared at Ryle. "Few people would do that, even for their best friends."

"I'm not most people, Paddy."

The cook stood. "Then if we're done, I will finish up preparations for your breakfast in the morning and take a stroll around the place before turning in. Good night, you two."

"Don't you even want to know what your salary will be?" Jazzi stopped the man from leaving the room.

He turned back and smiled at her then nodded at Ryle. "No need. I trust that man."

The two were quiet for a minute, watching Paddy move to the pantry, then Jazzi drew in a deep breath. "Wow. He's amazing."

"I agree. Jazzi, we've got our work cut out for us to make this man feel the most at-home he's ever been."

"I have a feeling he's comparing every place he goes to, to something from his past." Jazzi was staring at the doorway from where he'd disappeared.

"And he hasn't found it yet."

"No, he hasn't. Let's hope this is the place."

"We'll do our best to make it so." Ryle stood. "I called Toby, and he and Amy should be here soon, right before dark. I'm going to add a few more things I want to take down to the basement."

"Do you need help?"

"No, it won't be that much."

"All right, I'll see you later when the Gibsons show up. I think I'll go up and catch up on my reading till then."

How fortunate was he? He had Jazzi and now, Paddy, two maids already on the premises, and, hopefully, two gardeners/caretakers, and an assistant for Jazzi soon, they'd be ready, employee-wise, for opening day. All the remodeling was finished. There should be no reason for opening day to be postponed.

All was going as planned. Hopefully, nothing stopped the progress.

Not the mayor or unknown complainee nor

any ghosts.

Ryle chuckled at the last.

~*~

The Gibsons arrived promptly at nine that evening. Toby came in carrying a sleeping bag, a lantern, and a duffel bag which his wife, Amy, joked about being filled with snacks. "As if he's spending days down there instead of hours. If they last *that* long."

Jazzi chuckled at Amy's sweet, if teasing manner with her husband. That's the kind of relationship she wanted if she was ever able to find the right man. The big if. Amy had done a fantastic job of getting the husband she deserved.

She and Amy watched as Ryle and Toby lugged their gear down into the basement. When they'd finished, they'd called out good nights. Jazzi shut the basement door and teased whether they should lock it. In the end, they decided to be nice.

"Do you want some snacks before bed time?"

"I don't think so. We went to Apple Blossoms for dinner tonight, and I'm still stuffed. What I'd love is to have some girl-time with my sister."

"Okay, that works. Your room or mine?"

"I'm not sure I'm comfortable sleeping alone tonight, not with Toby scaring the wits out of me about ghosts haunting the place."

"That's nonsense. There's no such thing as ghosts. It's just some real-life thing that seems ghostly."

"Like a creaking house, you mean?"

"Yes. Ryle nor myself believe in ghosts. Whatever is causing the disturbance, Ryle will find it out. I'm not worried about that."

"What are you worried about?"

"Right now? Nothing. It's good to have a chance to visit with you, Amy."

"You'll see me a lot for a few days."

"That's nice. Ryle's looking forward to opening day."

"What about that mayor problem?"

"Haven't heard from him yet. Ryle says if he doesn't, he's opening. He has a lawyer who's checking out some things too, so that's good that he has someone who can stand by him legally, if need be."

"That's a shame that he has to have this problem now, after all the money and time he's spent on getting this ready."

"Yeah, I know. It upsets me, but there's nothing I can do except be here for him and try to do what I can to make everything run smoothly."

"Are you still happy about your decision to work here?"

Jazzi stared at her sister. Was she implying Jazzi would take off at the first hint of trouble? If so, Amy was wrong. She loved this place, loved the job, and...

And the only thing that could force her to leave was her past catching up with her.

"Yes, I am. It's quiet here and the perfect job. I love it."

"I'm happy for you, Jazzi."

A scream rent the air, and both of the girls froze. Amy whispered as Jazzi jumped to her feet.

"What was that?"

"Sounded like a woman screaming, but..."

"But what?" Amy's voice was still barely above a whisper.

"But I'm going to check on the cleaning girls and then the guys. Sounds as if it's stopped for now, but that doesn't mean..." Jazzi headed to the door. "Stay here. Lock the door if you want. I'll be back."

"Jazzi, you can't go by yourself." Amy grabbed her arm.

"Yes, I can. I'm not afraid, and I want to be sure the guys are okay."

"I'm coming with you."

Jazzi shrugged. "Then come on if you're coming."

She wasted no more time, only running through the large place, with Amy on her heels.

As she approached the maids' two rooms, down the hallway, Paddy stepped out of his room. "I heard the scream. They haven't stirred, and I'm keeping watch."

"Thanks, Paddy."

At the basement door, Jazzi cautiously opened the door and listened. No sounds. They peered down the dark staircase and saw nothing. Jazzi called softly, "Ryle, are you all right?"

No answer.

Jazzi looked at Amy whose eyes were as big as saucers.

Why weren't the men answering?

Chapter Seven

Ryle had never felt so sleepy. True, he'd taken that long hike today, but when had exercise forced sleep on him like now? He blinked and glanced at Toby. The man was sitting up with his back against a wall, eyes closed.

"Toby?"

"Yeah, Ryle?"

"Are you sleepy?"

"I am. Can't keep my eyes open. Whew." He sat up, shrugging and shaking his head. "We had a great dinner, but that usually doesn't put me to sleep so quickly."

Ryle stood up. "Me either. Do you think there's something in here that's sleep inducing?"

"If I had to guess, I'd say no one's been in here for decades. I mean, no one other than Toni's crew." Toby chuckled, eyes still closed. "Besides, there's no opening anywhere. Unless they couldn't find it. They may have overlooked—"

Ryle yawned and sank to the floor again. "You're right. We're just tired, I think..." He closed his eyes just to rest them a minute.

All was quiet as he felt the darkness of sleep overcome him.

A scream rent the air, but neither Ryle nor Toby stirred.

~*~

"I'm going down there, Amy. I have to see if they're all right."

Amy grabbed her arm. "Jazzi, it may not be safe. We'd better call that new chef of yours."

"You call him." Jazzi shook her head. "We can't wait that long. There's something wrong, I know it."

"Then take this scarf and cover your nose and mouth." Amy unwrapped the scarf from her neck. "Please. I'll go get the chef. We'll be back in a minute."

"Okay." Jazzi started down the stairs but looked at Amy. "I'll be fine. Stop worrying."

"I can't help it."

Amy's voice followed her as Jazzi descended the stairs. When her feet touched the floor, she shone her flashlight around the large room. The two men were lying still on top of their sleeping bags, and Jazzi was sure her heart had stopped. Were they...dead?

She hurried over to Ryle and shook him and was never so glad when he stirred. He didn't open his eyes, but groaned a little.

Leaning over him, she urged him. "Ryle, wake up. Now. I need you. Wake up, Ryle, wake up."

His eyelids quivered, then opened a crack. "Jazzi, what are you doing down here?"

"There was a scream, I hollered at you, and you didn't answer. I was afraid something had happened to you."

Ryle stirred, yawned and pulled himself up, running a hand over his face. "Whew, I was out like a light. Still feel woozy-headed, like I could sleep for a week."

"I want you to help me waken Toby, then you two need to get upstairs immediately."

"Why on earth?"

"Because I'm pretty sure someone's been spraying this room with sleep inducing spray. It's not toxic, but it's filled with ingredients that relax you and encourages you to sleep. Now, up."

Ryle stood and walked slowly over to Toby and shook him, ordering him to wake up.

It took a few minutes, but Jazzi was finally able to get the two climbing the stairs. In a matter of seconds, all three were upstairs. By then, Toby and Ryle had wakened fully.

"That's the best sleep I've had in months." Toby yawned. "What happened?"

Ryle explained what Jazzi thought might have happened.

"I used to make my own spray for my pillows so I could sleep at night. Worked like a charm." Jazzi motioned to Amy to close the basement door.

"What's going on here in the middle of the night?" Eddie, the police chief of Appleton walked in from the kitchen. "Your new chef called me. Got here as fast as I could."

He was tall, thin and had recently grown a mustache. He talked gruff at times, but he was big-hearted and knew everyone in Appleton. That was why he'd been the chief for so long. Everyone liked him.

While Amy explained what had happened, Jazzi studied the two men. What she hadn't told them was the question of whether the spray had contained any harmful ingredients. Someone who hadn't wanted nosy people to find something may have been behind this. Someone who was trying to scare Ryle away from this business.

Everything had gone so smoothly until lately. Was there something so important hidden in this place that whoever it was would do whatever it took rather than risk discovery?

If so, that person was serious and playing for

keeps. He meant business.

~*~

Ryle and Jazzi stood on the front part of the veranda that circled the entire bed and breakfast watching as Toby and Amy drove down the driveway. Paddy had prepared a select breakfast with plenty of fruits and his own special recipe for French toast. Coffee, tea and two kinds of juices were the drinks, and none of them had refused eating.

Without looking at his manager, Ryle spoke quietly, as his gaze switched to the fog covering the low land and the huge pond in the distance. "What were you not telling me last night, Jazzi? I haven't known you long, but I feel I know you better than most people. I know something was bothering you last night that you didn't share."

Jazzi didn't speak for a moment, her gaze on the fog too. "I wasn't trying to hide anything, Ryle. It was my own feelings that there's something behind all of this sudden disturbance in your plans. I don't know what it is. There's a reason for it all."

"Any guess what?"

"It doesn't make sense to point a finger at Maisie when she willingly sold you this place. And the mayor hasn't contacted you yet, which, if someone has a real concern about the place, why hasn't he? Then there's the problem with the timing. If this unknown person was so concerned, why didn't he speak up when Maisie owned the place? Why now?"

"Maybe because Maisie let the place go to ruins. I think you're right. Now that I've had it remodeled, there could be some reason why this person is worried."

"But about what? Is something hidden here?

Is there a body here? Are there jewels here that that person couldn't recover for whatever reason?" Jazzi shook her head. "It all sounds like nonsense."

"Like we're jumping the gun, looking for trouble."

"So what do we do?"

Ryle pressed his lips together as if thinking. "What's on your agenda today?"

"Not much." Jazzi shrugged. "Thought I'd get a head start on looking through the financial remodeling figures to make sure we're still in budget, but that can be put off if you need me for something else."

"I think I do. Let's set some fans to blow out any spray scents still lingering—if that's what it was last night—gather some more lanterns so we'll have plenty of light, and in an hour or two, you and I will go over that place with a fine tooth comb."

Jazzi's eyes sparkled. "Sounds like fun to me. I'll meet you at ten thirty then."

~*~

Promptly at ten thirty, Ryle and Jazzi began descending the stairs to the basement floor. Earlier, he'd placed fans in the bottom to make sure it was aired out. He'd carried down hammers, chisels and any other tools he thought they might have use for. He didn't plan on doing anything major—not without Toni's approval and presence, but he wanted to double check a few things, and Jazzi would be the perfect assistant.

"Where shall we start?" Jazzi picked up a chisel.

"I was thinking earlier that we might check each of these bricks. Look for loose ones or ones that weren't as old as the others. That sort of thing." He motioned at a wall farthest from the center of the house. "Let's start with that wall. If you'll begin at the left side, I'll take this one, and we'll meet in the middle. Okay?"

"Okay." Jazzi turned to the wall.

Ryle looked over his side of the wall, studying it, searching for any minute piece of evidence that would suggest altering of the wall. He stepped forward and began running his glove-covered hand over brick by brick.

Down the bricks they went one by one. But it was only when both had almost reached the middle, about half way down the wall, that Jazzi spoke.

"Ryle, I think I've found something. I think it sounds hollow behind this brick."

He glanced at her. "I think I have one too."

They stared at each other, then Ryle straightened. "Well, we'll never know until we try to get them loose."

"I agree."

He drew back his hammer and struck the brick. "Now take the chisel and try to pry it out."

She did as he asked. "I think this brick can be pulled out now."

"I think you're right. Let's do it." He lowered the hammer. "No, wait."

"What?"

"When Maisie was here the other day, she ran her hands over this wall as if looking for something."

"Really? Maybe she was casting a spell on the place."

Ryle chuckled and shook his head. "Maybe, but I don't think so. Whatever it was, I thought it was odd at the time."

"There's nothing we can do about her strange

ways."

"Right." Ryle lifted the mallet again.

"What about the structure? What about Toni? Shouldn't she be here just in case we need her?"

"I doubt one brick will cause trouble."

"Okay then. Here goes." Jazzi picked up a large set of heavy-duty tongs and inserted them so that she could grip the brick. She pulled at it, wiggling it a bit, and the brick slid out, along with a wave of dust.

"Good. Ready to see if we can see anything in that small hole?"

"You bet."

Ryle shone his flashlight through the hole and each took a turn trying to peer into the miniature hole.

He drew back. "Nothing."

"Don't be so disappointed. We're not going to see anything through that tiny hole. We've got to take out more of the bricks."

It took them twenty minutes to remove enough of the bricks to expose a space roughly eighteen inches wide and twelve inches high

They both knelt and stared, once again, into the hole.

But this time they were able to see something, and in seconds, Ryle had reached into the hole and lifted out a wooden box that looked as if it was a solid piece of wood.

"There's writing on the top of it." Running a hand over it to remove the dust, Jazzi bent down to stare at the writing. "I can't read it. We'll have to clean the box better to make it readable. Did you see any sign of a key?"

"I'll look again." Ryle searched the hidden area again but shook his head when he flipped the flashlight off. "Nothing. Unless it's buried under inches of dust and debris."

"That's a shame. I hate to damage it by smashing it open."

"We won't do that." He thought a moment. "I think I know of someone who can help us out here."

"You do? A locksmith in town?"

"There could be one, but Jazzi, I think you and I should keep this secret until we know what is inside this." Ryle laid a hand on the box.

"You're right. It could be something valuable or something important, like papers and such."

"I'll clean this mess up in the morning." Ryle stood, lifting the box as he did. "Let's quit for now. I want to see about cleaning this box, then I'll make a phone call to a friend and see if they can swing down here to help us get this open. Very talented in this type of thing."

"Are you talking about a burglar you know?"

Laughing, he shook his head. "Not at all. This person is a respectable business person, influential, rich and my best friend since college."

"Wow. He sounds amazing."

"She is."

"She?"

"She. Emilia Pavlo."

"That's a beautiful name."

"Emilia's a beautiful person with a big heart."

"When can she be here?"

"Unless she has an urgent matter to attend to, after I call she'll leave immediately. I figure she'll be walking through our entrance early tomorrow morning."

"Then I'd better make sure we have a presentable room ready for her."

"Don't go to any trouble. She'll be happy sleeping anywhere. That's her beauty. She's high class but not snobby about it."

"She sounds amazing. I'm in awe already."

"No need to be. She's as common as us for the most part."

"Still, I'm headed to that extra suite. I don't want her to think we're total bumpkins!" Jazzi gave him a little wave and left.

He knew Amy awhile back had been worried about her sister, but Jazzi seemed happy and contented here helping him get everything in order. He'd praised her, given her a generous salary and tried not to be overly demanding.

Still, once in awhile he saw something behind those deep azure-blue eyes of hers. Doubt? Confusion? Worry? No, more like someone feeling trapped.

He hoped she wouldn't run.

~*~

Jazzi wanted to hide in her room for the next few days. Or better yet, run. Could she face handling a sophisticated woman and put on a convincing act that she was thrilled to meet this paragon Ryle had painted a picture of?

Nope. She couldn't do it. Jazzi had never been sophisticated. Never been a society girl. Or even much of anything. Except a troublemaker. Not that she looked for it or desired it. It just seemed to spontaneously happen. She'd make a wrong choice, meet the wrong people, and on and on.

She was torn. She loved this place. It felt like home to her, where she was—for once in her life—important and valuable. Ryle praised her work, encouraged her and seemed to appreciate the company. He was easy to talk to—no airs, and well, she liked him. A lot.

But that woman. Even her name sounded exotic and beautiful. Emilia. Not just plain Em or

Emily.

She threw herself across her bed and groaned into the quilt. How stupid she was, how utterly stupid and pitiful. Why didn't she have the confidence of other women? Amy had been strong and confident in getting Toby to fall for her, in starting her own business, in becoming liked about town. What about all the other friends in town, like Toni and Starli, and even the third individual of the threesome, Caroline, who was more down to earth than the others, but still pretty and cute in her own way.

And her? She had no one to call a friend, except maybe Ryle, who'd been kind and sweet, but now? Emilia was in the picture and she'd be sitting in a corner, alone and too dumbfounded to know how to talk with this woman from New York.

She was pitying herself, and she hated that.

What a mess.

~*~

Early the next morning, Jazzi's walkie-talkie woke her when Ryle's voice interrupted her sleep.

"Jazzi, hope I'm not waking you this early, but just got a call from Emilia that she's landed and headed our way. Said she'd be here in about an hour. I hope you'll join me in welcoming my friend. Paddy's promised to make a sumptuous breakfast."

Jazzi rolled over and pulled the covers over her head. Not what she wanted to hear this morning.

Yet her manners and like of Ryle urged her to get out of her mood and *move*. She sat up in bed. Okay, if she had to do this, then she'd do it with a bang and put on a show of confidence even if her insides quivered like Jell-O. She'd be polite and as warm as she could be, but that didn't mean she had to be chatty.

Jazzi's shower took ten minutes, another fifteen to prepare her hair, then she walked to the closet and studied her small selection of outfits. She touched the aquamarine formal dress Amy had insisted she buy.

No. Way too much.

The classy outfit with its sharp details in navy and white and gold buttons?

No. Too stiff and business-like.

She ran her fingers over several others before stopping at the white sundress with its touches of soft blue and yellow flowers giving it a spring-like, country feel, yet—she thought—was warm and friendly.

This was the one. Not what she usually wore for everyday, but it would be perfect to meet this paragon of Ryle's. Hopefully, she would look like a professional manager of the country bed and breakfast in a mountain state.

Dressed, Jazzi stared at herself in the full length mirror then nodded her head. She'd do.

Drawing in a long breath, she headed downstairs. Ryle was pacing back and forward, stopping to stare out a window now and then. He must have heard her coming, because he turned just as they both heard the smooth sound of a limousine pulling into the driveway. But he didn't take his eyes off of Jazzi as she approached him.

"I think I hear Emilia's car."

"Limousine, no doubt. Jazzi, you look amazing. And..." He paused, a confused expression crossing his face.

"I thought I should look a little more presentable to meet your friend from New York. In fact, I will dress like this each time we meet

84

our customers."

"I like it. Very much."

The doorbell rang, but for a second Ryle ignored it, his gaze still focused on Jazzi.

"Shouldn't we answer that?" Was that breathlessness in her voice? *Calm down,* she instructed herself. *It wouldn't do. At all.* "Ryle?"

"I agree. We should dress up every time we meet a customer."

"I plan to." She smiled at him, the nervousness in her seething for relief.

An impatient doorbell—if doorbells could sound impatient—blared into their ears again, and Ryle's hand touched hers as she reached to answer the door.

She pulled hers back immediately, but she caught the enlightening expression on Ryle's face, and then it was gone. He opened the door.

In stepped the most beautiful woman Jazzi had ever seen. She was tall and elegant, composed and confident, as she hugged Ryle and chattered for a few seconds before stopping mid-sentence and turning to gaze at Jazzi.

She didn't speak at first then moved toward Jazzi. "So this is the woman Ryle's bragged about so much—"

Ryle uttered something, but Emilia ignored him and kept talking. "—I would be totally jealous of you had it not been Ryle and I knew long ago we were not compatible for a romantic relationship but only ever be life-long friends. I must say, you are beautiful and quiet, and I like that. Isn't she beautiful, Ryle?" Emilia asked but didn't move away from Jazzi.

Jazzi heard a tiny chuckle, almost like a choking sound, and knew Ryle felt cornered. Not fair to put him on the spot like that. What if he thought her ugly, or worse, ordinary?

"I'm sure, if I know him even a little, that he is too kind to say otherwise." Jazzi motioned to the chauffeur who'd carried Emilia's two luggage bags. "Please set them there, and we'll get them to Miss Pavlo's room. If you want to follow me, Emilia, I'll take you there now."

Ryle's friend nodded but spoke to him. "I like her. I think we're going to be very good friends."

Jazzi was headed to the stairs but caught Ryle's remark when he spoke, and glanced back.

"Don't overwhelm her, Emilia. I won't allow that."

"I just bet you wouldn't." Emilia gave Ryle a peck on the cheek. "I'll see you in a bit as soon as I change."

Jazzi faced the stairs again and didn't look back. She kept climbing.

Chapter Eight

Ryle stared at the two women who were climbing the stairs. Two beautiful women, but only one sent a sense of confusion to his brain. Why hadn't he noticed how stunning Jazzi looked before? And those eyes of hers.

He shook his head. He couldn't allow himself to get sidetracked over an employee. There was too much to do including getting that box opened that was hidden in the office safe.

Ten minutes later, Jazzi joined him, followed shortly afterward by Emilia.

"You said you had a box that needed opened, so important, I assume, you had me fly clear to West Virginia to do this for you?"

"Because this is a private matter. I didn't want to use anyone locally. I don't know what is in the box."

"I see. A secret. What if it turns out to be nothing more than a long-ago child's treasure?"

"So be it. Can you open this or not?" Ryle placed the box on top of his desk.

"Let me take a look." Emilia pulled up a chair close to his desk and drew the box closer. "Hmmm. Interesting. There's no key lock, and I assume, that's why you called me."

They sat in silence for thirty minutes, before Emilia gave out a chuckle, fiddled with the thing for a few seconds longer and sat back in her chair. "There you go. Easy as pie once you know how the puzzle box works."

"Puzzle box?" Jazzi leaned forward.

"It's a creative thing that people use to keep most people from opening it. Those who are good at solving puzzles find it fun and relaxing to find the right way to get it open."

"Jazzi, you want to do the honors?"

"Oh, no, Ryle. You should open it. You own the bed and breakfast."

"Let's not fuss, children. I'll do it." Emilia laughed.

"No, thanks. I'll do it." Ryle tugged a little on the box and lifted the lid. He stared down into the box until Emilia moved restlessly.

"What is it?"

Lifting out a small, homemade journal, quite a few crumbly, yellowed papers, a tiny, shabby and crudely made doll, and an old leather journal, Ryle spread them across his desk. "Maps, looks like some writing about this place—maybe—what's in this?"

Both Jazzi and Emilia leaned forward. Jazzi reached for the homemade journal, opened it and turned pages. "It looks like a child's journal. Scribblings and a few rough drawings."

"A child's? May I see?"

After Jazzi handed it to Emilia, the lawyer held it up to the light. "Interesting. Whoever reads through this will no doubt be quite entertained."

"It's also very sad." Jazzi leaned closer to stare at the small scribblings. "Something a child might love doing, especially if they didn't have many things to keep them happy."

"Why would you think that?"

Jazzi nodded at the box and items. "Because these things look like they were a child's objects.

Saved and cherished by, perhaps, a poor child. A child who kept whatever they could. Why? I have no idea, but I hope we can find out."

Ryle spoke up, interrupting the women's contemplation. "Or it could be drawings from an adult who couldn't draw. I know I can't draw a straight line."

Emilia and Jazzi laughed.

Ryle ran a finger over the journal. "And who's to say these cheap items weren't saved because of the loss of a child? A mother's few cherished items to remember."

Jazzi and Emilia were staring at him, sobered, but Emilia spoke first. "As always, thinking of the alternate explanation. That very well is the explanation."

"Maybe." Ryle reached into the box again. "What's this?"

"It's a ring missing the stone." Emilia took it from him. "Inexpensive and small."

"A child's." Jazzi's gaze went from the band to the open handmade journal and the rough drawings on the page. "The child lost the stone and kept the ring band, perhaps hoping to find it again sometime. She knew her father would e able to put it together again.

"Why would you think that?" Emilia's tone wasn't mocking but curious.

Jazzi smiled at her. "Because that's what I would have done as a child."

Ryle stood, gathered the papers and moved to a small table close to the window. "Come and take a look with me."

Both women hurried over to the table and took chairs on either side of Ryle. The three bent over the papers, studying them.

Ryle lifted one of them. "Do you two think this

looks like a rough draft drawing of a big house?"

"You're right, Ryle. It does indeed." Emilia nodded. "It surely isn't the drawing of a talented artist."

"Do you suppose it's a blueprint of sorts?" Jazzi's gaze was skimming over the drawing. "It looks like..."

"Like what Jazzi?" Ryle skimmed the blueprint again to catch what she was seeing.

She glanced at him then pointed at the drawing. "Like your bed and breakfast. See..."

And with that, she pointed at the different rooms.

"You're right. There's some difference, but that could be because of changes through the years."

"That's what I thought." Jazzi nodded.

"What's this?" Ryle pointed at a small, square shape a short distance from the scrawled blueprint of the inn. A dark line stretched across the lawn from the inn to that square shape.

"I don't know. There's lettering here, but it's been rubbed away, or disintegrated."

"I haven't seen anything like that around here."

"Did you look specifically for such a thing?" Emilia spoke up giving Ryle a glance.

"How could I when I didn't even know it existed?" Ryle sat back in his chair. "Jazzi, I have some business things I need to talk about with Emilia this afternoon. We're going to walk around a bit while I do so. Would you like to go over these papers for me and see what you can spot?"

"I'd love to. May I use your office?"

"You know you can. Just lock up when you leave it." Ryle and Emilia stood. "I made dinner reservations at Apple Blossoms for us three this evening at six."

Jazzi nodded, and Ryle gave her a quick smile then left the room with Emilia by his side.

~*~

"I'm pretty sure this place is going to be one of the best investments you've ever made, my friend."

In spite of Emilia's fussing over the phone last night about heading to the boondocks, Ryle could tell she was enjoying herself.

"This is beautiful country. I didn't realize West Virginia was so...so stunning."

"Of course, you didn't. You've never been here." Ryle locked arms with his best friend. Going through college, he'd fought like the dickens to keep his grades up topnotch. Second rate hadn't been his first choice, but when it had come down to him or Emilia, he'd given in and purposely missed that last test. It was just enough to cause him to slip behind her a half of a percent. She'd topped him out, and he hadn't minded at all. Her tear-drenched eyes at his generosity had been worth it. Her family would have been heartbroken had she not taken that place, and that had been the act that had placed him forever in their good graces.

Well, that and rescuing the Pavlo fortune. Which was nothing compared to giving place to her in highest grades.

That was all in the past, and he couldn't care less now.

"I told you about the mayor and what he said about putting a stop on my proceeding with the opening."

"You did. Has he made contact again?"

"No, he hasn't. Not a word. But that's one reason I made that reservation at Apple

Blossoms—you'll love the place. He usually eats there on Friday evenings. I wanted you to be able to size him up to determine how to handle him."

She faked a yawn. "I hardly think a small-town mayor will overwhelm me."

"I think there's more going on than we realize. But I haven't a clue yet what it is."

Emilia patted his arm. "Don't you worry. We'll get to the bottom of it and stop this nonsense. No one messes with my best friend and gets away with it."

"Vicious woman." Ryle laughed.

"You've got that right." She pulled away from him. "Let's see if we can find that building that was on the blueprint. After that, I need to do some work on the computer I can't put off. Then it's off to dinner at that Apple Blossoms restaurant."

"You'll like it."

"And what about Jazzi?"

"What about her?"

Emilia waggled her brows at him. "She's a stunning looker."

"And a very hard worker. I'm glad I hired her."

"But—"

"But nothing. We work together, respect each other and get along fine. That's it, and the subject is dropped." He gave her a severe look.

She moved away from him, but he heard her mutter. "For now."

~*~

Jazzi went over the papers that had been in the box with a magnifying glass she'd found in Ryle's desk drawer. Then she grabbed a large sheet of paper and sketched out a rough blueprint of the current bed and breakfast. She outlined any room that wasn't in the original blueprint.

- The basement seemed much smaller in the older blueprint.
- There was some kind of dark mark on one basement wall. What it was, she had no clue.
- The kitchen had been expanded—it looked like—after the bed and breakfast had been built. How much later was the question.
- This older version had not had bathrooms.

She sat back after listing her thoughts and stared down at the papers, tapping them. It wasn't much and this list might mean nothing, but who knew?

Stretching, she gathered them together and walked toward Ryle's desk to lock them up. She glanced out the window, and in the distance, near the wood line a figure stood staring at the house.

In the window where she was?

A trespasser?

Or the man who'd stared in her window days ago, scaring the daylights out of her? Someone she didn't want to see ever again? Someone who'd destroy what she was building here?

Security. A peaceful, happy life. Home.

~*~

There was a knock on Jazzi's door as she prepared to dress that evening. "Who is it?"

Which was a stupid question given it could only be one of two people on the property—not counting Paddy. She opened the door.

"May I come in? I cannot decide on what to wear tonight. This one...or this one? One's too formal, I think, but this one is too casual. Oh, dear, I didn't bring enough clothing. Help me decide." Emilia's plea was too earnest, as if pleading for her life.

Jazzi was pretty sure Ryle's friend was reaching out to her, not because she actually needed the help, but to encourage Jazzi's confidence in her. If that was the case, she'd do her best. She eyed the two garments. Hmmm. "If you shed the jacket on this one, and here, wear this black belt with your red dress. You do have black pumps with you?"

Emilia nodded. "Always."

"Then use this..." Jazzi grabbed one of her own black scarves and thrust it at Emilia. "And you'll be awesome. Perfect for a Friday night in Appleton."

"Wow. That was good, and I love the difference those touches give this dress." Emilia settled on Jazzi's bed. "What are you wearing?"

"I'm torn between this deep green—which I think is too dark for me. I'm not very good at choosing what to wear—or this pink? The skirt has a light brown lace overlay which tones down too much pink or this green skirt and patterned top."

"Girl, you just chose for me, and I couldn't have done it better. Tonight, go with the pink, although that shade of green will be lovely against those blue eyes of yours. And if you have brown heels, wear them."

"My sister has picked out most of my outfits after I decided to stay in Appleton."

Emilia's brows lifted. "You haven't lived here all your life?"

"No. I was raised here, but ran away and was gone for five years. I just came back last year. I found out I like it here after all."

"You do a lot of traveling?"

Jazzi snickered. "Hardly. I did rebelling. Almost ruined my life, but I finally, I think, got my head on straight. Ryle gave me this job, and I love it. I can't thank him enough for believing in me."

Emilia was quiet a moment. "He always helps people."

"I know."

"You do?"

Jazzi nodded. "He's always so helpful to everyone. His friends adore him."

"I meant, that's his business."

"His business? I thought—"

"He's smart, but quiet, doesn't pry in others' business, and expects the same respect. I've never seen him fall for a place like he has this community. In spite of denying it to Ryle's face, I was anxious to see Appleton for myself." She rose. "I've got to get ready. Don't want him waiting and growling at me."

Jazzi watched the woman hurrying out of her room then smiled. As if Ryle would lose his temper with her.

~*~

Ryle and Emilia sat in the front of Ryle's car, with Jazzi insisting on sitting in the back which, for some reason, irritated him. He'd refused the use of Emilia's limousine declaring that it would attract too much attention. If they went, they'd go in his smaller car, and Emilia had given in.

When Ryle pulled into the driveway of Apple Blossoms, Emilia spoke. "It's homey, but has a classy look to it."

"Wait till you taste the food."

"I'm looking forward to it. I figured we'd have a selection of bear meat and possum."

"Snob." Ryle stepped out of the car and headed to the other side to open the doors for Emilia and Jazzi then held out both arms. "Shall we? Let's hope there's no trouble."

"Why should there be? We won't allow it. Not while eating. Afterwards, then the gloves can come off."

Emilia sounded so outrageously tough that both Ryle and Jazzi laughed. "Can you believe this woman is really as gentle as a lamb?"

"I don't know. Not sure I'd like to meet her in a dark alley."

"What would we be doing in a dark alley, my new friend?"

Jazzi didn't answer, and Ryle changed the subject as they entered the restaurant. Manny met them in the lobby.

"Miss Jazzi. Ryle. We're happy you could join us tonight. And who is this lovely lady?" His gaze switched to Emilia.

"Emilia Pavlo, a friend from New York, Manny."

"How is the remodeling coming along?"

"Everything is almost completed." Ryle spoke up as he held out an arm to Emilia. "We are already booked through Christmas and hoping we have more business than we can handle."

"Is Starli playing tonight?" Jazzi loved watching Starli at the piano. She didn't always understand some of the more classical music, but she enjoyed it.

"Yes, she is. She's on break right now, but will return in a few minutes. With her toddler, she isn't able to entertain us as much as she used to." Manny held out his arm to Jazzi. "Come, my dear, let me escort you."

Ryle watched as Jazzi, who looked fabulous in that pink get up, took Manny's arm, the surprise feeling of wishing he was the one escorting her taking *him* by surprise.

Manny placed before them three elegantly created menus, and a casual glance at Emilia, had Ryle smiling. She was impressed. Good.

They had given their orders and prepared to enjoy Starli's piano selections, when Mayor Slater and his ever-present assistant, approached their table. From the inside of his jacket, he withdrew an envelope and tossed it down in front of Ryle, barely missing the water glass.

"I was going to have my secretary put this in the mail tonight, but remembered you usually ate here on Fridays. Since, as usual, my memory is excellent and you're here, you might as well take it and save the town the postage." He straightened and leaned back on his heels, giving the odd impression of a boasting, loud rooster.

Ryle wanted to laugh, but he wasn't in the habit of making a bad situation worse. But he did open his mouth to speak when Emilia stood. She snatched up the envelope.

"Thank you, but please don't interrupt us again while we're relaxing over dinner."

The mayor glanced at her then away as if she was of no interest, and Ryle saw the subtle stiffening of her body.

Whoa. The mayor was about to learn who he was now dealing with.

"I hope you understand that's a court order and you are under obligation to follow the decree. Do not attempt to open your business until this matter is resolved." The mayor drew his brows together, lowered his head, morphing into, Ryle thought, unable to keep from seeing the likeness, a belligerent bull.

Ryle waited.

"I'm sorry, who are you?"

Ryle figured she knew who the man was, but

it was a good ploy.

"I'm the mayor of Appleton, Melvin Slater. Who are you?"

"Emilia Pavlo, Attorney at Law, from the Pavlo Attorneys of New York."

She hadn't explained her company was the biggest and best in the state, taking for granted *everyone* knew that, even those from West Virginia.

The expression on the mayor's face was beyond a price. When he spoke it didn't add to his importance any. "You're a daughter to—"

Emilia cut him off and held out a business card. "I'm the founder and creator of my business, Sir. And now, I'd like to get back to my dinner and friends. If you have anything else you need to communicate, please go through my office."

She sat then but looked up for a final dismissal. "We will be checking this suspicious claim and give you our answer. I expect it will all be resolved before the end of next week."

With a glance at Manny, she nodded, and he hurried over to usher the two intruders to their own table.

"You did say the Garlic and Rosemary Smothered Cornish Game Hen is divine, didn't you, Ryle?"

"I didn't describe it quite like that, but it is just that good. Almost as good as my Chicken with Cider and Bacon Sauce and a side of broccoli plate will be." He winked at Jazzi. "Or Jazzi's Chicken Scaloppini with the Sugar Snap Peas, Asparagus and Lemon Salad."

"Are you saying your choices are the better ones?" Emilia didn't frown, but it was close to one.

"I'm teasing, Emilia. No matter what you order at Apple Blossoms, you'll be pleased."

"Good." Emilia sat back in her chair. "Who is the tall blonde at the piano? Is that your friend—you called her Starli? She's beautiful, with an inner quietness about her that is mysterious."

"She is all that. Very talented. She's married to a good friend of ours: Sir Joel Peterman-Blair. He's Manny's nephew from England."

"A Knight? I'm impressed."

"This place burned down awhile back, but the Deluca Construction Company built it back. After Starli and Joel were married, she appointed Manny as the new manager because they travel so much from here to England, she knew she couldn't do both. Besides, she's pretty popular with invitations to play at events. She likes to do that particularly for worthy causes she believes in."

"Don't forget about Joel. He's an international success as a chef who's used his talent as such to help third world countries. That's why he was knighted." Jazzi's comment caused Emilia's eyes to widen.

"I'd love to meet them."

"You will when we have an open house party. They've promised to be there—in fact, Apple Blossoms will be providing the food for that night."

"You really do have a tight group of friends in this community. No wonder you love it so much."

"You haven't heard the whole story. You know our friend Toni-Deluca Douglas' company is doing the repairs to the bed and breakfast, and, get this, Jazzi's sister has already completed the preparations for the planting along with all the indoor plants."

"Impressive. I'll definitely return for this opening party just so I can meet all your friends."

"I expect no less from you." Ryle gripped Emilia's hand and squeezed it gently. "I want you there at what might end up being my very favorite inves—"

Ryle didn't finish. He wasn't quite ready to let Jazzi know what all he was involved in.

~*~

Jazzi was enjoying herself immensely. Emilia and Ryle's entertaining remarks, their close friendship—which did make her want to squirm a bit—and their knowledge of a more elite world fascinated her. And she liked that neither of them forced her into conversation, except for an occasional remark or question to her.

Listening to them gave her an opportunity to learn more about Ryle and their friendship.

Her mind kept going back over Emilia's words at the inn about Ryle. His business was in helping people. What had she meant? She knew Ryle was quiet and spoke rarely about his previous life before becoming a part of Appleton. And she knew about the occasional periods when he'd leave and be gone for a variable degree of time. She'd never questioned him—it was his business. She didn't want to talk about her past so why press Ryle on his?

She looked up as Manny, along with a server, arrived. As the server began placing their food, with Manny quietly making a comment, Jazzi realized how well Manny handled the restaurant. All class, he was. Probably from that British background.

It was forty minutes later, when they'd finished and sat quietly listening to Starli's music, that Amy and Toby stopped by their table.

Amy leaned down to give Jazzi a quick hug after the introductions. "I got a phone call from

Mom and Dad. They're coming home for a few weeks and want us to spend time with them. They were totally thrilled that you'll be here. So keep some open dates."

When her sister turned to speak to Emilia, Jazzi looked down at her hands, fingers clutched into tight fists. It wouldn't be one family dinner or outing. They'd want more than that, and she wasn't sure she was ready for more from them.

A hand stretched across the short distance between their chairs and touched her hand. A husky voice lowered to a whisper. "Don't worry about it now. You'll figure it out one day at a time. You know, you are *very* busy at the inn."

Jazzi looked at Ryle, and he winked. She allowed herself a moment of relaxation. He was right. Why worry now about how much her parents would demand from her? One day at a time sounded good to her.

Her nod at him caused his lips to widen, and he stood. "I hate to break up this gossip fest, but Jazzi and I want to show Emilia around town a bit before heading back to the inn."

It was only when they'd stepped outside Apple Blossoms that Ryle asked, "Want to stroll around town, Emilia? Can you walk in those sky-high shoes of yours?"

Emilia gave him a scornful glance, but the smile on her lips belied the glance.

He turned to his manager. "You don't mind, do you, Jazzi?"

"Of course not. I love walking."

They walked arm in arm until they came to Toby's *Undiscovered Treasures* shop, and when Ryle and Emilia would have moved on, Jazzi stood still, staring in the window at the lamp that was featured in the window scene. It was gorgeous, an antique, and Jazzi was wondering if it would fit in the upstairs corridor on the stand which at present held nothing. With a small basket holding chocolate mints, it might just serve as the thing...

"Coming, Jazzi?"

Ryle had turned to glance back.

"Give me just a minute. I'll catch up."

He nodded and moved on.

It was then that a voice spoke from the corner of the shop.

"If it isn't Jazmine Sanderson, aka 'Purple Jaz'."

She knew that voice—unfortunately—and Jazzi's insides quivered. Not from excitement, but from fear.

Her past had just caught up with her.

~*~

Ryle suspected Jazzi's suddenly troubled face inside Apple Blossoms had been from Amy's declaration of their parents' return.

Ryle could read between the lines. And he'd automatically—without realizing he was doing so—had leaped to reassure his manager that she'd be okay.

He knew she hid things from everyone, including himself, but then he did the same thing, so he could understand, in part, her motivation to do so. To reveal his past, meant questions, looks and comments he didn't want to deal with, and he suspected Jazzi felt the same.

But there was more to her reluctance than normal. Whatever her past had been, she was afraid. He had no idea of what, but when it was time, he felt within himself, she would reveal what she could. For now...he'd be there to encourage.

He turned at the corner of the street to look back at her again and was startled to see her talking to a big—hawking-big—man. He faltered. Should he go back for her? But then, she abruptly turned and hurried toward him, the man she left behind walking slowly away.

"Is she all right, Ryle?" Emilia's concerned voice captured his attention.

"I think so."

"You care, don't you?"

He swept a glance across his friend's face. "Well, yeah, I do. She's my friend."

Emilia smirked at him but spoke to Jazzi as she hurried up. "We were about to go rescue you from that huge man. A friend?"

"No."

Jazzi's quickly-spoken denial alerted Ryle something was wrong.

"He...he wanted...he wanted directions." She reached for Ryle's arm and thrust hers through it. "If we want to see the lake before it gets totally dark out here, we ought to move on."

Ryle patted her hand and held out his left arm to Emilia. "You're right. Ready?"

That had been no lost traveler needing directions. Someone had threatened her, and it sent flood tides of anger through him.

No one would get by with threatening Jazzi.

His manager.

Chapter Nine

Jazzi was sure her heart was ready to explode from her chest. But one look at the man's face stiffened her spine a bit. "What do you want, Maxy?"

"The boss needs your help in a little something he has going."

"I'm not doing that stuff anymore. I've changed and living a totally different life now. I'm not going back, Maxy. Tell Frankie I'm done with all that."

"Is that so? Just forgettin' all your old friends who took you in off the street and gave you something good to do. Is that it?"

"Something like that." She stared up at him. "People change, Maxy. I've changed. I like it here and don't want to go back to the big city. Ever."

"Don't worry about that. The job is here in this hick state. One or two simple things, and it's easy, peasy. You're done. We'll leave you alone." The man's gaze drilled into hers in spite of the rolls of fat surrounding his.

"I can't. Please let me alone."

"Boss isn't going to be happy with your answer."

"I don't care. Tell him to get someone else. I've got to go before my friends come rescue me."

The man's gaze switched to Ryle and Emilia a block away who stood staring at them.

"Those your friends?"

"Yes."

"I hope nothing happens to them."

A sword of fear thrust itself deep within her.

"Why would you say that? This is *me* saying no. They have nothing to do with it."

"Yeah, right. I'll tell that to the boss." But the man's tone indicated what he really thought about it.

"Go away, Maxy. Leave me alone and my friends. Go. And please don't come back." Jazzi turned and walked away, knowing Maxy wouldn't hurt her.

Not yet anyway.

But the words he tossed at her retreating back did scare her.

"Don't you go talking to that FBI agent. You hear me? Frankie will know iffn you do."

She didn't answer, only kept walking, refusing to look back, refusing to give him the satisfaction of knowing how afraid she was.

She really wasn't worried about herself. Not much. But it was her friends she didn't want drawn into this mess. She didn't want them hurt no matter what happened to her. No matter what she had to do to protect them. And she definitely didn't want them to know about her past life.

Jazzi's feet felt as if they were encased in cement as she trudged toward Ryle and Emilia.

"A friend, Jazzi?" Ryle patted her hand.

"No. He wanted directions." Jazzi turned her head so Ryle wouldn't see her tears.

~*~

It was nearing eleven when Jazzi, Emilia and Ryle reached the bed and breakfast. They'd strolled around the lake, laughing and talking—at least Ryle and Emilia had—and then headed home. As they entered the building, Ryle looked at Jazzi.

"Would you have time to do some research on this place at the library and courthouse tomorrow? If you could see what you can dig up, I'll study the map some more and call up some historians about the background."

"Sure. I'll be glad to do it."

At that moment the landline telephone in Jazzi's office rang, and the three looked at each other.

"Pretty late for someone to be calling." Ryle suggested and rubbed a hand over his hair.

"Maybe one of our friends?" Jazzi felt her knees go weak. Had Maxy already started his threatening measures on her friends?

"Well, while you two debate the subject of the phone ringing at eleven at night, I will answer it." Emilia marched to Jazzi's desk and lifted the phone. Her facial expression showed surprise then puzzlement. She held out the phone to Ryle. "It's for you."

"Who?"

"Have no idea."

"This is Ryle Sadler." He spoke into the receiver.

"You the man who bought that old bed and breakfast outside of Appleton?"

"I am."

"You the one remodeling it?"

"I am."

"I've got to tell you. We're thinking that place is haunted by the deaths."

"What do you mean? What deaths?" Ryle tried to keep the sharpness from his voice. "Who are you?"

"Never mind that. Strange things happened at that old place. If you want the truth, if you want to help all of us who want the truth—find the

truth. It's there. We know it. Help us, Mister."
And the phone went dead.

~*~

That had to be the secret. After relaying the information to Jazzi and Emilia, first Jazzi then Emilia had gone to their rooms. Now he paced back and forth in his own rooms. Was this why the mayor's secret informant was trying to keep Ryle from opening this place? Was the man on the phone tonight the one trying to stop him?

But that made no sense. If the man on the phone hadn't wanted him to open the bed and breakfast, then why had he called him, seemingly urging him to look for the truth?

What truth?

He felt the unusual—for him—pressure of a first time failure on his part, but he turned his mental back on that. If he failed, it wouldn't be for lack of giving it all he had.

Ryle walked back and forth in his room, thinking, thinking, thinking. He needed no lights. The moon lit up his room like a summer evening fading away to night. The outside land—all he could see—was illuminated into shadowy figures of monstrous guards of his property. Limbs on the trees shifted with the wind, the leaves whispering words he couldn't discern, whether warnings or soothing platitudes of encouragement.

Since when had he become so poetic?

Ryle shook his head and focused on the landscape before him.

Deer crossed his property, stopping to feed, raising their shapely heads to stare around then moving on into the forest. Once he was sure he saw a red fox trotting at the edge of the forest. And then he heard it again.

That loud, yet distant, agonizing scream, and

Ryle's eyes narrowed. It only came once, then the nighttime silence filled the air. Nothing else stirred. No other sound drifted to his ears.

A vague, dark figure appeared at the edge of the trees—so vague there was little that Ryle could discern about it. The figure didn't move, only seemed to stare at the bed and breakfast, quiet and unmoving...

Ryle turned and hit his outside veranda door that put him on the front part of his veranda, running, hoping to catch the figure. Grab him and hold him till the police could arrive. Or, at the least, question him.

But he wasn't able to.

The figure was gone.

Ryle shook his head. Was he losing his mind?

~*~

Jazzi was wide awake when the scream came. In fact, she had yet to close her eyes. Now she lay there, unmoving, listening, wondering if Emilia would find her way to her room. But no sound came of a door opening and feet shuffling to her room. Until...

The faint sound of a door slamming open somewhere and running feet speeding across the veranda, reached her ears. Every sound, every second of them was an excruciating pound inside her. She knew exactly what they meant and who made them. What she didn't know was why those sounds were made.

She sat up in bed, tempted to follow Ryle, to make sure he was all right, that he wasn't in trouble. But she didn't move for the longest time, and only when she heard his quiet footsteps return to his rooms, did she lie down again and shut her eyes.

Maxy's face laughed at her soundlessly

behind her eyelids, and she rolled over to bury her head into her pillows.

Whether she slept or not wasn't the question. Ryle was safe. For now. Sleep wasn't important.

~*~

Jazzi had no more than left for town to do the research he'd ask her to do today, when a Cadillac pulled into and drove up the driveway. Ryle knew immediately who the well-dressed, classy couple who emerged from the vehicle was. No one could have looked more like Amy Sanderson-Gibson than this woman.

Amy and Jazzi's mother.

Ryle stepped out onto the veranda and spoke. "You have to be Amy and Jazzi's parents, I'm assuming."

"You're assuming correctly, young man." The man was not overly tall—perhaps five ten or eleven, but his confident manner made up for his shorter height. The woman was slim and smaller—like Amy. The couple was as elegant as any royalty might have been.

"I'm sorry you've made the trip here. Jazzi left to attend to some bed and breakfast business. You just missed her."

"Actually, we came to see you."

"We're not open for business quite yet, but you're welcome to join me on the veranda. I'm sure I can find some of Jazzi's delicious lemonade. Or some tea if you prefer."

Mrs. Sanderson looked at her husband, beaming. "Jazzi always loved homemade lemonade. I'd love some."

"None for me, thanks." Mr. Sanderson shook his head.

"Then I'll be right back. Make yourself at home." Ryle hurried to the kitchen, speaking before he ever entered it. "Paddy, is there any of Jazzi's lemonade left? And do you have anything light I can offer her parents? They're on the veranda right now."

"Surprise guests, heh? Never let it be said that Paddy is not ready to serve at all hours." He went to a cupboard and lifted out a covered tray filled with cookies of all varieties. "A few of these should convince these people to go easy."

"What do you mean, Paddy?"

"Parents that slip in right after a child leaves are after one thing. Information. You watch what you say now, understand, Lad? Nothing to hurt our young lass."

"I'd never do that. I care too much about Jazzi." When had Paddy grown so fond of Jazzi? He was behaving like a protective father.

Paddy scooted the small serving plate filled with six or so of his cookie delights toward Ryle. "There you go, Lad. Remember now, careful with the words."

"I will be very careful." Lifting the tray filled with the cookies, drink and napkins, Ryle headed back outside. As he stepped out the door, he spoke. "Remodeling is finished. A couple more days of work in the basement, and we'll be good to go. Your daughter, Amy, has begun on the landscaping and helping Jazzi decorate the inside. Target date for opening is September tenth. Hopefully, a warm, non-rainy day for an outdoor evening meal. Once darkness approaches, we'll enjoy a concert of piano music from one of the best, then a tour of the place."

"You've got a business head on your shoulders, I've heard." Mr. Sanderson sounded pleased. "I take it Jazzi's working out well?"

Here it came. The reason for the visit. "Very

much so. She is smart and intuitive, always with a good attitude and willingness besides having a remarkable talent of knowing just how to help without being obnoxious."

Man and woman stared at him as if they couldn't believe him.

"Jazzi?" Mrs. Sanderson's voice sounded more like a croak.

"The very same one. She's not afraid to try new things, is interested in all aspects of the remodeling, and is amazing at the business end of the place."

"Ryle—may I call you by your first name?"

"Of course."

"Are you sure you should trust her with the business end? You are talking about the financial?"

"I am. Of course, I have an accountant who she reports to every month and a lawyer who keeps an eye on all my business dealings. But besides all that, Jazzi has proven herself capable and trustworthy."

"I'm not sure—"

"James, I'm not sure we should say anything." Mrs. Sanderson placed a hand on her husband's arm.

Her husband patted the hand but spoke anyway. "Yes, we should. You see, Ryle, when Jazzi ran away, she took five thousand dollars from us. It's not that we couldn't afford it or wouldn't have happily given it to her as a start, but it was the underhandedness of hers that hurt. We've never mentioned it to her, never asked for it back. Five thousand isn't much, but the fact is..."

The man's voice quivered and his wife carried on.

"The fact is, she was so nonchalant about it

all when she'd make very brief interactions with us, as if she didn't care or didn't realize how much we were hurt. We love her so much..."

This time it was the woman's voice that broke.

Ryle was silent for a moment thinking how to best answer these two broken-hearted parents.

"I can't answer for her past deeds, but from the time I met your daughter, I've felt the urge to encourage and help her. She's hurting for some reason, and blaming you, but I really do believe that she's coming around. She seems to feel at home here and enjoys the work. If you are praying folk, then do so. Give her space and allow her to come to you. And never cease loving her. She needs that more than anything."

Mr. Sanderson looked at his wife. "Not only a business man but a counselor too."

"I'm not meaning to overstep you. Just telling what I feel about the situation. And I know little, only what I've seen from Jazzi."

"She broke our hearts. We want our little girl back."

Mrs. Sanderson's tears were real, and Ryle's compassion burst into play. He wanted to assure them it would come, that they could rest easy, but it wasn't his to make the promise. Only Jazzi could do that, and he wasn't at all sure she would.

~*~

Jazzi stared down at the two papers lying on the passenger seat of the bed and breakfast's SUV. She'd found little at the courthouse, only a list of those who'd owned the place from the early 1800s. There were only three names on it. One of them she recognized easily—Maisie. One was unknown to her, but then that owner had lived a long time ago. She'd lived all her life here in Appleton, except for those five years, so it wasn't surprising she didn't know every owner on the list.

The second name she only knew because— she was guessing—there was a person living here in Appleton with a similar name. How could it not be an ancestor of the current person?

Then there were the library newspaper articles. Articles that had built questions in her mind.

An early 1900's article with a picture of Appleton's business district.

Another few about different historical buildings in the neighborhood.

In one article there was a list of men, and the man living now in Appleton who carried the similar name as the possible ancestor.

She started the SUV as the thought of the years she'd been gone from Appleton ran through her mind again. The faces of her parents sprang to life as a vivid flashing image. When she'd left at eighteen, she never figured she'd set foot in Appleton again, but here she was with a job she loved and enjoying life working at the bed and breakfast.

Why was that? She stared out the windshield as she drove and thought about it. Ryle was an excellent businessman, she could tell, just the few months she'd worked with him. He wasn't overbearing or bossy, and he didn't demand superfluous commands that weren't important, but when he did ask, he expected his wishes to be carried through.

It was a perfect fit for her, this job.

Her parents. Her mind circled back to them. Yeah, she loved them, she was pretty sure, but they were so clinging, she felt smothered. But the biggest complaint she'd had at eighteen, that they favored Amy above herself, well, now...now she knew it had been stupid.

Yes, they smothered. Amy had handled that well. She, on the other hand, had wanted a little more privacy, a little more trust. But then, had she given them any reason to trust her?

Not so much. Sneaking out at night, hanging with kids who were known to be trouble, skipping out on planned family outings, and when she had attended her attitude had been far from perfect.

She wanted to groan with the sudden realization that she'd been the one, not her parents, who'd created the problems, but she wasn't the groaning type.

But all that didn't mean she was ready to have them barging into her life with their smothering ways. Amy's warning—Amy would never have described it as such—the other night had filled her with no joy. Worry? Maybe. Anger? Not so much. Dread? Yeah, that had been it.

She didn't know what to do around them, what to say, how to act.

Jazzi turned onto the driveway of the bed and breakfast and knew that she'd have to face the dread face to face. Sooner than she'd planned.

Her parents had arrived.

~*~

Jazzi saw the car immediately after turning into the driveway, and her heart sank. She knew she'd have to deal with them, make amends, she reckoned, but she wasn't prepared today. At all. Maybe she should just back out and drive off somewhere.

What would that accomplish? Tomorrow or the next day or the day after that, the same problem would be facing her, demanding that reckoning. So she kept driving, and when she'd parked, she took her time gathering the papers and exiting the SUV.

She straightened and turned, prepared to head to the veranda...and a sudden blur of a delicate pink outfit slammed into her, as her mother threw her arms around her, not crying out 'thank God,' but giving every evidence she was overwhelmed.

And Jazzi's heart melted. She tried to keep it from doing so, fought it, but her arms betrayed her as they slowly, carefully wrapped around her mother.

It was several seconds before her mother drew back, still clutching Jazzi's shoulders, but staring up at her. "It is so good to see you. We've missed you."

No reprimands? No scolding? No looks of pleading or accusations?

Nothing but love shown in her mother's eyes.

"You're looking well, Mother."

"As you are." Her mother slipped an arm through Jazzi's and tugged. "Come. Ryle's been talking about the bed and breakfast and fed us some of the most delicious cookies I've ever eaten. We didn't meet this chef of yours, but he is a cook..."

Jazzi didn't have to talk. Her mother chattered the whole way to the veranda, and she let her. She looked up as her father walked up to her, took hold of her shoulders and stared at her. He didn't speak, but Jazzi saw the approval in his eyes, and then he drew her close for a hug.

~*~

Jazzi had given in to her parents request to have dinner at their home that night. She'd hesitated, wanting to refuse, yet reluctant because of their reaction to seeing her this afternoon. Surprisingly, their reunion had been pleasant and low key. But, now...now that she and Ryle were almost at her parents' home, she was having second thoughts.

They'd included Ryle, and when they'd learned of Emilia, they'd included her, but she'd called off. Too much work she wanted to catch up on. So here she was, riding in the bed and breakfast SUV along with Ryle, who was as silent as that moon skidding slowly across the dark sky.

"I'm sorry you were roped into coming tonight."

Ryle glanced at her, a small smile widening those lips of his. "No worries. Your parents seem like a decent sort and caring. That's a big thing for me. Besides, I wanted to come with you."

"Why?"

He was quiet for a few seconds. "I didn't want you to be the odd-man-out. I wanted to be there for you in case you decided you needed to go home early. After all, we do have quite a bit to finish up before opening day."

Jazzi laughed. "You always know the right thing to say. And I am thankful you agreed to come. I'm always nervous around them for some reason."

Ryle didn't speak again until he turned onto their driveway and drove slowly up to the house. "I really don't think you have to be. I got the impression this afternoon that they care an awful lot about you. I doubt there's much you could do to change that."

He parked, swung open his door and walked around to open her door. When he took her hand to help her out, he spoke softly. "Relax and have a good time. You're smart, doing well at a job you chose, and beautiful, Jazzi Sanderson. Any sane parent would be proud to have a daughter like you."

Jazzi didn't answer him. She couldn't. An unexpected emotion of confidence seemed to be swirling inside her, almost choking her up, but not quite.

Was there ever a boss like Ryle Sadler?

~*~

Ryle studied the Sanderson family. Toby Gibson, sitting with James Sanderson and seemingly as much a part of them as the two sisters, looked as comfortable as any of the rest. He could tell James and Heather Sanderson loved Amy's husband as much as their girls.

Jazzi seemed far more confident than she'd been in the SUV on the way here, and he was happy for that. Her face and body were relaxed, and though she didn't radiate the bubbly personality that Amy showed, she was serene and elegant in that long rusty-brown skirt and floral top, her hair sleeked back.

He'd given Emilia a faint nod and look when Jazzi had worried about what to wear earlier today. And true to her nature, Emilia had offered to help her choose her outfit.

She'd succeeded far beyond Ryle's expectations. Few women could do justice to the look Emilia had encouraged Jazzi to wear. Tall, rail-thin, a facial bone structure that could carry that sleek look and make it look as divinely elegant as Jazzi was doing.

She glanced at him. He gave her a wide approving smile, and Ryle saw her cheeks turn a faint pink.

No matter what happened with the bed and

breakfast, he'd done a good thing in hiring Jazzi Sanderson.

Though the Sandersons had kept the meal simple and tasteful, it was still luxurious. But the atmosphere was a peaceful one, with little tension, quite a bit of conversation and laughter. All in all, it had gone off perfectly. He had no doubt Mrs. Sanderson wouldn't have had it any other way.

Ryle stood by the unlit fireplace watching the others, listening as Toby and James Sanderson argued mildly over some business aspect. Amy and her mother were chattering nonstop, while Jazzi sat quietly with them, saying little, but seemingly enjoying their conversation, if her smiles and occasionally lit-with-laughter eyes were anything to go on.

"Come over here, Ryle, and settle this question. I'm sure, if my instincts are right, that you are a man of business who knows the best way to handle this situation." James Sanderson motioned for Ryle to come.

He did as summoned, but slowly, laughing and disagreeing with the man's argument. "I'm not sure I do agree, Mr. Sanderson. I'm afraid that every man has a right to choose what he thinks is best for him, his life and his family. To choose, or be forced, into a job against his will, no matter the past precedence, is pushing that person into a place of unhappiness and perhaps unsuccess."

Mr. Sanderson eyed him, frowning a little. "You really think a son or grandson has no responsibility to carry on his father's work, to make it a continued success?"

"That's a delicate subject, Sir, and I understand where you're coming from. If it's at all possible, and agreeable, then by all means, a son should do so."

When Mr. Sanderson would have spoken, Ryle held up a hand. "But if that child has no talent, no desire and no liking for that kind of work, what good would it do for him to attempt to carry on the success his father gained? Under pressure he might be pushed to agree, then fail and ruin not only the business, but his own life. What would that profit? Wouldn't it be better for the young man to seek out his own desires in work, to use the talents he was given at birth?"

"And what then, if the child is a ne'er do well and does nothing?" Mr. Sanderson smiled a bit.

"Then I would think something was wrong somewhere, probably lying at the parents' door. They either didn't encourage, discipline and train the child right, or he inherited some trait from a long ago ancestor. I can't think of another reason."

"Are you saying that when a child fails, it's the parents' fault?"

"I'm afraid I am to a certain degree. Who can say how and what training from parents is good and right? Some parents do all they honestly know how to do and still the child may never follow that training. Humans are so...difficult."

"You've got that last statement right, at least. Not sure I agree with everything else." James Sanderson cast a glance at the women sitting across the room.

Ryle wondered if he was thinking of Jazzi. "You have much to be thankful for, Sir. Two beautiful daughters and a son-in-law who's successful and happy at what he does, besides having a wonderful marriage."

"I know I have with Amy and now, Toby. I'm

keeping fingers crossed about Jazzi."

"Give her some leeway and trust. I think you'll find Jazzi has found a plan for her life. She'll make you proud one of these days, I'm sure of it."

Though Sanderson's face showed a bit of doubt, he nodded. "I hope you're right. I really do."

Chapter Ten

Monday morning, Jazzi peeked into Ryle's office where he was sitting at his desk.

"Good morning, Ryle. You're up early. I can smell divine things being prepared in the kitchen."

"That must be why I keep getting distracted." Ryle looked up. "Come in, Jazzi.

Chuckling, Jazzi stepped into the room and sat in one of the chairs. "I think Paddy was a great choice."

"I do too. You think we have time to talk about all that's going on?"

"I do."

"Good. First, what's happening with the bed and breakfast? The rest of the furniture we still need is being delivered today, right?"

"Yes. All furniture should be here at eleven." Jazzi nodded. "Toby is delivering all the antique-ish pieces we've chosen from his shop which should help fill in the spots that need that special personal, warm touch. Since Amy and her crew started a day early, she thinks they'll finish the outside work today sometime. She'll be free in the morning to help me with the décor."

"And, tell me again, what all her crew is doing."

"Flower and vegetable gardens outlined and flower gardens prepared around the inn and along the driveway. Mulch, stones spread where needed. Bulbs planted for spring. Bushes and trees, that she knows will have time to settle in their new home before winter, will be planted. And anything else that she has on her list to make this place look like a million dollars."

"Perfect. I'm glad you've kept on top of these things." Ryle leaned back in his chair. "Now what about the third person we decided to hire? We agreed to have him or her work as a general assistant to you, right?"

"Yes. We have two applicants coming this morning."

"Could you do the interviewing? You know what you'll need and want from her."

"I can."

"All this sounds great, Jazzi. Let's talk about what's happening here."

Jazzi nodded. "We have the screams in the night and have no idea where they're coming from, why or who is screaming. There's the man who keeps showing up at the edge of the yard, staring at the inn—or us."

"And the man who called with vague information begging me to find the truth." Ryle clicked off the things even as he jotted on a tablet.

"And the wood puzzle box we found hidden. What do some of the things mean?"

"And who is trying to stop us from opening the inn?" Ryle straightened, his lips set in a firm line. "Someone behind the mayor."

"Definitely that." Jazzi nodded. "Do you think he's in cahoots with this person or innocent and trying to do what's right?"

"I think he knows him, whether he knows if the person is correct in his accusation or if he's standing with the person because of political or friendship sake."

"Will Emilia be able to stop him?"

"Of course." Emilia's voice preceded her entrance

into the office. "My detectives are working on getting the information I need, and thanks to Jazzi, who found all the deeds the courthouse has on past ownership of the inn. It will take me a day or so to put everything together. Then we begin putting a stop to this nonsense. After that, I'm afraid I'll be flying back to New York."

"So soon?" Just when Jazzi was beginning to feel comfortable around the woman.

Emilia smiled. "I'll be back for the opening, Jazzi. I wouldn't miss it."

"And who is this lovely lady?"

The voice sent chills through Jazzi. The man she feared more than her previous associates in New York. How had he managed to enter the inn without anyone hearing his vehicle or him?

Jazzi didn't want to look up. Didn't want the man to see her, but it was too late to speculate on idle wishes now. Unless he'd become blind since the last time he was here, he had to have already seen her.

She could run...No, that was an idiotic thought.

Pulling in a deep breath, she looked up—

Lincoln Tillis was not staring at her. His gaze was on Emilia Pavlo, and by the looks of that gaze, he was entranced. Maybe she could slip out before he noticed her.

She stood and edged toward the door.

"I'd like to speak with all of you."

This time he did look at her, and Jazzi froze. She glanced at Ryle, hoping he would intervene and politely tell the man she had too much work to do to sit around listening to him—or worse, answering questions.

No such luck.

Ryle was standing, quiet, and studying the

man at the door. He looked at Jazzi. "Would you mind getting us some coffee? And tell Paddy we may be held up a bit for breakfast."

Before Jazzi could agree, Linc spoke up. "Breakfast?"

"Are you inviting yourself?"

Emilia didn't smile, but there was something about her voice. Was she upset that the man had interrupted them? Or did she see something in him that set *her* alarm bells ringing?

No, it was more as if she was surprised.

Surprised? Maybe. Taken aback? Emilia sure looked like it.

Jazzi didn't wait to hear Linc's answer as she hurried out the door, but she did catch Emilia's continuing remark.

"I didn't think you would be—would be—"

What was Emilia trying to say?

She hadn't reached the kitchen when Ryle caught up with her.

"I don't suppose you heard them, did you?" His voice was lit with a smile.

"Not all of it, but I caught enough, I do believe they were both struck with each other."

Ryle gave her a sideways glance. "I think you're right. We'll give them five minutes or so to come to their senses. I'm going to get some air outside for a minute then join you back in my office."

"Suits me."

As much as she'd laughed at the sparks between Tillis and Emilia, she'd just take her time getting back to Ryle's office. Maybe, just maybe, Lincoln Tillis would be gone by then.

~*~

Ten minutes later, Ryle eyed the man still standing in his office. He didn't dislike the man, but he didn't exactly appreciate the fear he saw on Jazzi's face every time Tillis came around. He hoped she'd reappear, but he wouldn't blame her if she didn't. Whatever she'd been involved in—or knew—from her past, he would stand with her if need be. He wasn't about to let something happen to her when she was trying to turn her life around.

Not with his lawyer—the best in New York state—and his money.

He switched his gaze to his best friend. Emilia still looked star-struck, and that was something he'd never, never seen on her face before. She'd dated, but never gotten close to any of them. At least, not to where she looked like she did now.

Tillis raised a hand. "I'm not trying to start trouble, and I sincerely hope Jazzi is not involved in what I need to talk with you about. Not because I know her and can vouch for her integrity but because I can see how much you both care for her. That kind of loyalty means you know her better than I do, and I want that loyalty to be justified."

"Very well. You can talk, but, you're right, we are very loyal to her."

Emilia took a seat, but Ryle noticed Tillis didn't bother to sit.

Left standing, the man moved a few steps farther inside the room and leaned against a wall. "I'd like for Jazzi to be in here before I begin."

"Why?" Emilia's forehead creased slightly with a frown.

"Because she needs to know what I want, what I have to tell you."

"And who are you?"

His lawyer wasn't about to let up on the

pressure. At least she wasn't so enthralled with the man, she'd forgotten her training.

"I don't want to repeat myself. If Jazzi joins us that will keep me from doing so."

Ryle spoke up. "Then I'll go get her."

"Shall I?" Emilia glanced at Ryle.

"You stay and entertain *him*." Ryle smiled then, knowing full well Tillis and Emilia wanted that, whether either would ever acknowledge it.

He called out as he approached the kitchen. "Jazzi?"

She was sitting at the table. Paddy stood nearby at his cutting board, viciously chopping at the vegetables on the block. They both looked at him as he entered, Paddy frowning, Jazzi with tears in her eyes. Ryle's heart softened.

"Jazzi, Lincoln Tillis wants you with us when he explains his business. Do you feel you can do that?"

She said nothing.

"Emilia and I will both be there. You don't have to say anything if you don't want to. And I'm sure as anything not going to let something happen to you. He'll have to go through me and Emilia first. And it won't happen. Can you be brave enough to go back with me?"

"I—I—"

"Jazzi, my dear, you do as Ryle asks. Paddy will be here, the door open, and if I hear you scream, I'll come running...with this." Paddy brandished the large chopping knife he held.

Was that a twinkle in his eyes or did he mean it?

Ryle grinned. "See, Jazzi, we all have your back."

She stood. "I'll go, Ryle. Thank you, Paddy. I don't want to face my past, but with friends like all of you, how can I not?"

"It might not be about *your* past." Ryle turned to Paddy. "Would you mind bringing some coffee and cream for all of us?"

Paddy nodded.

Ryle reached for Jazzi's hand and held it all the way down the long hallway. She didn't pull it away, but her tense grip told him a lot.

When they stepped inside his office again, Ryle led Jazzi to the sofa positioned by the front window. Emilia swiveled her chair to face them, and Linc Tillis took the only remaining chair, scooting it around to join them.

"We have a busy schedule today, so I suggest you get right to it. If we can help, we're all ready to do so." Ryle crossed his legs as he studied Tillis.

"What I have to tell you is to be held in strictest confidence. None of you..." Lincoln Tillis hesitated a moment then glanced at each one. "...can speak of this to anyone outside this room."

"Are you a detective?"

"Not exactly." Tillis reached into a pocket and pulled out his wallet, flipped it open.

Ryle and Emilia stared at it, but Jazzi made no move to look. Her gaze was fastened at something outside the window, if she was indeed seeing anything.

"You're—"

"Not so fast. I'd prefer you continue calling me by my name."

"Because?" Emilia's tone held a tiny speck of awe, but more so skepticism. "Why would you need to hide your job, and more suspicious than that, why here in this hick—I mean, why here in West Virginia? A small, quiet community where everyone knows everyone."

"Because my...hmm...boss doesn't want anyone to know what I'm doing in this small, quiet community where everyone knows everyone."

That was a dry answer if Ryle had ever heard one.

"I'll need to check out your references before we say anything or answer any questions." Emilia's lawyerly mind was in operational mode.

"I understand. Today, I will explain why I'm here—"

"You mean you and your kids—do you really have any?—aren't really moving because you love the town but because of your job?"

Tillis had the decency to look a little abashed. "I'll admit it's mostly because of my job, but I have to insist, I wasn't averse to doing so. The little time I spent here was a restful time—for the most part—and in the back of my head, I realized it was an atmosphere I wanted my kids to grow up in. When my job seemed to be leading me to this area, I was pretty excited."

Ryle nor Emilia said anything for a moment, and he knew Jazzi wouldn't either. The man's story was logical. He needed to hear more.

"Okay, say we do accept what you've said, why is your job leading you here? As far as I know, there aren't any serious crime lords around here."

"That doesn't make it so." This time Tillis' tone was solemn.

"I think it's time for you to tell us what you're talking about."

"There's an under—"

The scream that split the air and echoed up and down the hallway outside the room, effectively interrupted Tillis' explanation. Ryle, Emilia and Lincoln Tillis jumped to their feet and moved to the hallway, each of them splitting up then heading in three different directions.

~*~

Jazzi stood too, but after watching the three disappear, she moved, walking quietly to her room, shutting and locking her door. She couldn't shut any curtains because the windows still had none. But she could and she did crawl into her bed and pull the covers over her head.

She could hear occasional shouts, and one time, she heard a couple of the landscaping guys talking outside her window. They must have joined the search. Everyone so busy trying to find out what was causing the screams, and here she was acting like a baby, afraid of her past, afraid of someone finding out who she really was.

Sitting up, she threw off the covers and sighed. This was stupid. She'd never been so afraid, but then she'd never had a reason to hope certain people would never find out about her past.

Now she had a reason. A good one.

But could she have respect when she didn't deserve it? Just as she'd felt that inkling of truth that her parents might not have been the cruel people she'd built up in her mind, now it was the time to face up to the fact, she'd made the life she'd had before returning to Appleton. Now she needed to man up and face the consequences. Only then would she deserve the respect she so wanted from...certain people.

Jazzi practically jumped from the bed, hurried to her door then returned to the bed and threw her covers over it again, smoothing the wrinkles from it. Finally, she unlocked the door and headed outside.

Almost running to the back of the inn, she started to climb down the steps—newly built by

Toni and her crew—when she met Ryle coming up.

"Nothing?"

"Nothing yet." Ryle shook his head.

"We're missing something. It's almost as if it's right in front of our face, but we can't see it." It was Jazzi's turn to shake her head. "I actually think we've been so caught up in everything happening here, including the remodeling, that we can't see the obvious."

"You're probably right about it.

They hurried toward their offices again and ran smack into Emilia and Lincoln Tillis. For just a second, the urge to retreat back to her room swept over her, but she gave herself a mental shake.

No. Grow up and stop acting like a fifteen-year-old. Drawing in a breath, she looked up and met Ryle's questioning gaze. She gave him a small smile and nodded, and the relief that flooded over his face was well worth her efforts at conquering her fears.

Tillis was talking on his cell, and seconds later he replaced it in his pocket and turned back to them. "I've got to go, but I'd like to talk with you all later, when I can."

"I won't be here. I'm leaving soon." Emilia handed him a business card. "My address and phone number if you need to reach me."

"Thanks." He turned away and swung back, making eye contact with Jazzi. "I'd appreciate it if you didn't leave town."

Jazzi didn't give Ryle time to bristle at the order. "I'm not going anywhere."

"Good." He nodded. "All I want is information. And I believe you may have that."

With another nod, he headed toward his SUV,

the three of them watching him leave.

"That's vastly disappointing." Emilia snapped her words, frustration edging them.

Ryle burst out laughing, and even Jazzi had to smile.

"Why on earth would you say that when we both figured he was going after Jazzi for something or the other?"

"Because I don't like to be kept in the dark about anything, but especially when it concerns a new friend for whom I care very much."

Emilia might have sounded somewhat lofty in tone, but Jazzi sensed the depth of her meaning and appreciated what was being left unsaid. The woman—her new friend—was determined to stand with her and protect her from undue harm.

Maybe there was a God who loved her after all.

~*~

Jazzi led the applicant for the assistant job to her office and nodded at her to sit. She studied the woman who didn't look much older than her. There was something about her that—well, troubled Jazzi, but she couldn't put a finger on the problem.

The woman looked decent, albeit a bit on the wild side—whatever that was, and Jazzi cringed. Hadn't she looked the same months ago? Wild, impossible hairdos, way too much makeup and actions that were better forgotten? Perhaps this woman was trying to turn her life around—just as she had.

"You're Creticia Moses?"

"Yeah. I mean, yes, ma'am."

"You don't have to call me ma'am. Jazzi will do just fine."

"Okay."

"Tell me a little about yourself, Creticia." Jazzi sat back in her chair.

The girl shrugged. "What do you want to know?"

"Where have you lived? What jobs have you had? What do you like to do in your spare time? Do you know anyone in Appleton? What are your hobbies? What do you consider your talents?" Jazzi ticked off each question on her fingers. "Those sort of things."

"That's an awful lot of questions to answer. Do you have to know the answers to all of them?"

Was it worry or fear causing that anxiousness in her eyes? "Answer whatever you feel like. If I need to know anything else, I'll ask. I want to get a feel of what you're like."

Creticia sat silent, staring at Jazzi for a moment. "I've lived in, uh, around quite a bit. I don't have hobbies and I've dealt in selling, mostly. I don't know anyone from around here—"

"How did you hear about the job?"

"Someone mentioned it to me." She shifted in her seat.

"Have you had experience in management assisting?"

"No. Yes. Some."

Jazzi raised her brows. "Which is it?"

"I'm not much on hard work, but I was order—I mean, I need the job and will work hard doing what you ask."

...but I was order— What had Creticia almost said? Had someone ordered her to get a job here in Appleton, here at the inn? If so, why? Trouble for Ryle?

Or was someone from New York ordering this girl to come here to deal with her—Jazzi? There would be only one person who would do that, and Jazzi hoped with all her heart it wasn't him. She wanted to have nothing to do with that man. Nothing.

"Who do you know in New York?"

The grin on Creticia's face was spontaneous. "I know lots of people there..."

She must have realized what she'd just said. "I mean—"

"What do you mean, Creticia? I can't consider hiring someone who hides things..." Jazzi cringed inside at her own words. Wasn't she doing the same thing? "...and who isn't to be trusted."

"I can be trusted."

Maybe. Maybe not. Jazzi sat forward. "Tell me the truth, Creticia, or walk out of here. Why are you here?"

"I need a job."

"Were you ordered to come here?"

"No."

"Who sent you?"

"No one."

Jazzi stood. "Creticia, I've dealt with a lot of people. Some liars. Some who wouldn't tell a lie for any amount of money. I'm a fairly good judge on who is sincere and who isn't. I'm pretty sure you aren't telling me the truth."

"But I am."

"The thing is, we have to have employees we can trust to do what we need and ask whether we're in the room or not. I'm not convinced you're one of those persons. I'm sorry, but we won't be able to use you."

"But I have to get this job." Creticia still sat in her chair, a sudden alarm in her expression.

"Why? Tell me."

"Because I need the money."

"And what else?"

She sat silent, lips pressed together. Then, lips opened in a snarl. "You'd better watch out. Frankie's got his eye on you, now that he knows where you ran off to. He was not happy that you did that, you know. Did you think you couldn't be found?"

Jazzi stared down at the still-sitting woman. Terrified. Tongue-tied. Weak and sad. That's how she felt right now. Yet...

Something—Jazzi didn't exactly know what it was—was running through her body, steadying her nerves, strengthening her body, calming her brain, clearing her thoughts.

"I figured he would. Hoped he wouldn't." Was that her voice speaking those defying words? "Because I'm not going back. I'm done with him and his work. I have a different life now, better and satisfying. I'm staying."

"Not when he gets a load of what you're planning. He's been steaming ever since you ran. Hasn't been the same. Short-tempered, restless. He depended on you more than even he realized."

"I'm sorry for that, but I won't change my mind. Not for him or anyone else."

Creticia stood. "Then look for the fireworks. Now that he knows you're here, he won't stop at anything..."

"What?"

"Whether it's to coax or force you back...or kidnap you."

"He can't do that."

"Then you're a bigger fool than even I took you for." Creticia headed for the door. "If I were you I'd get a bodyguard. Someone bigger and meaner than Maxy—if you can find someone like that."

She left Jazzi staring after her, reeling from

her words. Probably a scare tactic, but what if...what if the girl was serious?

Walking to the door, Jazzi invited the second applicant into her office. And as the interview progressed. Jazzi realized this woman would be a perfect addition to their staff.

She was quiet but confident. Polite and reserved, yet open with her answers to Jazzi's questions. Certainly knew the business. Agreeable to the hourly schedule and ready, she assured Jazzi, to move in whenever she was asked.

"You're hired. We have rooms near the kitchen area that we've planned for our staff who want to stay on the grounds. They're not huge rooms, but we've made them into comfortable and homey places for our staff to relax in. Two of our maids—who aren't working yet, but will begin next week—and our chef are already moved in. We'll serve breakfast and lunch here daily. Suppers will be on your own. You have a small fridge in your room for sandwich materials and drinks if you prefer that than going into town."

"Sounds wonderful. My son wanted me to move in with them, but I'm not quite there yet, in mind or age. This will be a perfect solution. I've already downsized, can have the rest of my things stored and tomorrow bring what I'd like to have with me."

"I think we're going to get along just fine. Welcome, to our inn, Barbara Sizemore."

"Thank you." At the door, she turned back. "Do you mind me asking? What's the name of the inn?"

Jazzi's mind went blank and she laughed. "I have no idea. Ryle Sadler, the owner, hasn't said. I suppose I'd better find out if our sign is to go up in time for our opening."

"I'd say you're right. I'll see you early tomorrow to get settled in. Oh, and I don't mind starting early if you need me."

"Great. I'll let you know if we do."

Jazzi settled back in her big desk chair and closed her eyes. That had gone perfectly.

"Taking a break, I see."

Jazzi opened her eyes at Emilia's teasing comment. "I certainly am."

"How did the interviews go?"

"One not so good. The other couldn't have gone better. Barbara Sizemore is my new assistant. I think she'll be a great asset to the inn."

"Have I told you yet that you're the best thing that's ever happened to Ryle?"

"No."

"Well, then. I've said it. And it's true." Emilia smiled and turned away. "And I don't make statements I know nothing about. I'm glad you're here, Jazmine Sanderson. But don't you go breaking his heart."

The sudden breathlessness that swept over Jazzi took a second to overcome, then she croaked out, "Why would I ever do that?"

But her friend was gone, and she was left wondering if Emilia meant what Jazzi suspected she'd meant.

Chapter Eleven

Jazzi was still awake, sitting up in bed with a light on, reading, trying to finish the last few chapters of Carole Brown's second WWII book, *A Flute in the Willows*, when the moans started.

It'd been a good day, in spite of the fright she'd had when Lincoln Tillis showed up. Even then he'd been soothing, insuring her he wasn't out to cause her trouble. Did she believe him? She wasn't positive about that.

Emilia had left right after supper. The interview with that Creticia girl hadn't been enjoyable, but Barbara Sizemore, she was sure, would be a great employee for Ryle.

Everything else was happening right on time, and a week from Saturday, their opening party would herald in the opening of the inn.

Everything was perfect.

Except for these screams and moans. It was upsetting Ryle, she knew. And they really couldn't continue, especially when guests were here.

Another distant but decidedly loud moan interrupted Jazzi's thoughts. She swung her legs from the bed and stood. This was getting annoying rather than frightening.

They'd searched the basement. It seemed too far away to be in any of the rooms—even empty ones.

She opened her door and stepped into the hallway, almost running into Ryle.

"You couldn't sleep either?"

"I wasn't asleep yet." Jazzi frowned. "But who could sleep with that going on?"

"Yeah. And Paddy or the maids haven't said a word. Do you suppose they haven't heard it?"

"How could they not?" Jazzi shook her head. "It's hopeless. I have no idea where to even begin looking again. Whoever did this, they were very creative to hide it."

"I'm afraid we're going to have to use our investigative juices in figuring it out."

Ryle's usual confident, serene face was anything but that. Jazzi's heart ached for him. He was such a good-hearted man. Who would do something like this to him?"

"I was thinking. Don't they seem kind of far off? At first I didn't pay any attention. I was just creeped out, but now..." Jazzi shivered.

"You're right. From the first time I heard them, I felt something off. I'm missing something." Ryle rubbed a hand over his head then turned abruptly toward Jazzi again.

"I suppose I should tell you..." Ryle drew in a breath then studied her face. "...I invited your parents here for supper tomorrow evening."

"What? Why?"

"They called while you were interviewing today and wanted us to go to some concert or other with them. I knew we were too busy to do that, and rather than upset them, I encouraged them to eat with us, and they accepted. I hope you won't be too angry at me. I should have asked, but at the time, I was trying to avoid you wiggling out of their invitation and upsetting them—and you. Was I wrong?"

Jazzi drew in a long breath. "Of course, you weren't. You made the best choice of the matter. I'm surprised they didn't pressure you."

"No pressure. They were surprisingly agreeable. Perhaps excited would best describe your mother's attitude."

"I guess that's a good thing considering their normal stubbornness."

"From what I've heard, parents are usually a bit stubborn over certain things."

Ryle's dry remark brought a smile to her lips. "Well, I haven't heard anymore moaning, so maybe we can get a good night's sleep after all."

"Maybe. I mentioned to Paddy we'd have company tomorrow evening. Would you check to see that everything would be to their liking?"

"Do we have to? I was thinking fried bologna sandwiches."

Ryle laughed. "Better not. *I* might get blamed for that one."

Him? Jazzi seriously doubted it. "I will. Good night, Ryle."

"Goodnight, sweet Jazzi." Ryle turned and walked away.

She stood rooted to the floor. No one, *no one* had ever called her sweet before. Cute, A bundle of curiosity, active, and some descriptions that weren't so nice.

Sweet. She kind of liked that.

~*~

Early the next morning—just about sun up, Jazzi dressed quickly and decided to go for a run. She wouldn't go far, afraid of who might be hanging around, but she'd stay on the inn property where she'd feel a minimum of safety. She finished tying her running shoes, opened the door of her suite and almost bumped into Ryle as he walked past.

"Whoa." Ryle stretched out a hand to steady her. "You're up early. Out for a walk, are you?"

"Looks like you almost beat me to it." Jazzi grinned as she scrunched back her hair into a ponytail.

"Want to run together?"

She propped a hand on her side. "Are you sure you can keep up?"

"Huh. You'll only see my back, sister."

Sister. Where had the *sweet Jazzi* gone overnight?

She moved ahead of him and tossed back her comment. "We'll see about that."

Ryle caught up with her as she headed down the driveway. "Wanna run into town, around the park and back again?"

"Is that where you want to go?" She shrugged. "Fine with me."

As long as Ryle was with her, she wasn't worried. He might be half Maxy's size, but Ryle was strong and smart.

Side by side, they ran, talking little, but sharing smiles, pointing at a redbird, scaring a fawn and its mother from a meadow into a stand of trees. They avoided downtown Appleton although Ryle did joke about stopping for breakfast.

"And have Paddy angry at us for not eating his cooking?" Jazzi grinned, but kept heading toward the park. "You're slowing me down with your wishful thinking."

And then she saw him.

Frankie? And, of course, the big, big man was Maxy. What was Frankie doing in Appleton? She could see him sending Maxy to force her back to New York, but Frankie in this small town? Didn't make sense, but then, he definitely wouldn't be here unless it made sense to *him*. That's all that really mattered.

She should know.

Ryle was still talking, laughing, but Jazzi couldn't

focus on what he was saying. The fear winding its way through her heart nearly caused her to black out. She knew it, wanted to stop it, but couldn't.

Finally, she edged closer to Ryle, gripped his arm and turned around, gasping. "Let's go back this way."

"What? Why?"

He wasn't fighting her statement, but she could see the puzzled glance he gave her, see the confused look on his face.

Jazzi shook her head. "I can't go that way."

Ryle didn't speak, and Jazzi didn't look at him. But she saw—from the corner of her eyes—the casual glance he shot behind him.

~*~

That was pure terror in Jazzi's eyes. Ryle recognized immediately someone or something had caused it. Only one thing was different from any other time he'd been around the park, and that was the two men lounging against the back of the park bench.

He only spared them a casual, quick glance, but years of reading and studying humanity gave him an advantage. That quick glance told him plenty.

One, the big man was the same one who'd talked with Jazzi when she and Emilia and himself had strolled down the street after a dinner evening. Secondly, the other man was smaller, but he was the one in charge, and if Ryle had been a betting man, he'd place that bet on him being the dangerous one.

He had no interest in tackling either today. That's why he'd turned his back to them and trotted beside Jazzi back toward home. His tackling of a questionable, possibly a troublesome person, was to do his research first—with the capable help of Emilia.

That look of fear in Jazzi's eyes bothered him. A lot. He didn't like it. At all. And he meant to get to the bottom of it. He could, of course, have Emilia's investigators check out Jazzi's background, particularly when she lived in New York. But...he'd never cared for searching for information about a friend.

And Jazzi was that.

Ryle felt an unfamiliar, uncomfortable stirring inside his chest. He thought about that even as he ran beside the best manager he'd ever had.

And then he decided *not* to think about it.

For now.

~*~

Later that morning, Jazzi stood at the front window of her own small office staring out at the landscape. Amy and her crew were working on the landscaping, and their figures moving around the yard area gave her a sense of security—minute that it was. It was ridiculous, this feeling of fright at the thought that Frankie was here in Appleton. Why? What other reason could it be than he'd come for her?

Or maybe it was revenge on her escaping his clutches without him having a hint of where she'd fled to. Or what her real name was.

Either way sent shivers of terror through her.

It was hopeless to allow it to rule her like this. She needed something to do besides enduring her own company.

Slipping out of her office, she hurried to Ryle's, hoping he wouldn't be there.

Futile hope.

He must have been following her trend of staring out windows.

Ryle turned as she entered. "Looks like—the

way Amy's crew is working—they'll be done ahead of time."

"She loves her flower shop, but the landscaping business part gives her an extra boost mentally, she says. Helps keep her creative juices flowing." Jazzi wrinkled her nose but grinned. "She's quite talented. I'm just a bit jealous of her, you know."

Her boss gave her a look. "You have no need to be. You're quite talented yourself besides being..."

His voice trailed off, and he swiveled to glance out the window again. "We never had a chance to talk about your research at the courthouse. Did you come up with anything profitable?"

"Maybe. Let me grab my case, and I'll go over it with you, if you have the time."

"I do."

"Be right back then." Jazzi hurried to her own office where she'd locked the papers she'd gathered the night her parents had surprised her.

Jazzi placed the items methodically on the large table in his room. "Here are some pictures I thought were interesting of different places in this area. Then I did find a list of three of the previous owners, one dating back into the early eighteen hundreds. What really caught my attention was this person who has a similar name as—"

"I see. But it's spelled so differently. Why would you think they could be related?"

"Many times names are changed through the years, sometimes by a mistake, other times by lack of education, and a few times for nefarious reasons."

"Could be a coincidence because I'm sure I heard Toby mention awhile back that he was actually a fairly recent addition to our town. If that's the case then—"

"Right. That probably is the case."

"We'll keep it in mind though. Now Maisie... how did she come to own the place? That interests me more than the other. I wonder why there was no mention of who owned it before her family. Look at the dates. There's no one listed during these years. Do you suppose she was married and a deed was in his name?"

"I never thought to check that."

"It's okay, Jazzi. We can't think of everything. Why would we?"

Ryle replaced the deed ownership list. "Have you had a chance to check out that old map of the inn again?

"That's why I came by. Thought I might study it again."

"Great. Help yourself." Ryle moved toward his desk. "You think everything is going okay?"

"Sure. Once Amy's done this week, we'll have a few days to make sure all things are ready for the private party, and then the open house. I've checked with Starli and Manny, and they have the menus all planned and ready. The furniture has been delivered. Amy will help me with the final decorating touches inside, and Paddy's ready to assist as needed. Barbara Sizemore moved in early this morning, and the two maids have their things moved in and will begin work first of next week, if not sooner."

She grinned at him. "Paddy's agreed to train them in their duties, although I'm pretty sure all of them already know the ropes."

"Great job, Jazzi, as always."

Jazzi headed to the locked safe where Ryle had stored the small chest. "Then, if you have nothing else for me right now, I'll go study this some more. I'd like to get this thing untangled before opening night."

"You and me both." Ryle ran a hand through his short brown hair. "We haven't had anything unusual happening lately, but that doesn't mean something else won't pop up."

She lifted the chest a little. "That's why I'm going to give it another go. I'll talk with you later."

He waved a hand, and Jazzi hurried to her office again. Now to tackle this thing and figure out if it even meant anything.

Jazzi settled in her desk chair, smoothed a hand over the age-old chest and admired the handiwork. Whoever had made this had done a remarkable job. The brass around the edges of the scrolls was tarnished from age and dampness, but all in all, the box was unique in design. Had the maker created it especially? Maybe for a wife? A daughter? A lover?

She drew out the map and carefully opened and spread it out on her desk. Her glance drifted over the whole thing then settled on the main part that seemed to be the inn itself. With one finger she traced the drawing, up and down, side to side, following the lines. Everything seemed to be close to what the inn was now, although there were changes here and there of the structure.

She stared, looked away, and back again.

Nothing.

But...

Maybe she was focusing on the wrong thing. Instead of the inn holding the answer, could it be something else? Something on the grounds? But what?

The big what. Hmmm.

Her gaze swiveled back to the map and stared at the small dark square drawn away from the inn. No one had found any hint of a building. At least, Ryle hadn't given any hint of it. If it was a significant building, then surely it would have been mentioned to him before he bought the place.

Should she try to find it? Her stomach tightened. What if Maxy was out there? Or worse, Frankie?

Nonsense. They already knew she knew they were in town. Why would they be skulking around in the woods here at the inn?

Jazzi stood, gathered up all the papers and replaced them in the chest. Marching to Ryle's office which was next door to hers, she put the chest in the safe, and headed out. Where Ryle was, she had no idea.

It was exceptionally warm for early-September, the sun was shining down on her world, and a pleasant sense of contentment swept over her. How different her life was now compared to the last few years.

She'd already decided she wouldn't go deep into the woods, only wander around the edges of the cleared area and a bit of the woods. She was careful to keep track of her surroundings and always be on the lookout for anyone who shouldn't be on the property—like her two nemeses from New York.

Most of the land beneath the trees was fairly clear, but occasionally, a few spots were filled with briars, thick, wild plants and bushes that kept her from beelining toward what she hoped she'd find. Back in her office she figured what the possible distance according to the size of everything, but whether she was right or not, she had no clue.

Not too far from the back of the inn, she found the worst tangle of briars she'd ever seen. Could it be hiding a small secret building? She propped her hands on her hips, wondering what to do about it.

There was no way to tackle those briars unless she was willing to allow herself to get ripped by the thorns. She didn't want that—she could imagine her mother's face tonight if she saw her arms streaked with scratches. So, the next best thing would be to keep circling the area until—and if—she found a large enough hole to get through or, at least, look further into the area.

As luck would have it, she found what looked like a better opening than any other place would be. It was on the far side away from the cleared lawn, and still looked harder than she was willing to tackle. Some of the overgrown vines and branches were almost impossible to trim with anything other than a large tool.

Jazzi huffed and gave up. Time to head back to the inn and return when she had more time— and after locating a tool big enough to do the trick. Turning, she wiped at her face and caught a glimpse of...

Frankie.

And Maxy standing only a few feet away. Maxy had a hand propped against a large Oak tree trunk. Frankie leaned against that same tree, arms and legs crossed, the smirky grin on his lips showing her—just like he had many others—his contempt for her attempts at escaping his clutches.

Jazzi froze. Frankie wasn't a large man, but his attitude ranked his self-importance. But he didn't need size when he had his right hand man, Maxy. That man had kept Frankie's flunkies in line. No man talked back to Frankie. No one.

"What are you doing here in Appleton?" She wet her lips. "I am not going back."

"You don't have to."

"I don't?"

"What do you see in this place anyhow?" He straightened.

She shrugged and flicked a strand of stray hair out of her eyes. No doubt she was a far cry from her looks in New York. Maybe he wouldn't want her back cause of that. Suited her.

Still, she needed to be careful how she phrased her words. "I was tired of that life. I was afraid. Every. Day. Of. My. Life."

"I'd never let anyone hurt you, Purple Jaz."

"You say that, but you don't know that for sure."

"You doubting me?"

"No. But you and I both know what we were doing was dangerous. I woke up one day and realized I wanted something different."

"And you found it coming back *here*?"

The scorn in his voice sent the blood rushing to her cheeks. "I did. I just want to live a normal life and be left alone."

"Well, now that might be a problem." He edged closer to her. "Got a little project I need some help with, and you're the girl to do it."

"Frankie, no."

"You expect me to beg?" His smirk widened. "You know I can't do that. What kind of leader would I be begging you to do one little thing for me and the boys?"

Yeah, right. Whatever he wanted wouldn't be little or easy. Dangerous, and definitely not something she wanted anything to do with.

"Go away, Frankie. I won't be involved in anymore of your—your deals."

He didn't say anything more, but Jazzi knew what that flick of a glance and bit of a nod at Maxy meant. *Convince her she's not being smart.*

And Jazzi felt the fear strangling her.

Chapter Twelve

"**W**hat's going on here, Jazzi?"

Jazzi's face paled at Ryle's question. He stepped into view. His question was aimed at her, but his gaze remained on the two men six feet away. He tilted his head their direction. "Are they bothering you?"

"Yes. No. I'm okay, Ryle."

He did look at her then. "What are you doing out here alone?"

"I was out walking."

His gaze slid down to the long scratch on her hand. "I see. Did you find what you were looking for?"

"No, the briars and honeysuckle vines were too thick. I'll have to find something big and strong to tackle them next time."

He opened his mouth and shut it. Now was not the time to inform Jazzi she would not be coming here alone again. Instead he gave the men another look. "Well, guys, sorry to intrude but we need her back at the inn."

Maxy growled. "Boss isn't done talking to her."

"Boss? Not mine. Not Jazzi's." He held out his hand. "Come, we have people waiting on us."

Jazzi hesitated, glanced at the men then hurried to Ryle's side. But before they left, she spoke. "I meant what I said, Frankie. I'm staying."

She moved in step with Ryle as he walked away.

Ryle had no idea if the two men—who he was positive might try to stop them—would come after Jazzi. He sure could feel their eyes on him. And hopefully, that's all that would be hitting his back in the next few seconds.

They'd barely escaped out of view when Ryle couldn't hold back his question. "Jazzi, I'm not trying to butt into your business, but who are those men? Why are they here? They are why you didn't want to walk all the way around the park, aren't they?"

She looked at him then, and Ryle saw her eyes, glistening with unshed tears.

"Ryle, I'm so sorry. I didn't mean for this to happen."

"Unless I'm missing something, how could you prevent something like this from happening? My guess would be those two don't take orders from others."

A spontaneous giggle escaped her. "Very true."

"Can you tell me?"

She turned her head away. "I can, but I don't want to."

He said nothing for several seconds. "Then you don't have to, Jazzi. I won't pressure you. If you ever decide you can, and you want to, then share with me. But I can't protect you if I don't know what I'm protecting you from."

She didn't look at him for the longest time, but just before they approached the inn, she murmured, "I'm afraid you'll get hurt."

He stopped walking. "I'm stronger than you think."

"You haven't come up against the likes of..." she tilted her head back "...them."

At that moment, sunlight streaming between the overhead clouds stroked Jazzi's tilted face, giving it a gentle, innocent look, and Ryle drew in a long breath. He swallowed hard before he could comment.

"What makes you think that, Jazzi? You know nothing about my past."

Her startled gaze rested on him again. "That's true, but..."

"But what?" He spoke as gently as he could. He'd figured when he'd first met Jazzi that she'd been running from something, that she'd gotten herself in a bit of trouble by running from the life she knew and thought she didn't want or like. When it'd seemed that God wanted him to get involved in her life, he'd obeyed and hoped it wouldn't be a mistake. But the changes he'd seen in her since hiring her had been impressive. He believed she was not only happier, but stronger in spirit.

He hoped he wasn't wrong.

"I've seen too much. I don't want you to get hurt. I couldn't live with myself if that happened. You're too good of a person—"

"Stop." Ryle laughed a little, but felt that prick to share what he *never*, ever shared. "I've not always been good, Jazzi. My mother died when I was young, I never knew my father, and I eventually, as a teenager, hung around the wrong crowd. My only saving was the promise I made to my mother before she died."

"Really? You're not just saying all this to make me feel less guilty?"

"Why should you feel guilty? You didn't ask them to come, did you?"

"Of course not. I'm done with associating with them."

"And I'm telling you what my life was like when I was growing up."

"What was the promise you made your mother? Do you mind telling me?"

He hesitated but smiled. Here he was sharing things he'd told no one—not even Emilia. "She asked me to stay in school, not to neglect my studies, and I promised her I'd honor that request. How could I not when she was the best and only light I'd had in my life?"

"Ryle, that is so—so sweet. And now look at you. A wonderful, successful business man."

She didn't know the half, and he wasn't about to tell her. Not yet, at least.

"I'm trying."

"You are. This bed and breakfast will be very successful, I know it." Her smug, carefree exclamation had him chuckling inside.

"Because I won't let it fail. I'll work myself to the bone to make it happen. You've given me a job I love, one where I can start over and maybe be something someday. It will happen."

He looked at her, at her straight shoulders, her set lips—all showing how determined she was to make it happen for him, and he felt something happening inside him. As if his insides were chocolate and melting from the heat his heart was producing.

They stepped onto the first step of the four that led to the veranda. No signs that the men had followed them. Only Amy and her crew were finishing up touches of the landscaping they were doing to create an awesome outdoor welcoming décor.

They were crossing the veranda preparatory to entering the inn when Ryle stopped her. He reached over and tucked a bit of hair behind her ear. "Jazzi, you are the best thing that has ever happened in my life. I can't thank you enough for your confidence and hard work to make this come to pass."

He leaned toward her and pecked her cheek with a kiss.

~*~

Shock ran through Jazzi when she heard Ryle's comments. The best thing that had ever happened to him? Really? What about Emilia? Comparing her with Emilia—well, no one would have second thoughts of who would be the best.

But when Ryle kissed her—cheek, yes, but still a kiss—Jazzi thought she might faint.

The next words which he tossed at her as he hurried inside, caused her to hesitate.

"I really do think you deserve another raise. I want to make sure you'll be with me when I move on to another project."

Her heart sank. Another project? Move on? He wasn't planning on staying? Living here forever? She hadn't given a thought that he might leave, and she'd be...

Alone again.

Stupid tears were filling her eyes. He had no obligation to keep her happy. Why should he when she jumped to conclusions and couldn't even keep herself in a modicum of happiness?

Swiping at the unwanted tears, she marched inside the inn and straight to her suite. She was tired, hot and bothered. Time for a soak in that huge whirl-tub and a few hours alone to rest for the dinner tonight with her parents. Maybe she'd regain her senses.

~*~

Ryle stood in front of the huge fireplace, a fire burning in its cavity after a sudden evening chill had followed the earlier rain. Paddy had promised a meal for the Sandersons Ryle would be proud of. Almost everything had been finished except for the final touches tomorrow when Amy joined Jazzi to finish the indoor décor upstairs. Downstairs, everything was warm and inviting. Just what he'd hoped for.

He was answering one of James Sanderson's questions when, through the wide doorway, Ryle saw a vision—Jazzi—pausing outside the room. Her velvet blue eyes were wide, her dark hair sleeked back giving her face a classical look, her long neck elegant and slender.

He'd never seen a more beautiful woman.

"Jazzi, come join us." He stretched out a hand. When she reached his side, he turned to her parents. "My very valuable manager, Jazzi Sanderson. I think you both know her."

Everyone laughed, even Jazzi, and she leaned forward to hug her parents. "Paddy, our chef, has promised us an out-of-this-world menu tonight, so we're hoping you enjoy it."

"If he's anything like he sounds, we might try to bribe him away." James teased.

"That might be a little hard. I'm afraid he's fallen for Jazzi."

Sharp glances swept her way. "What?"

"He's teasing you."

"Truth." Ryle winked at her. "Truth, but he is very protective of our Jazzi and constantly gives me orders how to take care of her."

He saw the red climbing her cheeks. "I am teasing her a bit, but I'm pretty sure our chef has his cap set on her."

"Ryle Sadler. Stop!" She slapped at his arm.

The Sandersons were grinning. Whether it was from seeing their second daughter like this, or the thought that someone might have stolen her heart, he couldn't tell. Either way, he enjoyed the comradeship between them.

At that moment, Paddy stepped inside the room. Ryle stared at the man's transformation. Usually, he wore a plain shirt and jeans when serving him and Jazzi for breakfast and lunch. Tonight, he'd donned a stark white shirt, with tie, and black trousers. He was as immaculate as any chef in a big-city restaurant.

"Dinner is served, Mr. Ryle."

Ryle walked toward Mrs. Sanderson and held out an arm, and they strolled toward the now-furnished dining room, leaving James Sanderson to escort his daughter into the room.

When they were settled, Heather Sanderson asked a blessing, then Paddy served them.

Everything was top-notch, as good, if not better, than anything Ryle had eaten in the best restaurants in New York. Paddy had certainly outdone himself with the Grilled Salmon and Avocado Salsa. Just one more item to his list of reasons why he was glad he'd obeyed that push to buy the place.

Everything had run like a well-oiled piece of machinery—until that bit of unwanted news Mayor Slater had shared. Still, with Emilia on his side and Jazzi declaring her determination to fight till the end—he grinned at that—he was pretty sure that whatever came up, they'd conquer it.

"Do you think we could postpone our trip till after Ryle and Jazzi's opening, James? I would love to be here for it." Heather Sanderson turned to Ryle. "That's if we're invited."

"Of course. You're always invited to our functions, Mrs. Sanderson."

"Please, call me Heather." When Ryle nodded, smiling, she returned her gaze to her husband.

"James?"

"Whatever you want. I'll have my assistant adjust my schedule."

"Thank you." Jazzi's mother smiled at her husband then turned back to Ryle. "Is there anything I can do to help?"

"You'll have to ask Jazzi that question. She's the one who has everything organized."

"Jazzi?"

Ryle heard the doubt in Heather Sanderson's voice and knew Jazzi heard it too but the daughter didn't show it. Good for her.

"I think not. Everything's in place now, except the pictures and inside touches. Amy is helping me tomorrow to put those final touches to everything. We've got it covered."

Heather's face was a little blank at Jazzi's refusal, Ryle figured, and opened his mouth to thank her, when Jazzi spoke again.

"Amy has been such a help in teaching me a few decorating tips, but, Mother, thank you so much for offering to help. You've been a wonderful example through the years, and though I haven't always...appreciated you, I do now. I hope someday to become someone you can be proud of."

Ryle stared at this beautiful woman. If her mother didn't see the change in Jazzi, he sure did.

There was an emotion rolling through him that was unfamiliar. Something warm and strange and alluring. He shook his head slightly. Whatever it was, he wasn't ready to face it, accept it, or even acknowledge it.

He didn't have to worry about Heather Sanderson's reaction to Jazzi's words. She'd stretched out a hand to touch Jazzi's. Her soft words were like the icing on a cake.

"I already am proud of you, my daughter. I certainly am."

~*~

Jazzi and Ryle stood at the front door of the inn watching the Sandersons drive down the driveway.

"That went well."

"It did. I feel..." Jazzi's voice trailed off.

"How do you feel?" Ryle made sure to keep his voice soft and not too inquisitive.

She shrugged. "Confused. Happy. Pleased. I don't know."

"Want to sit on the veranda for a bit?" When she nodded, he stepped out and motioned for her to follow. "Come sit with me on the wicker loveseat. Look at that moon. That much more wonderful after the earlier shower. I wonder why people are afraid of a full moon?"

"Depending on how you look at it, it's a big light in the darkness. It could be too much for certain people who have things to hide, but just enough for those who love the nighttime." Jazzi settled on the loveseat beside Ryle.

"Do you, Jazzi?"

"Do I what?"

"Love the nighttime?"

"Most times. It can be scary if you're running for your life or there are things you're afraid of."

Ryle said nothing for a few minutes. "Can you believe I'm craving a cookie or two Paddy made earlier. Want one?"

"I could do with one, maybe. I'll go grab a few. Drink?"

"Let's have some of your lemonade if there's any left." He held out a hand as she started to rise. "Wait. I'll get it. You stay here and relax.

Enjoy the quiet sounds of the dark."

"Sure?"

He rose and smiled down at her. "I am."

It took less than fifteen minutes for him to gather the drinks and cookies. As he stepped through the front doorway, he spoke. "I think Paddy hid the cookies. It took me a few minutes to find them. Must have wanted—Jazzi?"

Jazzi wasn't sitting on the loveseat. She must have walked around on the veranda.

Ryle set the tray on one of the small tables nearby and strode around the veranda, making a complete circle. At the front again, he called softly, "Jazzi? Where are you?"

No answer. Had an octopus from the ocean managed to get to West Virginia and land on his property? Because his insides felt as if something was squeezing the life out of him.

He turned and trotted through the inn. When he reached Paddy's room, he pounded on the door, and only seconds later, the man opened it, his hair standing on end.

"Ryle, what's wrong?"

"We were sitting on the veranda out front when I went to gather a few late night snacks to nibble on. I returned, and Jazzi had disappeared."

"She may be strolling around the yard." But Paddy was pulling on a shirt.

"I know that. I'm probably worried over nothing, but after that meeting with two men from her past, I want to be sure. Could you help me look? Just in case."

Paddy shut his door. "Let's go. She's strong, lad. We'll find her."

Ryle didn't speak, only half-ran down the hallway. Outside, he motioned for Paddy to take one side while he headed for the opposite.

The cleared property was large. Big enough to build a future pool and maybe a tennis court or basketball area. The small lake was on the opposite side and would do perfectly for future fishing enthusiasts. But his hasty search yielded no Jazzi, and Ryle whirled to return to the veranda, when he heard Paddy's voice.

"Ryle."

Ryle went, running as fast as he'd ever run before. What was that on the ground?

As Ryle slowed to a walk, he realized what it was—or who.

Jazzi Sanderson lay motionless, her feet in the water, her eyes closed.

Was she dead?

Nearby stood two men. Paddy and Maxy, and they weren't having a friendly discussion. As he approached, he caught bits of their conversation, if it could be called that. More like taunting. Or arguing.

"Really? I big man like you hurting a delicate woman. Man up."

Paddy was standing still, arms at his sides, but the expression on his face told Ryle a lot. Quiet. Deadly quiet. He was angry, but his chef hid it well. And though this Maxy, before now, had come across as tough and mean, he wouldn't bet on him, if he was a betting man. Ryle had his vote on who would come out on tops.

But Ryle didn't stop to watch the two. He headed straight to Jazzi and gathered her up in his arms. As he strode away, he heard Paddy's warning. "Don't let me see you anywhere near Mr. Ryle's inn again. In fact, I don't want to ever see you again. I told you once before what would happen if I did, and here you are, pushing whatever luck you think you have."

There was a splash, and before Ryle entered the inn, he cast a quick glance back at the two.

One was striding toward the inn.

The other man was wading out of the river.

~*~

"Calm down, Ryle. She's okay." Paddy caught up with Ryle as he neared Jazzi's suite.

She didn't look okay. So quiet, no smiles, no movement.

He might be smart in his business and intuitive in what to invest in and what to avoid like the plague, who to help and who to refuse, but when it came to illness, he felt as useless as a baby.

"I'm pretty sure someone used pressure points to knock her out. She'll awaken soon. Breathing is fine, and she's already moved some." Paddy rested a big hand on his shoulder. "I'll go get some tea warmed and have Barbara come to help you. She needs to be in something more comfortable."

Ten minutes later, Ryle waited outside Jazzi's door as Barbara prepared Jazzi for bed. Five minutes later, when the woman stepped out of the room, Ryle questioned her with raised brows.

"She'll be fine. She stirred, mumbled some but didn't wake fully yet. I'll stay with her, if you'd like, but you can go in if you want to check on her."

Ryle nodded, entered and stood by Jazzi's bed, staring down at the woman who'd come into his life unexpectedly. "Jazzi, you wake up, you hear me? You be okay tomorrow, and I promise you, I'll not let this happen again."

Touching her hand, he felt a finger twitch, and he smiled. Her eyes fluttered open. "What happened?"

But before he could answer her again, she murmured, "I'm so tired. I'm going to rest for a bit, then I'll get up and help you."

She'd drifted off to sleep. A fighter, she was.

Outside in the hall, he met with Barbara again. "I'll sleep outside her room. If you need anything at all, just wake me if I'm asleep."

Barbara patted his shoulder, stepped inside Jazzi's room and shut the door.

Ryle slumped on the floor, vowing not to sleep.

~*~

"Ryle, why are you sleeping outside my door?"

Ryle jerked awake and jumped to his feet. "You're awake."

She was smiling although her face looked a little wan. "Why wouldn't I be? I have work to do."

"You, my young assistant, are not working today. You have today off. You will spend the day lounging, reading, or whatever else suits your fancy." He was shoving her gently back into her room, but he felt her stiffen. "Please, Jazzi. You scared me to death last night. I thought—I thought you were—well—gone."

She'd stopped resisting his gentle push and moved to one of the arm chairs, pulling a throw over her and drawing her knees up to wrap her arms around them. "It was them, or at least, I think it was Maxy. He's big and strong and mean. I was always afraid of him, but knew he wouldn't hurt me unless Frankie ordered it."

"Jazzi—"

"I'm okay, Ryle. He only applied enough pressure to barely knock me out. I heard you and Paddy talking last night when you—you carried me back here."

"You did?"

"Yes, and I woke fully probably fifteen minutes after Barbara shut the door and settled in her chair. I drank some of that delicious tea that helped me go back to sleep later on. Didn't realize you were sleeping outside my door, or I would have sent you to your suite."

"I wouldn't have gone."

"I believe that." Jazzi chuckled.

"Why is he doing this?"

"Why?" Jazzi switched her gaze to the window nearest her. "Because Frankie is used to having his way. Always. He doesn't take no for an answer, he doesn't put up with those who disobey his orders, and he knows how to make someone pay."

Ryle jumped to his feet and strode back and forth several times before he spoke. "He'd better not touch you again. I made a call to Chief Eddie last night who said he'd be here this morning to talk with you."

"I really am okay, Ryle. I don't need to talk with Chief Eddie."

"Are you *refusing* to talk with him?"

She didn't answer him. Instead she fidgeted with her throw, took a sip of what he knew would be cold tea, and then sighed. "Yes, I guess I am. Please call him and tell him I'm fine."

It had been a long time since he'd been this upset, and what shocked him was his intense worry about Jazzi, the woman he'd championed, who he'd hired because he'd thought it was the right thing to do. He wanted to keep her safe but she was refusing his help...

He jerked around and headed for the door. "I won't call him. If you don't want to speak with him, then you call and tell him not to come."

"Ryle—"

But he was done talking. He'd been almost physically sick last night, worrying about her, and now she was brushing it off, almost as if she was protecting that thug from New York.

How much did he really know about Jazzi Sanderson after all?

Chapter Thirteen

What had she done? She was only trying to protect Ryle, but, obviously, he'd misunderstood her intentions. She knew how mean Frankie could be, and he wouldn't think twice about taking out Ryle, or anyone, out. She wouldn't let that happen—if she could help it—no matter how angry Ryle got with her.

She laid her head on her hand, wishing she could restart the morning. Really, would it have hurt to talk with Chief Eddie? Maybe. Or not.

Jumping to her feet, she knew what she could do. Ten minutes later she was dressed and headed to the kitchen. She called out to him before she entered his domain. "Paddy, I need to talk with you. I said something to Ryle and now he's angry at me. I didn't mean..."

As if she'd run into a huge block wall, Jazzi stopped. At the kitchen table sat Paddy, and he wasn't alone. Ryle sat across from him, and by the looks on the younger man's face, he was not happy.

For just a second, she froze, then she began backing out. Her tongue felt as if it was glued to the top of her mouth.

Paddy lowered his head a little and motioned. "Come, Jazzi. You might as well join us. Let's see if we can straighten the misunderstandings."

"I didn't misunderstand. He did."

"When I'm trying to protect you?"

"I wanted to protect *you*."

"Protect *me*?"

"If you'd only listen."

"Enough."

Paddy's voice was too quiet, but somehow it rang with a strength and power that bode no argument. Jazzi stared at the man who'd seemed so mild, yet a champion to her.

"Enough of the piddly arguing. You both are strong people with definite opinions. The problem is…" he paused and gave each of them a searching glance. "…you are both wrong. And right."

"What do you mean?"

"We will take this one at a time. We'll let the lady go first."

When Paddy nodded at her, she opened her mouth to speak. "I know Frankie. I know how he works. Am I afraid? Yes, I am. I've seen him have Maxy beat men—and worse—because they didn't fulfill his demands or failed. I think he wants me back just because I out-tricked him in leaving. I hoped he wouldn't find me, but now that he has, he won't stop at anything—anything, Ryle Sadler—to force me back to New York."

"We can understand that, can't we, Ryle?"

Jazzi looked at Ryle. He was staring at her, but it wasn't that that caught her attention. It was the emotion in his eyes. She had to swallow down the tears that begged to be released.

"I think we can agree, Ryle, can't we, that Jazzi did and said what she did because of her concern about you, right?"

Ryle gave him a nod.

"All I can see in my head is a disaster. A looming, huge disaster which, of course, doesn't end well for anyone. I don't want you involved in this mess, Ryle, because—"

"I was just trying to protect you." Ryle's voice had lost its forceful tone.

"I'm trying to protect *you*."

Their comments blended together as did the sudden sheepish smiles on their faces.

And when Paddy nodded at them, Ryle reached across the table to grasp Jazzi's hand and whispered. "I'm sorry. I should have understood..."

"Me, too." Jazzi tightened her fingers around Ryle's.

~*~

Jazzi had agreed to take it easy today. He was almost sure it'd been that goon of Frankie's who'd knocked Jazzi out. He'd have to keep watch she didn't go out by herself—and not give her any suspicion he was doing it.

He might have to have a talk with Chief Eddie or maybe...Lincoln Tillis, depending.

Ryle gathered a couple items he needed and headed out. He wanted to walk around the inn property and see what all Amy and her crew had accomplished. What he had seen was amazing. If the rest proved the same, he'd definitely be using her business again.

Twenty minutes later, Ryle had seen enough, and he was impressed. The place looked exactly like Amy had promised. A million bucks. One more thing to do before he returned to the inn.

He'd brought ribbon to tie onto the tree he'd chosen for the single swing. A child's swing, some might call it. But he'd never had one as a child himself, and he was determined this place he'd fallen in love with would have one. Even if no one ever swung on it, it'd be there.

Only one tree stood out to him as the perfect place. Close to the inn, it would get the morning sun and afternoon shade.

He lifted his gaze to pick out the sturdiest branch he knew would hold the swing and caught sight of a dark box in the midst of the leafy branch.

What on earth was it?

He'd need an extension ladder, and he knew just where to get one. Amy's landscaping manager had asked, and been given, permission to store one in the inn's huge garage, temporarily, until he came for it in a few days.

Fifteen minutes later, Ryle had the ladder propped up against the large oak tree trunk and began climbing. Ten minutes later, after studying the box, he realized there were buttons on it to program it to send out signals. Or voices, or closer to the truth, screams-in-the-night. Someone was either programing this thing to automatically send out the screams, or doing it live when they thought it would be to their best advantage.

Why?

After so long, so much searching and thinking about it, he'd realized something. The sound wasn't coming from inside the house, just as Jazzi had thought. It was loud, true, but it wasn't a shrieking loudness that made you want to cover your ears. It was coming from *outside* the house.

Were they really that concerned that Ryle had bought the place? Did they think a few annoying screams would do the trick? And more important, why? It was all very immature, if this was the case.

Ryle reached in his back pocket for the snips he'd brought with him. If he was right, and he was pretty sure he was, he could clip this wire and though the scream might happen, it would be silenced to listeners. And as long as no one checked the box, they'd never know, Ryle and whoever else lived in the inn, wouldn't hear the screams.

And the big question, who was doing this? Frankie and Maxy. Maybe. But why? They were stationed in New York. Would they want some small place in West Virginia, for whatever reason?

Who else then? Appleton's mayor? Ryle shook his head. That sure didn't make sense. Unless he knew something Ryle didn't know. Or could be he was working with someone else for some reason or other.

And then there was that phone call late one night from a stranger insisting something was wrong. Why call if he wasn't going to share details?

Too much to think about right now, especially when it was just days before opening.

Ryle walked a pace away, turned and glanced high up in the tree where the box sat hidden now that he'd walked away. No one, unless they were looking for it, would have ever guessed it was up there.

Ryle headed back to the inn when he saw a police car pull up the driveway. He frowned.

Chief Eddie stepped out of the vehicle as Ryle approached. His unhappy face was proof enough that he wasn't about to share good news.

"What's going on, Chief Eddie?"

The man looked down at the envelope he held. "Not good news, I'm afraid, Ryle."

"Is that for me?"

"Yeah, I'm afraid so." He handed it over. "Hate doing these things, but gotta do it sometimes. This is one time I'm tempted to defy the law, even if I vowed to keep it to the best of my ability."

Ryle didn't answer the man. He was too busy

scanning the paper. A cease and decease order. Signed by no other than Mayor Slater.

When he looked up, Chief Eddie asked, "Trouble?"

"Afraid so. Seems someone is trying to stop me from opening the inn."

"What?"

That was real concern—or was it anger on the Chief's face. "Why? Who on earth would want to stop you from improving this rundown place? That's plumb crazy."

"Isn't it?" Ryle glanced at the paper again.

"Want me to keep an eye out for what's going on?"

"Yeah, I'd like that, but Chief Eddie, I have a feeling I'm dealing with something serious here. Screams in the night, but I found the equipment sending that out, so I think I've got that stopped. A strange call warning me there's trouble here. Two men from New York who are threatening Jazzi. And then this." Ryle tapped the paper in his hand.

On purpose, Ryle didn't mention Lincoln Tillis. Right now, it was better no one knew that an FBI agent was sniffing around town.

~*~

Jazzi was taking it easy. If Ryle caught her following Amy around, and the one man she'd brought with her to help with the heavier decorating things, Ryle might suspect she'd done more than he'd wanted her to. Which she had, but she'd been careful. After their argument yesterday about her talking with Chief Eddie, she sure didn't want a repeat of that. It had hurt too much to have him upset with her. Nope. She'd be very careful.

And, really, Amy and her help had done

almost everything. She'd been asked what she thought, whether she liked what Amy suggested, and she had. What was surprising was Jazzi's own tastes were quite good. The couple of times she'd suggested something different, Amy had agreed and seemed totally in approval.

So she had no qualms bothering her when Amy finally took her leave, and Jazzi stopped by one of the large front windows and saw Ryle and Chief Eddie beside the driveway talking. They weren't laughing. In fact, Chief Eddie looked a little angry and Ryle—well, she really couldn't tell how he was feeling, except she knew it wasn't a happy emotion on his handsome face.

Before she could even speculate on what was happening outside, the phone rang in her office. She hurried to answer it.

"Is this the person who bought that ole bed and breakfast in West Virginia?"

"Ryle Sadler is the owner. I am his manager, Jazzi Sanderson."

"Well, then, Miss Sanderson, has that owner found out anything?"

"No. I mean, we are investigating some things, but we don't know what's the problem yet. Can you give us some clues, some idea of what to do?"

There was a pause, and Jazzi heard a long sigh as if the man was weary with the burden of memories he was carrying.

When he didn't answer, Jazzi pressed him. "We could really use your thoughts. We're in the dark here."

"I had the rest of my family to think about." The voice was low, almost sad. "But I'll tell you this, I didn't stop looking. I tried. I really did, Miss, and everything pointed at that place. But I wasn't smart enough or rich enough to stop it. No one would listen—"

"Jazzi, where are you?" Ryle's voice preceded him into her office.

"Who's that?" The voice on the other end of the line sharpened, suspicion and anxiety wrangling over which would come out on top.

"It's just Ryle, the owner—"

"Gotta go. Don't stop looking, Miss."

The man hung up as Ryle entered the room.

Jazzi hung up the phone and stared down at the instrument.

"What's wrong, Jazzi?"

She lifted her gaze to his face. "It was him. Again."

"Him?" The frown on Ryle's face deepened. "Frankie?"

"No, not Frankie. The man on the phone who warned you something was wrong here."

"He called?"

"Yes. Just now."

"What did he say? Did he give you any idea what he was talking about before?"

"Not really. He said he'd tried, but he wasn't strong or rich enough to do anything. No one would help him." Jazzi did her own sighing. "He sounded so sad and hopeless. My heart is breaking for him, and I have no idea what all this is about."

"He could be pulling this to stop us opening the inn."

"Maybe. But I hope not."

"Things are worse." Ryle pulled the paper from his pocket Chief Eddie had given him. "We just got ordered to cease our plans for opening the inn."

"No."

"Afraid so."

"Can Emilia do something?"

"Probably. I'm on my way to talk with her now."
He headed to his own office but turned back. "I just
caught a glimpse of the interior decor. Everything
looks great. I'll check out the whole inn after awhile
when I have more time."

Jazzi didn't have time to answer him. He was
already in his office, and he shut his door.

~*~

"Emilia, I need your help again."

"What, no polite hellos or wondering how I'm
doing?"

Emilia was teasing, but he figured, in some
ways, she meant it. She was loyal, and faithful to
his business needs. She'd never let him down,
not once, and he guessed she wouldn't this time
either.

"I don't have time for that. You already know
you're the only friend I trust."

"Of course. That's a given. But I am your
lawyer. That could have something to do with the
trust."

"Maybe. But I trusted you before you finished
your lawyerly studies."

There was a smile in her voice when she
spoke again. "I know. How can I help you?"

"Two things. First, our town chief delivered a
paper, just minutes ago, halting the opening of
the inn."

"I told him—" Her voice hardened to steel.

"I know. Just fix it please."

"Right. And the second thing?"

"I need you to check out a man from New
York—hold on. I forgot to get his last name." He
pressed a button, and spoke into his phone
again. This time it was to Jazzi.

"Hey, can you tell me Frankie's last name?"

"No."

"Do you mean you don't know? Or you won't tell me?"

"Of course not. I don't know. Have never heard it spoken. Not by anyone. None of his pals and not even Maxy ever spoke it, that I know of."

"But how did he get credit cards or sign up for anything? There has to be some way to find out."

"If there is, I wouldn't have any idea."

"Ok. We'll work with what we have." Ryle started to hit the button to talk to Emilia again.

"Wait!"

Jazzi's sudden order stopped him. "You've thought of something?"

"Once I heard him called Frankie G. That probably won't help."

"You never know. It might. Thanks, Jazzi. We'll talk later." Ryle switched back to Emilia. "She has no idea what his last name is, but she did say she'd heard someone once call him Frankie G."

"What are you talking about?"

Ryle hesitated. He didn't want to violate Jazzi's trust by telling information about her that she'd shared—reluctantly, true—with him, but then he wanted those men gone. He shoved his concerns aside. Her safety was much too valuable to hesitate now. "I'm going to tell you something, Emilia, but I want it to be kept as quiet as you possibly can. And please don't mention it to Jazzi. Ever. Okay?"

"You know I'll do as you ask."

"Then here's the info. Jazzi was adopted by a couple here in town. She grew up feeling as if she wasn't loved as much as their own daughter—

which, by the way, wasn't true. She ran away at eighteen, but returned last year determined to turn her life around."

"That's good." Emilia sounded hesitantly positive.

"It is. But, the problem is, some people she associated with in New York, have shown up here, determined to take her back to New York. She doesn't want to go, seems to love her job here and her new life, but they won't stop bothering her. She's been physically attacked and threatened."

"Ryle, that's awful."

"It is."

"Tell me what you want me to do."

"I want you to find what information you can about this man. His name—as much as we know of it—is Frankie G."

"That's it? You want me to find someone with no last name, and you have nothing else?"

"That's about it. Frankie G. from New York. He has a bodyguard called Maxy, and I believe this Frankie is in some unpleasant work."

"Meaning illegal?"

"Yes, or criminal."

"I see." Emilia was quiet a moment. "You haven't given me much to go on."

"No, I haven't. But you haven't failed me yet."

"I haven't, have I? And I won't fail this time either, my friend. I'll have my investigators on it as soon as we're off the phone. And I'll take care of the other business immediately."

"Thank, Emilia. You've lifted a load off these broad shoulders of mine."

"I know." She laughed. "I'll send the bill in an email this evening."

"You're a harsh, cruel woman."

He could hear the laughter in her voice when she spoke again.

"Good-bye. Don't forget to get that check out to me ASAP." She hung up.

Ryle shut off his own phone and swiveled his chair to stare out the window. It was only when Jazzi thrust herself halfway into his office after knocking, that he looked away.

"Sorry to bother you, but Barbara just stopped by and asked if we'd like to take a walk this evening after supper with her and Paddy. She said Paddy mentioned you and I needed some cheering up and wanted to prepare a nice supper for us. You too busy? Want me to make excuses?"

Leaning back in his chair, he shook his head. "No, let's go with them. I'd like to find out more about these two employees of ours."

"Really?"

"Yep, and of course, we do need that cheering up." He winked.

"Right." Jazzi laughed and backed out of the room. "I'll let them know."

~*~

Paddy had prepared a simple supper when Jazzi and Ryle entered the dining room that evening. Barbara was just lighting candles, and she gave them a bright smile. "Hello, you two. Have a nice day?"

Ryle nodded. He wasn't about to tell her the bad news. "It was fine."

After a supper of what Paddy called the best Philly Cheese Steak sandwiches in the country—because of the special ingredients he added to the steak, along with a simple salad with his homemade dressing, Ryle was ready for that walk. Once again, he was thankful God had sent the man to his inn.

They met Paddy and Barbara outside on the front veranda.

"Barbara needs to pick up a couple of things from that small shop just outside of town. Are you two game on walking that far?"

Ryle glanced at Jazzi, and at her enthusiastic nod, he agreed. "Sounds good to us."

By the time they'd reached the store, Ryle was glad they'd accepted Paddy's invitation. It had been a short period of relaxation and peace. He could tell by Jazzi's laughter at some of Paddy's tales that it'd been good for her too.

Jazzi entered the store with Barbara while he and Paddy wandered around a little outside, finally leaning against the side of the store. They didn't talk at first, only studied the stars and surrounding area, enjoying the quietness together. Paddy was fast becoming more than just their chef. His friendship—with no nosiness attached—and acute intelligence was impressive.

"Paddy, I haven't had a chance to thank you for saving Jazzi last night."

"No need to. It needed done, and I was the one to do it at the time."

"It means more than you—"

"What is she doing here? She's trouble and you know it. No common sense and no ability at pulling off what I want. Just because you think you need her, doesn't mean I want her here, spoiling my plans. She—"

The hushed voices came from the front of the building.

Ryle glanced at Paddy who met Ryle's with one of his own.

"...said you ordered her to get here...possible."

Someone snorted, and then there was the

sound of scuffling.

"Ouch."

"Have that giant of yours get...of her then."

"He's gone." The voice sounded panicky.

"What do you mean? Where?"

"Don't know. When I woke this morning..."

Paddy shifted his feet, and even in the midst of listening to the covert conversation, Ryle wondered how such a big man was able to move so quietly.

"Get out of my face. Don't want to see you till...straightened out."

Paddy's raised brows questioned Ryle, but he shook his head.

The smooth sound of a modern vehicle interrupted their silent communication, and Ryle stepped closer to the corner of the building to catch a glimpse of the vehicle.

But as luck would have it, the girls came out of the store at the moment, and all Ryle caught in his rush was the tail end lights of a car a block away. Worse, there was no sign of anyone strolling down the street—or even running.

Ryle didn't say a word about what they'd overheard on the way home. In fact, neither of the men said much at all, but neither Jazzi nor Barbara seemed to notice. The women said their good-nights. Jazzi gave him a smile and a wave as she headed toward her own rooms.

"Jazzi." Paddy approached her. "I just want you to know, you have no need to worry about that man ever again. He'll not bother you."

She stared up at Paddy, her face questioning but trusting.

"You believe me?"

"I do, Paddy." She smiled, gave the men a casual wave and headed to her rooms.

Paddy turned back to Ryle, his voice quiet and low. "I need to talk to you a moment."

"You have coffee still hot?"

Paddy nodded and went straight to his domain. By the time Ryle stopped at his office a minute then arrived at the kitchen, Paddy had poured two cups of the brew and settled in a chair. Ryle joined him.

They sat silent for the first few minutes then Paddy spoke. "I don't like to bring up past happenings especially when they're not anything to be proud of, Ryle, but I think this needs told to you, and now's the time."

"You don't have to tell me anything."

"I know Maxy."

"You do?"

"Several years ago, I worked at a place. Maxy would hang around there nearly every night. But one night things went wrong."

Paddy's gaze was fastened on something across the room, but Ryle wasn't about to interrupt his contemplation on whatever he was contemplating.

"There was this sweet little thing, no bigger than a minnow. He was trying to drag her out of the place. She was struggling, and when I saw it, I took care of it. I warned him I'd better never see him again, and gave him a thrashing."

"Did you?"

"Did I give him a thrashing?"

"Did you ever see him again?"

"Not until last night. He had our Jazzi in a choke hold. She couldn't do a thing. I saw red, and that's when I went after him."

"I can't thank you—"

His chef looked at him. "I know, Ryle. I know."

"I thought she was dead."

"We caught him in time. I think he wanted to kidnap her, not kill her, but regardless of his intentions, I saw that same red I saw that night years ago. He saw me coming and backed away from her. After making sure she was okay, I headed for him. He knew what I could do. He's a big man, but last night, he was afraid."

"You wouldn't have killed him." Ryle was sure of that.

"No. I'm not a killer, and I don't go around beating people. But I gave him what he was asking for, and then I asked questions."

"You did?"

"We need to know why he's hanging around."

"Right."

"So he talked."

"Just like that."

Paddy's crooked smile told Ryle all he needed to know.

"It doesn't make sense, but he said there was a deed that was a fake, and it has to do with the inn."

"A fake deed." Ryle frowned, thinking about it. Was that what Mayor Slater's secret person was using as evidence to stop him? He leaned back and nodded when Paddy stood, then offered more coffee. "I guess I need to do some explaining too."

"Go ahead. I'm listening." Paddy sat again.

Ryle explained about the unknown man— through Mayor Slater—ordering a halt on the opening of the inn, the phone call from someone who seemed genuinely concerned. And then there was the concrete situation. "I do have people working on the problems, so I have help. But this new news sounds troublesome."

"Can I do anything?"

"Just help me keep watch over the women and our inn, but don't get yourself in more than you can handle."

"Don't you go worrying yourself about that. I reckon Paddy McKinney can handle himself."

"Then I'll see you in the morning. I think I need to soak in what we heard tonight. Maybe tomorrow something will click."

"You're probably right. Night, Mr. Ryle."

Ryle rose and left the kitchen. He wondered what Paddy thought about their conversation.

Chapter Fourteen

Ryle rose at daybreak, did a quick run around his property and almost beat Jazzi into the breakfast room.

She grinned as she slipped inside just before he did. "I guess I get first dibs of which homemade donut I want."

"Don't touch the chocolate one!" Ryle gave her shoulder a nudge with his own.

She reached for that exact one, winking at one of the maids as she did.

Ryle promptly reached for his favorite—since Paddy's hiring—a Scottish Cream Bun.

Jazzi frowned at him. "I thought you wanted the chocolate donut."

"Oh, that. It was just a ploy to keep you from deciding on the Cream Bun."

"Not nice."

"I know, but I couldn't resist."

"What is it?"

"A buttery bun filled with sweet cream. Delicious, especially with my morning tea."

"I'd like to taste it..." Jazzi eyed the confection.

Ryle held it out of her reach, but it was a futile attempt.

At that moment, Paddy set another small plate carrying the second Cream Bun in front of Jazzi. "For you, my dear."

Owner and manager laughed.

"Am I in time for breakfast?"

Ryle, Jazzi and Paddy turned in unison.

Emilia stood at the entry door to the breakfast nook, her smile as lovely as it'd been days ago.

"Emilia, why are you here?" Jazzi spoke before Ryle had a chance. "Not that we aren't thrilled to see you."

"I've got news." Emilia took a seat at the end of the table, between Ryle and Jazzi. "I have an appointment at ten thirty this morning."

"You didn't tell me." Ryle raised a brow at her.

"I know. Didn't know myself until last night. I wasn't about to refuse it. Besides, I was thinking I'd take a few days to explore the town. You did say your opening is this weekend, right?"

"It is. So does this appointment have anything to do with our problems?"

"It does. Why else would I be here in this state, although, I'll have to admit, Appleton is charming."

"I do think we've almost convinced Miss New York to move here." Jazzi spoke to Ryle, but her gaze remained on Emilia.

Emilia laughed. "I'm afraid not. I wouldn't mind owning a cottage somewhere around here just for short vacations."

"Meaning a mini mansion." Ryle's dry words had both of the ladies chuckling.

Paddy set down a fresh pot of tea and a scone in front of Emilia.

"Thanks, Paddy." She nodded, forked a few chunks of pineapple onto her plate, scooped up a couple of the grapes, then stirred a touch of sugar in her tea. "We did some extensive research on the title. There was a minor question about it at one time, a few years ago, but it seems fine , from everything we could find, that all is in the clear. Unless something is brought up at the hearing, everything should be fine, Ryle."

"That's a relief. Want me to go with you?"

"No, I won't need you. I'm sure you have final things to deal with."

Ryle scooted his chair back. "I have a man coming around nine with his GPR equipment to see what that cement is about, out back."

"That should be interesting."

"Where does a person have to go to find a friend around here?"

Ryle jumped to his feet. "Athan, what are you doing here two hours earlier than you said?"

"You seemed to need me sooner rather than later, if I recall your words." The man's words were dry, yet the amused smile on his face gave him away. He was happy to see Ryle.

"I certainly do. Athan, this is my manager, Jazzi Sanderson, and you remember my friend and lawyer, Emilia Pavlo and our extremely talented chef, Paddy McKinney. Our househelp by the windows are Lana Taylor and Liz Graham. And Jazzi's very capable assistant is Barbara Sizemore.

Athan nodded. "Good to meet all of you."

"My friend, Athan Meadows, is a genius, so be careful what you say when he's around. The little girl who is a mini-me of his aunt is Georgiana Meadows, and I do believe the boss of the family. His aunt Fay Anna Meadows is a talented teacher and cares for her niece when Athan is busy with work. She's interested in moving back up north."

"I hate to interrupt, but I have to run." Emilia turned to Jazzi. "Same room work for me?"

"Sure thing. You know where it is."

"Jazzi, would you mind showing Athan's aunt to her room?"

"Of course, I will." Jazzi followed Emilia out of the room with Aunt Fay Anna and Georgiana tailing her.

Ryle watched the three women and Georgi leave.

~*~

Emilia chattered as they climbed the stairs, and Jazzi listened, but if pressed, she would have had to confess, her mind was on the man who'd called yesterday. She did so wish there was some way to help him.

When she'd deposited Aunt Fay Anna and Georgi in their room, she'd gone with Emilia to hers. "It's good to have you here, Emilia. I'm sure Ryle is happy to see you again."

"Probably happier to have me here solving his problems." Emilia leaned forward to give Jazzi a hug. "The only thing that makes me happier than my work—not counting the pro bono work I do as a ministry—is spending some time with Ryle Sadler. That man has a heart of gold. If you knew what he does, how much he does for others—"

She swung away, but Jazzi could feel the depth of emotion in the other woman's voice. "I haven't known Ryle long, but I can see and sense what you're saying. I've never known another man like him."

Emilia turned slowly. "And I've never seen him so—so taken with anyone like he is with you."

Jazzi's throat closed up. What could she say to a comment like that? Better yet...*don't even think of it*. Thinking about statements like that led to dreams too good to realize, to disappointments that led to trouble, to heartache.

"I've got to run. I'd love to watch Ryle's friend when he uses his equipment on that cement."

"I'll hopefully have a good report tonight for Ryle and you." Emilia opened her suitcase, not looking at Jazzi. "You can't run from the truth, Jazmine Sanderson—"

Yes, I can.

Jazzi didn't stop to answer her friend.

~*~

Ryle had never considered himself heavy, but he'd never seen anyone eat like Athan Meadows and stay stick-thin. As his mother used to say, *a strong wind would blow so-and-so away.* The man had just finished two bowls of mixed fruit, eaten three different donuts and drank two cups of Paddy's coffee. With cream and a nugget of sugar.

He was a good man and a loving father. There were rumors that Athan and his wife had served a period of time as missionaries before Georgi was born, but Ryle had never asked, and Athan had never spoken of it. True or not, Ryle liked the man. He'd seen him hold up in the midst of a financial crisis, worried, yes, but steady in his belief that it would work out.

Now, Athan stood. "That was some fine dining. Ready to check out this cement?"

"I am." Ryle stood.

Ten minutes later, Athan had gathered his equipment, and Ryle led him outside to the back of the inn.

"Shouldn't take long. We'll see what we can see."

"You're staying busy?"

"More than we can handle. We do sub some out to other businesses at times."

"I appreciate you coming to my rescue. I'll make it worth your while."

"Like I said, I owe you and haven't been able to return the favor."

"You brought your GPRslice with you?"

"Naturally. Scanning unknown territory always requires noise diminishing equipment." Athan grinned. "You ready?"

"I am." Ryle watched as his friend switched on the machine and began running it over the ground, moving forward slowly. But it wasn't twenty minutes later, that Athan turned off the machine.

"Ryle, did you say this was a very old inn?"

"I did."

"Then I'm guessing you won't know what's under the ground here?"

Ryle stared—he hoped not open-mouthed—at Athan. Beyond the man, climbing down the steps from the veranda was Jazzi and following her was Aunt Fay Anna and Georgi.

"What did he say?" Jazzi walked across the short span of grass, her eyes wide.

"Athan was just about to tell me—us—what he's discovered, what that cement is about."

"It appears to be larger than Amy and Kory thought." Jazzi was eyeing the six foot length Athan's GPR had already spanned. "What is it? Not a grave, I hope."

"Nope. Not that."

"Then what could it be? Do you know?" Jazzi eyed first Athan then Ryle.

"Remember that long black line running from the house to the woods?"

Jazzi nodded.

"What if—could it be—" Athan hesitated, obviously uncertain about his own suspicions.

"A tunnel?" The childish voice came from a grinning Georgiana.

"I think you're absolutely right, little lady. Your daddy's been making us guess. Do you think you could coax him into verifying your guess?"

Ryle smiled down at the precocious child.

The little girl eyed her father, hands propped on her hips. "Daddy, you must tell us right now, or Mr. Ryle will be very angry."

"Do you really think so?" Athan knelt down in front of his daughter.

"I do." Her head bobbed up and down, and as if it was an afterthought, she added, "Please."

"Then I think I must do that." He rose. "We've found you an honest-to-goodness tunnel. Georgiana is exactly right."

"A real tunnel and not just a room?"

Jazzi's confusion was perfectly understandable. Ryle felt the same. A tunnel?

"Pretty sure. We'll keep going and see how long this thing is."

"But we've found no opening."

"Probably hidden. These old places have more hidden spots than a normal person can think of." Athan leaned down a little to check his equipment. "I'd suggest you check out your basement. That would be a good place to start looking for a hidden door."

Ryle glanced over at Jazzi, whose eyes were as big as the proverbial saucer. "Want to help me look after lunch?"

"You know I do." Jazzi looked at her watch. "Only two hours to wait."

~*~

Before the two hours had passed, Athan found them, a grin on his face. "I think you'd better come have a look at this place."

Ryle and Jazzi both jumped up from their desks and followed Athan outdoors.

In the back of the inn, to the left, was the woods and if one walked far enough through it, that person would run into the river. It was a nice distance away. Far enough that any owner of land close by wouldn't have to worry about flooding.

Now, Ryle and Jazzi hurried after Athan with his long strides, and all three entered the woods...

Athan stopped walking. Glanced around. And pointed. "I suspect, if you cut down those briars, you may find the end of the tunnel.

Beside him, Jazzi gasped. "Ryle, this is where I was at the time Maxy and Frankie found me. Remember?"

"How could I forget?"

"Right."

Her firm answer sent Ryle's next question straight at his friend. "So the tunnel stops there?"

"It does."

"Are you sure?"

"I am."

"Maybe your machine is not reading it right." Jazzi tossed in her comment, wary of what the man had found.

"This is the end of the tunnel."

"Are you sure? Have you—" Ryle repeated his question.

"I've gone over all the area around it and nothing else shows up. This is the end of it."

"Could we dig here and go back toward the inn?"

"Maybe, but my guess would be there's damage if this tunnel is as old as I think it might be. My personal thinking is, find that door—wherever it's at—and begin there. Even then you need someone to make sure it's stable. Left to themselves, tunnels have a way of falling in, of deteriorating over time."

"Then I think you and I, Jazzi, need to start checking out that basement again."

"I have a better idea." Athan motioned for them to follow him. "I have just what you need in the truck."

"And what would that be?"

"More equipment."

Ryle, Jazzi, Fay Anna and Georgi followed him back to his truck.

He opened the back of the truck and pulled out a small, handheld item and handed it to Ryle. "I wasn't sure what I might need so I brought two different pieces."

"How does it work?"

"You slowly run it over the blocks, cement or bricks. It will alert you to whatever is behind that wall."

"Nice. May I try it too?" Jazzi leaned in closer to study the machine.

"Of course. Let's go, and I'll give you an example of how to use it. Then you're on your own. Georgi's been begging to go into town. She saw something in that antique shop that caught her attention. I promised her I'd take her, and you can handle this just fine. It's easy as eating pie."

Twenty minutes later, Jazzi and Ryle were alone in the basement.

"I'm thinking we should start with this wall." Ryle patted the very back wall. "This is the one that is closest to where the tunnel begins.

"I agree." Jazzi nodded.

"You first or me?"

"Go ahead, Ryle. You can make the first mistake."

"Ha, watch me." Ryle turned on the machine and began scanning the brick, starting at one end of a wall. When he'd scanned half of it, and nothing showed but more dirt, he turned it off and handed it to Jazzi. "Your turn. Maybe you'll have more luck."

"Okay. Here goes." She lifted the machine then hesitated. "Do you think we should call Toni in case we need to reinforce anything?"

"I'm thinking we'll see what we find. If our curiosity is too much, we'll open it up a bit and see what's beyond. Then we'll call her if we decide to remove more brick."

"Okay then." Jazzi lifted the machine again and began scanning. When she found nothing after scanning the second half of the wall, she sat down on the bottom step of the stairs. "Nothing. Maybe we're not doing it right."

"Maybe. Wait."

"What?"

"We didn't check inside that small room where I stored Maisie's items."

"Yes, and remember how she acted so strangely? She didn't want you in there or even to look inside it?"

"Right. Let's see what we can see."

Stepping inside the room, they both stared at the back wall, the only one in the small room that was against an outside wall. Jazzi walked closer to it and placed a hand halfway up the wall. "I remember when we looked at the hand-drawn map of the place, there was a mark on the wall, and if I remember right, it was about here."

"Do you think...?"

Jazzi nodded. "We won't know unless we check it out."

Ten minutes later, the machine began reading, and Jazzi nodded at Ryle as she turned it off. "There's a space behind this wall."

"Looks like it. Let's see what's behind it, if we can."

"I have goosebumps."

Ryle stopped his reach for a chisel and mallet.

"Are you afraid. We can wait for—"

"No, I'm not afraid. Just excited. Let's do this."

Unlike their search days earlier, when they'd found the puzzle box, digging away the mortar from these blocks turned out to be much harder. Ryle guessed the brick—although not new by any measure, was still newer than the tiny section they'd opened before when discovering the puzzle box. Placing the chisel against the freshly painted mortar joint, he gave it several hardy strikes.

The mortar began crumbling until the brick was easily removed.

They moved from one to another until the space was big enough to step through.

"Do you think the tunnel will be collapsed, Ryle?"

"I have no idea, but I hope not." They shone both of their flashlights into the hole.

Jazzi straightened. "It *is* a tunnel, and it looks fairly clear. Are you thinking what I'm thinking?"

"I think I am. Are you game? If we do this, we've got to be really careful or we'll be in more trouble than either of us want."

"I'm not sure *I* can wait." Jazzi's tone was low and bordered on excitement and cautiousness.

"Well, then, get us some drinks, if you will. We'll give the tunnel a cursory study and later have Toni and her crew frame in the opening."

"Extra batteries? What else?"

"Maybe grab the walkie-talkies. Leave one with Paddy, just in case. Jackets?"

"Will do. I'll see you in fifteen minutes."

Fourteen minutes later, she was back. He took the bottle of water Jazzi handed him and drank half before replacing the cap.

"Ready?"

"I am."

Ryle edged his way through the opening. He turned and held out a hand to Jazzi. "Come, and I'll help you through. We've got to be really careful from here on."

Jazzi shone her flashlight around the area. There wasn't a lot of debris lying around, and at least this part of the tunnel was fairly clear. She took a deep breath. "Let's see how far we can go. I can't imagine what this tunnel was used for."

"Who knows? Until we find some evidence of that, we'll have to use our wits and imagination. Keep a sharp lookout for anything that might give us a clue."

"Maybe it was used during the Civil War."

"Or used as an entry for illegal smuggling."

"You think so? Drugs?"

"I have no idea." Ryle swept his flash along the roof of the tunnel.

"It could be whoever owned this land—"

"Or inn."

"Right. Or inn, used it as a method to deliver supplies. Completely innocent and reasonable."

"And when it was no longer needed, it was walled up in the basement."

"Good possibility." Jazzi hoped with all her heart it was true. But who knew? That elderly man who'd already called twice kept insisting something or someone needed found. But with no idea of where to look, his wish might never get answered. Her sigh caused Ryle to shoot a quick question at her.

"Are you okay? Is something wrong?"

"I'm fine. Just thinking."

"About all that's happening? Regretting your decision to work here?"

"Of course not. I've already told you, I love the

job. I even enjoy the mystery, but I can't help wondering what we might undercover. And why did Maisie run a hand over each wall?"

"Maybe she knew something. Maybe she felt something."

Occasionally there would be a large rock at the side of the tunnel or a decaying tree root that had managed to survive enough to cause a minor hindrance in passing, but nothing major hindered their progress to wherever this tunnel was headed.

"Jazzi, do you get the feeling that this tunnel might have been used a lot in the past, but it also seems as if it's been used recently too?"

"I do. I didn't say anything because it seemed such a crazy idea. I mean—"

"Yeah." Ryle laughed aloud. "Are we both crazy?"

It was only another few hundred feet that they came to the first large blockage. Debris—lots of it blocked their passage, and even a minor study of it, gave them no assurance they'd be able to move on.

Ryle was irritated, and his voice showed it. "Guess we'll not find out what's at the end of this now."

"Doesn't look like it. But, Ryle, look how far we've come." Jazzi's light caught the glimmer of something in the pile of dirt, boards and other things. "What's that?"

"What do you see?"

"I saw a flash of something. Right...there. See it?"

Ryle leaned forward. "I do. Let me see if we can retrieve it."

"Be careful."

"You bet." Ryle shone his light around, then

grabbed a long, thin twig. With care, he eased it into the pile and wiggled it inch by inch through the mass of wood-ish earth. "I think..."

"Do you have it?"

He pulled again, dragging the end of the twig from the mess. And at the end of the twig, being carefully drug from the mess, shone a tiny gold button. After he picked it up, Jazzi reached for it.

"What is it? Oh-h-h." Jazzi turned it over and over in her fingers, studying it. "Do you suppose some genteel person wore it?"

"Then lost it? Why would they be inside a tunnel?" Ryle took hold of the button—what use to be, no doubt, shiny and bright, the edges of it, dull and tarnished.

Jazzi's forehead wrinkled in a frown. "I don't want to think about it, but possibly a youngster from the mid-eighteen hundreds, escaping with her parents?"

"From what? The only people I know of who tried to escape were the slaves, and why would they have a gold button? "What would a child be doing in a tunnel?"

"The book didn't describe anything specific happening here."

"No, not unless you count the mild, general comment about strange happenings after the inn closed in the early nineteen hundreds."

"I wonder what that meant?"

Ryle turned the button over and studied it.

Chapter Fifteen

Fortunately, Toni-Deluca Douglas knew of a smaller excavation company that agreed—when Ryle talked with them and offered a bonus above the cost—to begin work on cleaning out the tunnel that afternoon. Ryle insisted on carefulness with the work, but urgency in getting it done. Who knew what might be found or how it could be used as an attraction—possibly.

Now, he and Jazzi stood watching as the men began clearing out the tangle of briars and honeysuckle that engulfed the spot above the tunnel ending.

"I put the button in the safe for now. Wrapped it in a clean white handkerchief to try to preserve any—if there is any—evidence. We'll examine it later when we have more time. And I did contact Chief Eddie about it."

"I probably should go through those books and the material I found and printed out at the library. I'd love to have this mystery solved before opening day."

"You've been busy, but now, that everything is ready for opening day, if you want, I'd like that. We really need to know more of the history of this place."

"I'll do that this afternoon." Jazzi gave the working men a glance. "I wonder how Emilia's doing."

"I didn't get a chance to quiz her, but she'll fill

us in when she gets home. Looks like we may have a full inn for this weekend with everyone showing up determined to celebrate the opening with us."

"I know. I'm so excited. So pleased that everything is going as you planned."

"I don't like failure and do all I can to prevent it."

"I don't like failure either, but I've certainly experienced it." The moment she spoke the words, Jazzi wished she hadn't. Why bring up her failures now?

"Who hasn't?" Ryle shrugged his shoulders. "It's hard, embarrassing and emotionally depressing, but strong people fight through it, and Jazzi, you're a strong person because of it. I've watched you overcome everything that wasn't great in your life."

"I'm learning, I hope." Her sigh was a breath of released tension. "I think I'd better have a look at those library books and information. I'll let you know if I find anything pertinent."

He sketched a wave at her, watched as she walked back to the inn, then returned to watching the excavating team who were making rapid progress. All of this might not mean a thing, but he didn't want to leave even a minor detail unchecked. He wanted answers. He wanted peace restored to this place he was sure he'd been nudged to create. And, for once in his life, he wanted a life he'd never imagined having.

~*~

Jazzi spread the books out across one side of her work table, the individual papers and files on the other. Picking up a book that looked as if it might be helpful, she flipped through the pages and, finally, laid it down. She reached for the second book on the stack. It looked as new as the day it left the printing press. She opened the book and began skim-reading it. She wasn't past the first few pages until it gripped her attention.

It wasn't a boring detailed fact book, but a real live history of Appleton. Midway through it, she came to the chapter that talked about a fancy inn at the edge of town. The picture that was included didn't look much like what Ryle's inn did today, but the veranda and the structure were similar.

Jazzi kept reading.

~*~

Three hours later, Jazzi had managed to finish the book. She flipped through it, the pages fluttering slowly, one after another, finally coming to the end of the book. Turning it over, she opened the front cover and stared down at the black and white photo of the man who'd written it.

And kept staring at it.

Rushing over to the desk, she rummaged through it until she found a magnifying glass. Holding it over the image, she studied it, scanning each part of it then returned to the one thing that'd caught her attention the most.

When she finally laid both book and magnifying glass on the table, she drew in a deep breath, her heart beating a stampede.

She spent another hour going through files and papers that gave her nothing. Only that one chapter in the new-looking book called *The True History of Appleton, West Virginia* and the photo, gave her information that might prove valuable.

Jazzi gathered up everything she'd borrowed from the library in a neat pile to return, but the book she laid on her desk. That would be what she'd share with Ryle later on.

Heading to Ryle's office, she retrieved the key for his safe, unlocked it, and withdrew the puzzle box. She made sure everything was locked and secure again before carrying the box to her office. It'd taken awhile reading that Chapter Thirteen in the book—unlucky number? Not by her calculations—when a thought hit her. They—she and Ryle—had been studying the wrong item in the box. Instead of the map of the assumed bed and breakfast, she should have been focusing on the pictures they'd both deemed unhelpful.

There were only three of them. She spread them out in front of her and zeroed in on the one of the inn. The identical picture in Chapter Thirteen of the book.

She picked up first one then the other and flipped them over. Grinning, she wanted to dance across the floor in excitement. She did jump to her feet just as Ryle entered her office.

"Whoa, didn't mean to startle you."

"You didn't. I'm just so excited I could barely wait to tell you."

"Tell me what?"

"Look." Jazzi spread the pictures and pointed at the one of the inn. "This picture was in the puzzle box. This exact same one is in this book. Chapter Thirteen."

Ryle lifted the single photo first and studied it. Then replacing it on the table, he flipped through the book until he came to the same picture. Settling in one of the chairs in her office, he did as she'd done earlier: skim-read through the chapter.

When he'd finished, he closed the book and replaced it on the table. "I see why you're excited.

How does it help us though?"

"Don't you see? Whoever wrote this book..." Jazzi tapped the book with one finger. "...and whoever created this puzzle box had to have been the same person or two people who are connected somehow."

Ryle stared at her. "Jazzi, that sounds very reasonable. And if that is true, perhaps that person is still alive. The published date is current."

"Not only that, but did you catch what all this inn was used for in the past?"

"Y-e-s, I did."

"One of the stations on the Underground Railroad. And the tunnel was used to hide those escaping."

"I think perhaps it was, and maybe that's all it is about."

"Maybe." Jazzi stared out the window, her imagination soaring higher than even she could usually dream about. "But why did the writer—this MB Slate—write about strange happenings? Why is he or she so mysterious in the last third of the chapter? It's almost as if he was rambling."

"Exactly. That brings up the question: Is the person a knowledgeable writer? Or just some wannabe who used already known information to try to reach a certain level of fame?"

"Who knows—yet? But there's something else." Jazzi was so excited she barely could stand still.

"More?"

"Yep. Look." She opened the cover and pointed. "Do you see it?"

"The same man again."

"Yes, but look what he has on." Jazzi handed him the magnifying glass.

Ryle took the glass and studied the picture. A minute later he straightened. "His coat buttons are the same as the one we found."

"Exactly the same."

~*~

Another three hours passed before Ryle and Jazzi ambled outside to see what progress had been done. They met the supervisor halfway across the lawn.

"All finished. It really was a fairly quick job. The only serious part was making sure we didn't cause any more cave in."

"Can we take a look?"

"Sure. We cleared away the remains of a small building that had mostly rotted away. And it seems the ground around the hole is secure enough, but the stairs leading down to the bottom are a mite wobbly. You'll want to be careful if you plan on using them."

Ryle nodded. "Will do. Let me do a quick check to make sure everything's finished while you're loading up your equipment then I'll get your check to you."

Minutes later, Ryle stood at the bottom of the steps and spoke. "Come on down, Jazzi, if you want. Just be careful. The steps aren't nearly as bad as I thought they might be. Here, I'll stand at the bottom and make sure you don't fall."

"I'm not afraid. But if you insist—"

She was laughing, probably at his offer, but he didn't care. Her safety was more important than her current amusement at his protectiveness. At least she wasn't protesting it.

Once on the tunnel ground, they took their time going through it, flashing their lights around, until they'd covered all the part they hadn't already gone thru from the other end.

"I'm ready to go if you are. We've already searched the rest of the tunnel." Jazzi whirled back to the steps just as the overhead light streaming through the hole at the top of steps darkened.

"Ryle?"

"I don't know what happened, but I suspect someone covered it over with something that will prove to be too heavy for us to move down here. Fortunately, we have our flashlights and another way out. Let's go."

"If we hurry, maybe we'll be able to see who did this."

"Maybe, but I wouldn't bet on it." Ryle gripped her arm and they made tracks toward the inn. "Whoever it was, wouldn't tarry around."

"Do you think it was Maxy again?"

"If it was, it's a very inept act of foolishness. They surely know we've already found the entrance in the basement."

"And if that's the case, it sounds as if they're the ones behind our troubles."

Ryle motioned for her to go first into the basement. If it had been Maxy, then Jazzi was right. He and Frankie were indeed his trouble makers. And Maxy hadn't learned his lesson from Paddy.

~*~

That night at supper, Ryle asked Athan. "I'm thinking I need you to work on another section of our land."

"What do you have in mind?"

"I need you to do some land scanning around the end of the tunnel."

"Are you thinking there's more tunnel?

Remember, I did a bit around the opening already."

"No more tunnel, but I suspect there's more mischief farther away than you looked."

"The opening is in two days. Think about it. If we discover anything, we're going to have all kinds of people roaming over your land. Not a good prospect for the opening."

Ryle eyed his friend. "You're right. Are you thinking waiting till after the opening?"

"Yes, but even then if we find anything at all controversial, you'll have a time with guests arriving. Not sure that would be good for business." Athan shook his head slightly at his daughter who was playing with her food. "Georgi, that's enough."

"I'm not sure there will ever be a good time."

"True. I'll tell you what. Let's take a look at it. If we see anything, we'll make a determination then whether it's important enough to call in the cops."

"I agree. I don't want to put it off if there's something—if you find anything disturbing."

"Could be nothing."

"Could be. I'm going with my gut right now."

"Never has failed you before, has it?"

"Always a first time."

"True. But I hope you're wrong."

Ryle nodded but didn't answer his friend. He really, really hoped the same.

~*~

Early the next morning, Ryle met Athan outside. "Ready?"

A nod was Athan's answer. "Ready if you are. Show me what you want to scan."

Ryle pointed out the area. "Let's start here."

"Got it."

Ryle backed out of the way while Athan went

to work scanning the area. After twenty minutes had passed and Athan was still scanning, Ryle edged up to his friend.

Athan looked up and switched off the machine. "Don't ask."

"What do you mean, don't ask?"

"Just trust me on this."

"Athan Meadows—"

"No, Ryle. I've always admired you for your ability to know how to go about helping. But this time, you need to trust *me*. If not for your sake, then for that exotic girlfriend of yours."

"You're making no sense. Is it that bad?"

"Yes, but I want you to wait till after opening, for sure. When you call in the authorities, you're going to wish I'd never found what I've found."

"I think I should at least call our detective here in town. He's discreet and works with the citizens."

Athan cocked a brow. "You know him. If you think that's best."

"I do."

"Whatever you decide, I'll stand with you."

"Is it that bad? I don't see how I could be blamed for it."

Athan didn't answer. His silence said it all.

~*~

Opening Day

Ryle stood at the end of the hallway on the first floor where the three suites were located, watching as the final touches were being put on the pavilions. A movement to the right caught his attention. Was that—

Athan and Chief Eddie disappeared into the woods. What was Athan doing, especially after urging Ryle to wait till after the opening to talk with authorities?

"Ryle, are you okay?"

"I'm fine." He smiled at the woman who'd been there whenever he'd needed her. But no reason to worry her over his unsubstantiated suspicions. "Are you sure we're good to go with our opening?"

"All's good, Ryle." Emilia thrust her arm in the crook of his. "The judge threw out the case, saying that the plaintiff failed to prove his case."

"That's a relief. How did the opposer take the judge's ruling?"

"He wasn't there, and his lawyer spoke to no one after the ruling." Emilia gave him a smile that would have conquered the hardest heart. "Who cares? We won. Enjoy yourself tonight and relax. You've turned this project into another success."

"The prospects look great, but we'll see how the rest of this year goes." Ryle rubbed a hand over his head.

"And what's next on your work schedule?"

"I have businesses who've requested help right here in West Virginia, and a couple other places I'm considering. I've giving this place most of my attention for a few more months, but with Jazzi's help, I think I can sneak away to work with a few businesses in the near future, then take on more that I feel are important."

"After that? What about Jazzi?"

Emilia's smug glance both irritated and amused him. "What about her?"

"Really? Are you going to leave her hanging? You know she's crazy about you, but too shy to show it."

"You're imaging things. She's been a great

help, organizing, taking care of so many details, making sure deliveries are both on time and correct. She's interviewed, helped research, and worked almost as hard as I have getting this place ready to open. She's lifted a ton of weight off my shoulders. I couldn't do without—"

"Ah, ha! I thought so."

Irritation made a swift track through his body. As much as he loved this friend, she could be— annoying. Very much so, when she was determined to win their minor touchy subjects. Like this one.

He cast a swift glance out the window, but there was no sign of Chief Eddie or Athan.

Throwing her a quick smile, he walked away. He wasn't ready to face up to his feelings about Jazzi. Not yet. Maybe never. He was so used to being a loner, it was hard to imagine Jazzi being in his life as a—

Nope. He wasn't going there today.

The surprise he had planned for his manager was as far as he would go with his emotions.

For now.

And maybe forever.

~*~

Heather Sanderson showed up early in the afternoon of the day of the opening. She walked straight to Jazzi's room, knocked lightly and called out. "Jazzi, are you in there?"

"Mother? Is that you? Come in."

Heather opened the door, and smiling entered the room, carrying a small box.

"You're here early..."

"I'm not staying right now, but I wanted to drop this off to you and hoped you'd like it well enough to wear tonight. You did say you're wearing that white dress with the blue shrug Amy picked out for you, aren't you?"

"I am."

"Then, if you like it and want it, this is yours." Heather thrust the box toward her daughter.

"What is it?" Jazzi took the box, turning it slowly in her hands.

"Open it. It was James's great grandmother's and has been handed down through generations. I can't imagine it suiting to anyone better than you."

Slowly, Jazzi opened the box and stared down at the beautiful sapphire-studded hair comb, lying on the satin covered, tiny pillow. Something— was it emotion?—swept over her, forcing tears to fill her eyes.

"Mother—"

Heather went to her. "It's yours. I hoped you might consider wearing it tonight. It matches those deep blue eyes of yours perfectly, and with that white dress—how could anyone not see what a beautiful person you are?"

She went to Jazzi then, and as tiny as she was, gave her daughter a firm hug. When she released her, Heather settled in one of Jazzi's plush chairs in her suite. "Your father gave me that comb after he proposed and asked me to wear it on our wedding day."

"It's beautiful, and I will certainly wear it tonight." Jazzi placed the box on her dresser.

"You and Ryle have done a marvelous job of creating this place. You'll have more business than you can imagine."

"You really think so? I hope for that, for Ryle's sake."

"Well, your father wouldn't tell you, but he put up his own money for an announcement in some of the biggest cities' newspapers."

"Did he really?" Jazzi had always known her father was the toughest nail to crack. Obviously, Ryle had cracked her father, if he was willing to do such a thing.

Heather stood. "I have to run, but I'm glad we got to spend a few minutes together. I doubt we'll have much time tonight to talk, so I wanted to make sure you had the comb beforehand. Love you, Jazzi. See you tonight."

And Heather Sanderson swept out of the room after blowing a kiss at Jazzi and leaving behind a trail of her chosen brand of expensive perfume.

Jazzi moseyed to the window to watch her mother leave in the newest model of Cadillac, and when she'd disappeared from sight, Jazzi took in the yard, the two rows of beautiful ornamental pear trees flowing in a curving sweep beside the driveway. Growing beneath the trees were samplings of different shade plants including hostas, colorful caladiums, stately coral bells, a variety of ferns and shy bleeding hearts, along with a mixture of spring flowers for that upcoming season.

And then her eyes caught sight of someone sneaking from out of the small bunch of trees to the west of the property. They seemed in no hurry nor showed any furtive movements as they strolled toward the inn.

Who was it? And more important, what had they been doing on Ryle's property?

Maybe nothing. Maybe someone thinking it was state property or someone just being nosy.

The knock on the door interrupted her musings. She hurried to answer.

"Miss Jazzi, Paddy needs you in the kitchen.

Could you come?"

"Of course, I can."

~*~

Preparations for the event began early that morning. Because of the large number of those invited who'd accepted their invitation, Jazzi had suggested, and Ryle had agreed, to hold the evening meal and piano concert by Starli Peterman-Blair, outdoors. Amy had created the flower arrangements, and Paddy and Apple Blossoms newest chef was preparing the food. Chief Eddie and his two deputies were offering protective duty throughout the evening. Just in case certain unwanted persons tried to interrupt the proceedings.

All was in order, and Ryle smiled in satisfaction that, so far, things were going as planned.

One hour still to go. Plenty of time to take a few minutes rest and then dress for the evening.

His thoughts drifted to the part of the forest where he'd disconnected the device delivering those howls and screams. So far, it had been quieter. There'd been no more signs of Maxy and his boss. Other than the idea they'd come for Jazzi, why else would they have been in Appleton?

Thank God, he had Chief Eddie and his men on guard tonight. That should keep mischief-makers at bay.

Besides all of his Appleton friends, the new pastor in town, Jazzi's parents and quite a few of his business associates who'd turned out to be good friends, FBI agent Lincoln Tillis had given him a quick phone call last night sharing that he believed he was narrowing down his suspect list and vowed he would be there.

It was going to be one of the best celebrations he'd ever had over what looked like was going to be a stunning success.

Mentally crossing his fingers, he headed to his suite, hoping to catch a fifteen minute catnap.

Chapter Sixteen

Ryle barely made it downstairs and out on the veranda that evening before cars began pulling into the driveway. The large canopy—big enough to seat the fifty or so guests—was elegant in its whiteness. Tables were set close by to hold the hors d'oeuvre that Jazzi, Paddy and Starli Peterman-Blair had chosen. The dinner itself would be served on dinner plates by the waiters from Apple Blossoms.

Of course, Starli had agreed to provide the music.

And then there was the surprise he'd planned for the evening. Someone—he hoped—would be impressed.

He walked down the steps of the veranda and began greeting the first arrivals.

Where was Jazzi? She should have been here with him, sharing this moment. But it was twenty minutes later before he caught sight of her hesitating at the top of the veranda steps.

Ryle drew in a sudden breath of shock. Jazzi stood quietly confident, seemingly unaware of the picture she made. She'd dressed simply in a white gown with its dark blue, lacey shrug, her black hair a stunning contrast. And even from where he stood, he could see the sapphire-blue of her eyes. And the expensive-looking comb encrusted with what had to be real sapphire stones, adorning the right side of that black hair—well, he'd never seen a princess look any better.

Before she could take one step, he hurried toward her, holding out a hand to guide her down the steps. "What did you do with my manager?"

Jazzi laughed. "Oh, I'm sure she's hanging around somewhere. I don't think you'll have to look too hard."

"You're right. No one will pay any attention to anyone else tonight. Everyone will be gazing at you, I'm afraid."

She laughed again. "Silly. Once they get a taste of those hors d'oeuvres they'll forget about the likes of your manager. And let me tell you, those things are scrumptious."

"Nevertheless, you are, my dear manager, the belle of the ball tonight."

"Thank you, Ryle." Her quiet statement wasn't finished. "I need to thank *you* for believing in me, for the opportunity to make a difference in my life, and for giving me a chance to do something I love. I've never been happier."

He stared at her for a moment. "Jazzi, I feel the same thing."

"You do?"

"I do. I've always loved what I do, but there was always this vague sense of void, as if I was missing something." Ryle stared down into her eyes. "I think I've found it."

Faint pink crept up in her fair skin, but he had no time to study it. A male voice interrupted. "Looks like you've got a bang-up event planned for tonight."

Lincoln Tillis.

Ryle gave a quick glance around. Most everyone was here. Time to officially begin the event. "Glad you could make it, Tillis. I need to talk with you later tonight. You are spending the weekend?"

"Planned on it."

"Good." But when he started to release Jazzi's hand, her's tightened, and he glanced at her. She didn't say a word, but he understood the sudden plea in her eyes. *Don't leave me alone with* him.

"Let's go, Jazzi. I want you with me when I welcome everyone."

When Ryle walked onto the platform, he pulled Jazzi with him, ignoring her low protests.

"It's your night, Ryle."

"No, it's our night. I couldn't have done this without your help." He let go of her hand, moved to the microphone and spoke. "Welcome, my friends! It's good to have you here celebrating with us on the newest bed and breakfast in West Virginia. We hope you'll enjoy this evening so much you'll plan on visiting us again..."

Ryle kept talking for another few moments then motioned for Jazzi to come to him. "I'll have my very capable assistant join me here as we wow you with another of *the* Andrew Carrington's famous works of art. He consented some time back to do our indoor pictures as well as our outdoor sign and...well, before we get to that, I want to share a special tribute to one of the best I've ever worked with. When I felt God wanted me to ask Jazmine Sanderson to come work with me, I hesitated. I was used to working alone, and Jazzi and I didn't really know each other. How could I know if we would be work-compatible, and that was not even considering her feelings on the matter. But she's proved to be an amazing manager and friend who's helped to turn this place into what it is today."

The sudden applause, started he was sure by

her parents, gave him pause, and he waited. Jazzi was staring at him, and he knew it was time.

"I wanted her to know how much I appreciated her, so I decided to honor her by naming the inn after her. And here it is."

With Jazzi's help, they uncovered the sign sitting on an easel, and Ryle was pleased when gasps of approval floated to his ears. It was an inviting, welcoming sign.

Welcome to
The Flowering Blue Jazmine
Bed and Breakfast

Andy had done a beautiful job.

But most of all, the look on Jazzi's face, the wonder of happiness in her eyes warmed his heart.

No, that wasn't right. It set his heart on fire. A feeling he'd never felt before. And if there hadn't been a multitude of watching eyes, he'd have lifted her and swung her in circles.

When the applause died down, he held up a hand. "Now it's time for you all to mingle. Our chefs have prepared a variety of appetizers for your enjoyment which are now ready for you. Feel free to mingle over the grounds. Once dinner is served, the renowned and accomplished Starli Peterman-Blair will share her musical talent with us. After that, the inn's doors will be unlocked, and we'll finish the evening with a tour of the inn. Enjoy!"

~*~

Jazzi was stunned by Ryle's action. The sign was absolutely beautiful, true, but why would

Ryle do this? After all, she was an employee, someone who'd accidentally entered his life. Someone, she was sure, because of his good nature, had hired her. Just because she loved the job and strived to do as good as she could, didn't mean she should be rewarded like this, did it?

She ran a hand along the edge of the sign.

"Do you like it?" Caroline Carrington—Andrew's wife—spoke from behind her.

Jazzi swung around. "It's amazing. I can't believe Ryle did this."

Caroline chuckled. "Why wouldn't he? It's an outstanding name for the inn, and he does seem to care a great bit for you."

"As an employer."

"Maybe, but I've heard rumors there's more to your relationship than that."

She'd never associated with Caroline as much as Toni Deluca-Douglas or even Starli Peterman-Blair, but she'd always wanted to as Caroline seemed more approachable than the others. She'd heard Caroline was rather—uh, forward—with her remarks, and now she wondered if she should put a definite stop to this supposed rumor or ignore it.

What would Ryle do?

Ignore it unless forced to make a statement.

She made her decision when she changed the subject. "I'd love to have a tour of your husband's art sometime."

"Come by anytime. He loves showing off his work." Caroline took her arm and walked off the stage just as Starli sat at the piano. "Hey there, Starli."

The quiet one of the bunch raised a hand and gave both Caroline and Jazzi a smile.

"Miss Jazzi." Paddy called to her in a low voice as he strode toward her. "Can we talk?"

"Of course." She promised Caroline she'd stop by soon to view Andy's artwork, then moved on to speak with Paddy. "What's wrong?"

"Someone's destroyed all the trays of the Raspberry Brie Tarts. I have no idea how this could have happened. All was safe when I checked late this afternoon. I gave the help an hour's break and took a short one myself, but when I returned, there they were—every one of them on the floor, smashed, as if someone in anger had stomped them."

"No! Paddy, I'm so sorry." Jazzi thought for a second. "Obviously, you don't have time to make more. We've planned for eight items to be served. We have the fruits and cheeses. That will have to do."

"I'm sorry, Jazzi. I should never have left the kitchen. But I'm also angry. It's a good thing I don't know who is responsible."

"We will be fine. We have more than enough other options. No one will notice. All will be fine." Jazzi patted the man's arm.

Paddy breathed out a sigh that was both disappointed and frustrated. "You are right. I need to get back to make sure everything else goes well."

Jazzi watched as the man stomped off, muttering to himself. He was such a nice man, seemingly loyal and protective of Ryle and herself. But he wasn't fond of trouble and those who caused the trouble.

She hadn't said anything to the chef, a little fearful of what he might do, but she was pretty sure who was behind this. She wasn't guessing because she'd seen the person do similar things before.

Frankie. But how had the man known the kitchen would be empty at that specific time? Paddy's quarters were close by. Frankie would have had to be very quiet.

But then, he wouldn't have done the act himself. Some flunky of his would have been ordered to cause destruction, and how much easier could it be than this? Just to convince her to return? To do another job for him.

And if it hadn't been his doings, then who else was targeting the inn and Ryle?

Who was that? Someone—was it a *woman*? Whoever, was walking briskly across the lawn behind the cars parked in the parking lot. The same woman she'd seen earlier.

~*~

Ryle wandered among the tables, stopping to speak at each one, sharing memories or warm comments to each of the attendees, but his favorite quick stops were to his Appleton friends— and Emilia, of course. There was no sign of Jazzi. Where had she disappeared to? He wanted her here. With him. She should be sharing the happiness this venture seemed to be promising.

Was that—it was! Jazzi was running across the back part of the lawn behind the visitor cars, the white of her dress like a beam of moonlight in the evening's dimming light, giving her an airy magical look.

Ryle stood quietly, staring at the woman who'd helped make this current project real and successful. Suddenly—he had no idea what was happening to him—he'd never done such a carefree—or was it harebrained—thing in his life? He was running across the lawn to join her in whatever she was up to.

She was fast, but he was faster, and when he came close, he called out softly to her. "Jazzi, where are we headed?"

With an abrupt stop and whirl, she was facing him, panting lightly. "Ryle, what are you doing away from your friends?"

"You were running. I wanted to join you. Where are we going?"

"But you have on dress clothes."

"So do you."

Her eyes were wide with questions, but she must have decided it was useless to argue.

"I'm chasing someone."

"I hope it's not a man."

She gave him a look that said plainly, *are you serious?*

He ignored the look. "Are we trying to catch this person?"

"I doubt that will happen now that I've been interrupted." She cast a glance behind her.

He reached for her hand. "Let's go see."

He took off, and she followed, her hand still snug within his. Minutes later, they burst out onto the country road.

A car was parked twenty feet or so down the road, and a young girl was climbing into the driver's seat. She hesitated, glanced back at them.

Was that a smirk on her face? It was hard to tell from this distance, but it sure looked like it. Why would she be smirking back at them?

"Who is that?"

Jazzi's face was a study.

"That's Creticia, one of the young girls I interviewed for the assistant position."

"And you didn't hire her."

"No, I didn't."

"Why didn't you hire her?"

Jazzi didn't answer.

"Jazzi?"

The car in the distance started, made a slow turn in the road and headed away from them. A hand shot out of the window and flipped a wave at them.

"That's why." She pulled her hand from his and turned, walking briskly, back to the inn. "You need to get back. What on earth will your friends think?"

"Jazzi, stop." He gripped her arm and forced her to stop. Running away from his questions? Probably. Running away from him? He hoped not.

She looked up at him. "What?"

Were those tears in her eyes? He gently placed a hand under her jaw to study her face. "Why are you crying?"

"It's all my fault. I ruined all the raspberry tarts."

"Nonsense. What are you talking about?"

"Someone tossed all those luscious-looking tarts Paddy and the maids made onto the floor and stomped all over them. Ruined. When I saw Creticia sneaking across the lawn, I knew who was behind it."

"Frankie. What did Paddy say?"

"He wasn't happy." She grimaced. "The problems you've had. It's all because I'm here. Frankie and Maxy, those sounds, then he sends Creticia. She warned me I couldn't get away from Frankie."

"Come here." He pulled, and at first, she resisted then fell against him, crying. When the sobs had slowed, he spoke again. "It's not your fault, Jazzi."

'It is."

"No, it's not. Do you think I care about all those minor things they've done to try to stop me? I've faced more difficult, scarier things than that, Jazzi Sanderson. I haven't let any of it stop me, and this hasn't either. No matter what faces me in doing the work I feel called to do, no matter what failures I have, I won't be frightened out of doing my work."

She looked up at him, her eyes still damp, but a small smile on her lips. "You really feel that way, don't you?"

"I do. With the mother I had who worked herself to the bone to give us what we needed, I had a great example of what people can do—if they want to."

"You know how to do everything, don't you?"

"No, I don't." He began walking, pulling her along with him. "Come on, let's walk."

"You'd better go on. I'll have to go inside to repair myself." She snickered.

"I'm fine. Emilia will see I'm missing and will take over if needed. She's my friend, remember."

"How could I forget?"

He laughed as they approached the inn. "Run along and get tidied up, but don't be long. I want you to help me with the tour of the inn."

She nodded, ran up the steps and disappeared inside.

Ryle turned and headed back to the pavilions. Time to mingle a little more before guiding his guests on the tour.

~*~

It happened just as the two groups of guests

separated, one to follow Ryle, and the second one, Jazzi. Ryle held up a hand to quiet the two groups when a deafening scream literally split the air. No one moved. No one spoke.

Ryle caught Jazzi's quick, questioning glance.

Before the scream was over, the clapping began. Laughter broke out. Then as the scream ended, calls of approval came from the groups.

"Way to go, Ryle!"

"Perfect!"

"Love it!"

And the last one was especially enthusiastic coming from a tall, rather dignified black man. "I couldn't have planned it any better, Sadler, my friend."

Friend? He'd never seen the man.

~*~

How had that happened? That scream. Someone had snuck back and reconnected the sound. Just at the wrong time—or was it right time, given the response from his guests tonight?

Ryle sat on the side veranda later that night, close to his suite, alone, his body relaxing, but his mind in full galloping mode. That scream, those raspberry tarts, that woman who'd could have been the culprit-maker tonight—all of it had been engineered to destroy the evening. It'd failed, of course, for which he was utterly grateful, and Ryle cast a glance upward toward the heavens, thanks in his heart.

"I think I have some explanations to make."

Ryle didn't look toward the voice. He knew who it was.

He'd not had a chance to question Athan Meadows about the trip he and Chief Eddie had made into the woods. Now he spoke without looking at his friend.

"I kind of wondered."

"You saw us?"

"Yeah, I did."

Athan sat on the second chair and leaned forward. "After we talked yesterday, I changed my mind. I'd heard Chief Eddie was a good guy, understanding and easy to work with. I worried that you might get in trouble by not telling someone what I'd found, even though it was my doing. I'm the one that found it, I'm the one who warned you not to share it until afterward."

"You decided the easiest and safest way would be to talk with the chief."

"Right. I figured he'd understand my concern, and he did. Although he was hesitant at first, he agreed we could safely wait until after the opening of the inn. It might still be a distraction, but he figured you could handle it."

"So what is this thing you discovered?"

Athan didn't speak for a moment. "I'd rather wait till morning to show you."

"Fine. But not an hour later. I'll see you at breakfast, Athan." Ryle stood and headed indoors.

Time to get some rest. If he could.

~*~

Early the next morning, Ryle, Jazzi, Athan, Chief Eddie, and surprises of all surprises, Lincoln Tillis met in the dining room. No one said much, and only Jazzi met Ryle's gaze with a puzzled look.

"What's going on, Ryle?" Her soft whisper barely reached his ears.

"We have another situation here on the grounds, Jazzi."

"Ryle..." Athan didn't say anything else.

Lincoln Tillis looked from one to the other. "I

think someone needs to tell me what's going on and why I was asked to stay over."

"You'll find out soon enough." Athan was either unconcerned it was FBI asking the question or more worried over what he was about to reveal to all of them.

"Athan, I'm not hungry. Let's get this over with now." Ryle stood. "Jazzi, will you inform Paddy breakfast has been cancelled, but to be ready in case someone is hungry for brunch."

Jazzi hurried to the kitchen while the men went outside.

Athan stopped them. "I need to get my equipment. I'll be right back."

Minutes later, the men were gathered in the woods, past the end of the tunnel, not too far from the river.

"I hope this is worth my time." Tillis mumbled.

"I wish it wasn't." Athan mumbled back at the man. He gripped his machinery and flipped it on. After a deep breath, he began swinging it back and forth.

No one had to wait long. With a steady noise coming from the GPR, it was evident, it'd picked up something. Athan motioned to the others to have a look.

"Hold it right there. I'll shoot anyone who attempts to look at that thing."

It was the same girl who'd driven off last night after Jazzi and he had followed her. And by the looks of the steady-aiming gun, Ryle was pretty sure she meant business.

"It's Creticia, isn't it?" Ryle moved forward one step.

"Yeah, it is, and unless you want me to plug you a hole, you'd better not come any closer."

"Even if we leave, what's to stop us from coming

back to have a look?"

"I don't care how many looks you have once I'm gone and after I get what I've been told to collect."

"You're outnumbered. You can't stop all of us."

"How do you know I'm the only one here? I wouldn't take the chance if I were you." Her mocking words didn't ease Ryle's worry.

"What do you want?" It was Tillis this time.

"Jazzi Sanderson."

"Are you kidding? That's not going to happen." The sudden intense fear for Jazzi almost—but not quite—overwhelmed his reasoning. "Why do you want her?"

Another smirk greeted his questions. "Because her boyfriend wants her, that's why. He means business, and nothing will stop him. She was the best in his line of work—his words, not mine."

"We'd like to help but you're going to have to be more specific than that." Tillis' firm words and no-nonsense tone indicated he'd done this type of negotiating more than once.

"Can't. He—"

"Who's he?"

"That information, Mr. FBI agent, you'll have to find on your own."

"It's Frankie, isn't it?" Ryle moved another step closer.

Creticia swung the gun toward him again, and Ryle saw her finger tighten on the trigger. She was still smirking, but the look in her eyes didn't bode well for anyone who refused her demands. But no matter what, he wouldn't give her what she wanted.

Jazzi, stay at the inn.

Even as he thought the words, his heart lifted

in a prayer.

"Guys, I think we can take her." It was Athan speaking in a low voice.

She heard. "Yeah, probably—if there's no one lurking nearby. I will get one, two, maybe even three of you before you tackle me. You willing to risk that?"

"Stay put, Meadows." Tillis ordered in a brisk voice.

"Wise man." Creticia flicked a glance at him. "Now, you..."

She pointed the gun at Athan. "Drop that thing you're holding, get to the inn, and bring Jazzi to me. You've got three minutes. After that, I'm going to start shooting the rest one by one."

When he hesitated, she screamed. "Move!"

Athan dropped his equipment, turned and ran as if running a marathon. In seconds he was gone from view.

"Creticia, why don't you take me?" Ryle pleaded.

She snickered. "Yeah. You and I would both be dead then."

"Is this guy—Frankie?—forcing you to do this? What's he got over you?"

She laughed then and seemed almost consumed by her laughter. "Nothing. Absolutely nothing."

"Miss, I never aim to be unreasonable. Why don't you talk to me? I'll go off a pace with you, and we can talk this over." Chief Eddie swept off his hat and swiped at his forehead.

"You're the town police chief, aren't you? You sound like a decent, reasonable man, but I don't want to talk, *Chief*. And if you don't shut up, you'll be the first to get plugged." She glanced at the expensive-looking watch on her wrist. "One minute to go. Who wants to volunteer to be first?"

"You don't have to do this." Ryle spoke before anyone else could. "I've got money. How much do you want to leave us alone?"

Appearing to study on his question, she then burst out loud laughing. "No thanks. Thirty seconds."

She motioned with her gun at Chief Eddie. "I hate cops. How about you?"

"No. If you must shoot someone, then I should be the one."

Before she could answer, Athan burst into view. "I can't find her."

As if a tornado cloud had suddenly covered her face, it turned dark with anger, her lips snarling. Her gun lifted. When...

A whirl of color burst from behind Creticia and before she could turn, it hit her full force from behind, causing her to stagger forward, right into Lincoln Tillis' grip.

Chapter Seventeen

Creticia was screaming, cursing and fighting like a wild creature, but with three of the FBI men—where had they come from?—ganging up on her, she was soon stripped of her weapon and tied up.

As for Ryle, he ignored his friends and the screaming Creticia, and headed toward Jazzi. Pulling her from the ground where she'd tumbled along with Creticia, he asked, "Are you hurt?"

"I'm fine." She was brushing at her clothes, but her gaze remained on Ryle.

He didn't wait for more. With a strangled moan, he pulled her close. He didn't speak, didn't loosen his hold, didn't hear any of the remarks coming from those behind him.

Jazzi's hand crept up to his cheek and stroked his cheek. "I didn't intend to make you cry."

"Men don't cry."

"Oh, right." she wiped her hand on her own clothes and settled her head against his chest again. "I'm really okay, Ryle. I'm not hurt."

He pulled away from her then and gripped her arms. "What on earth were you thinking? You *could* have been hurt."

"But I wasn't. I knew what I was doing, and besides, I wasn't taking a chance on you getting shot. Not when it was my fault this all happened."

"Really? That's all you can say? I thought my heart would stop when I saw you creeping up on her."

"Ryle, I really am all right. I've handled the likes of her before. I knew what I was doing."

"Guys, we're headed back to the inn. I'm going to have Chief Eddie put her behind bars. We'll continue our investigation later."

"Fine." Ryle answered Lincoln Tillis, but didn't bother looking at him. When silence surrounded them, Ryle led Jazzi toward a fallen log, and they sat. "Jazzi..."

"Ryle?"

"I want to take care of you. You mean a lot to me, and I don't want to worry about someone coming along and coaxing you away by bribing you with more money or a better, more important job. I want to do that myself...

"Give me more money and a more important job?"

"No, that's not what I meant—"

"Are you guys all right?" Paddy's voice preceded him.

Ryle pulled away from Jazzi and shifted on the log. "We're fine, Paddy, no thanks to Jazzi's reckless action."

Paddy's gaze shifted to Jazzi. "Are you all right, Miss?"

"I am, Paddy. Ryle's making mountains out of mole hills."

"Never mind that. Chief Eddie and Tillis have taken that woman to the town jail until they can sort out what she's involved in." Ryle ignored Jazzi's comment.

"Good. I figured that daft cow was up to no good the first time I laid eyes on her." Paddy sniffed his disapproval. "Now it's time for you two to come inside and grab a nibble to stave off hunger pains. You have fifteen minutes. And in case you want to tarry, Ryle, Miss Jazzi hasn't had a bite to eat since lunch yesterday. If you don't want her to faint away where you'll have to carry her inside again, then she needs food." Paddy stared at him a moment before walking away.

The man didn't seem to understand who was boss of the place, and probably didn't care.

But he didn't either. Paddy could boss them around all he wanted. His concern for them gave Ryle the unusual feeling of experiencing some fatherly concern. Not that he'd ever admit that to anyone.

He stood and held out a hand to Jazzi. "We'd better go before our chef decides to ban me from his cooking forever."

Jazzi laughed. "He wouldn't ever do that. He likes you too much."

"I don't know about that." His fingers closed around hers and kept them there all the way back to the inn.

~*~

Jazzi's heart had settled down from the outrageous thumping it'd done ever since Ryle had clasped her to his chest. What had he been trying to say? That he wanted to promote her? To what? Pay her more?

Or something more...interesting? Her heart had leaped and waited, pounding with excitement, but the explanation hadn't come. Now she wasn't sure how she felt. Disappointed? Discouraged? Frustrated?

Probably all of them. She knew it was silly to wish for what she'd never have. Gratitude from Ryle should be all she expected from the man. Should be enough.

But it wasn't.

She wanted more, and as much as she scolded her foolish heart, it just would not change its mind. She sighed.

"You okay?"

"I'm fine. Great." Was that the truth? Sort of. Yeah, she was great because she still had a job she loved, she still got to see Ryle almost every day, and Creticia was, hopefully, gone forever from her life.

"Tillis, as he was leaving, indicated he'd be back right after noon. Athan's leaving tomorrow so Tillis wants to see what he's found before he leaves. You want to come along?"

"Of course."

"Then let's get you to the breakfast room before you faint away and Paddy has my skin."

"I think I know the way by now. You go ahead and get whatever you need to do today done." Jazzi withdrew her fingers from his.

"Are you sure you're alright? You didn't get hurt any?"

"I'm fine. A couple of scratches won't keep me down." She gave him a gentle shove. "I'm going to wash up in the help's bathroom then eat enough to keep Paddy happy."

He nodded and left, but Jazzi stood still, staring at the man's strong back, his lengthy strides, his burnished brown hair that was starting to curl a bit from waiting too long to have it trimmed. He was smart, and gifted with an intuition that had created an aura about him that was both sweet and gentle and well as illusive and quiet. And he drew her attention like a firecracker on a warm summer night.

She just hoped she wouldn't get burnt.

~*~

Jazzi didn't want to, wanted to hide from talking to Agent Tillis. She wasn't blameless, and now, when she knew she had to confess up and talk to the man, she felt—not afraid, but resigned. If she went to jail, then so be it.

Jazzi saw that big, black SUV pull up in the driveway, but felt no emotion. Her body shivered, but her chest felt as heavy as a stone. She couldn't hide her past any longer, couldn't fight the questions she knew were coming, the possibilities she would be facing.

She had to do it.

She had to face FBI Agent Lincoln Tillis.

~*~

Lincoln Tillis arrived back at the inn just as Chief Eddie followed him onto the driveway. Ryle met them at the bottom of the front steps. The expressions on their faces clued him in something was wrong.

"What's going on?"

"Creticia."

"What? Did she escape?" Jazzi's voice from behind him was resigned, and was that a bit of fear in it?

"How did you know that?" Tillis' tart question shot at her.

"I didn't. You just now told me." Jazzi's voice was low and quiet.

"Do you know anything about this?"

"How could I? I've never met her before."

"No? Seems like you're kind of hesitant about that."

"Well, once, when I had to interview her, but no other time."

Ryle almost spoke up. Tillis was laying it on kind of rough.

"I am hesitant. I'm afraid of Frankie, I don't

know much about Cretecia, but I know Frankie. I sensed the whole time in New York that someone else was pulling his strings. I never saw anyone, never heard him or Maxy speak of anyone, but the calls from someone—he never shared with me who it was, and Frankie shared just about everything. Then there were the times when he'd leave for short periods and never let me know where he was going. None of that made sense."

"Doesn't seem like much, Jazzi." Chief Eddie spoke up. Was he trying to soothe over her past?

"I think it was. I was his errand girl, his confidant, more so than Maxy who was all brawn and brainless. It was like when Frankie was troubled or irritated or whatever, he'd call me to listen while he whined, growled or just shared his irritation with me. I didn't have to answer much. Just soothe his troubled spirit, and eventually he'd drink himself to sleep."

"You have any idea who these people were? You think it was someone higher up pressuring him?" Chief Eddie asked.

"Could have been. I didn't pay much attention to him other than when he wanted to vent. After I was there for awhile, I was always glad when he was gone."

"How did Creticia get loose?" Ryle decided it was time to interrupt Jazzi's tale of her previous life.

Chief Eddie's face grew red. "That no-good-for-nothing new deputy I hired turned out to be all that and more. After we interrogated her, we entrusted him to lock her up. Instead, he escaped with her through the back door."

Ryle shook his head. "Did Creticia say anything to help?"

"Sort of. She hinted that something was happening this afternoon close to the river, and—get this—not too far from where you're located."

"Why would she give up this information?"

"Because she hinted at two other locations that were possibly sites where suspicious actions were happening." Tillis' disgruntled voice was no promise of favorable results. "So, although we have multiple teams checking out these sites, she could have been lying to steer us away from the real site—if there even is something."

"We've got the patrol out on all the main roads. If they are foolish enough to try leaving the state on those roads, we'll catch them."

Chief Eddie wasn't allowing any negative thoughts get him down, if one could go by his tone.

"So you two are the only ones headed to this place close to here?" Ryle stared at first one then the other of the two cops. "I'd like to volunteer my services."

"No, I think—" Tillis didn't get to finish his sentence.

"Why not?" Chief Eddie glanced from Ryle to the FBI agent. "He's smart, strong, and sensible. He'll be a help if we run into serious trouble."

Tillis shrugged. "Fine. Come along. Don't get in the way."

As they started out, Ryle saw Jazzi begin to follow them, and he stopped, facing her. "Jazzi, I'd rather you didn't go."

"I won't get in the way."

"I don't know..." He hesitated, studying her face. "Promise?"

She nodded. "I promise."

"Jazzi, if something happened to you—"

"Nothing will happen to me."

"You don't know that."

"I do know it."

Staring at her, into her blue eyes, he was doubtful. It could happen, and he'd never live with himself if it did.

"Come then. Stay behind me."

It took them a good thirty minutes to reach the place. There wasn't a sign of anyone around. No stirring, no sound.

"Think we've got the wrong place?" Chief Eddie spoke in a low voice.

"Maybe." Tillis' gaze remained fixed on the house. "Let's give it a little longer."

No one spoke, but it wasn't ten minutes later that a door eased open. It was a rundown shack that looked uninhabitable. Brambles ran criss-cross over the front and sides of it. Shutters drooped with age. The weathered boards sagged from years of neglect.

No one showed. Then...

Someone's stringy, blond head appeared. And another and another. One after another, five, ten, then twenty young girls stepped outside and paused, huddled together, obviously terrified.

Ryle heard Jazzi's gasp. "Child trafficking."

Tillis was on his phone. "Park away from the site and come in quietly."

Ten minutes later, his men arrived, and while Tillis instructed his men, Ryle watched the girls, standing dejectedly and quiet.

The FBI agent returned. "You two stay here. Don't move."

"I can help." Ryle offered.

"No. Stay where you are. We don't want any accidental shootings."

"I think they'll feel safer if a woman

approaches them." Jazzi touched the agent's arm to get his attention, making sure to keep her voice soft.

"No. We can't risk it. You two, stay here."

Lincoln Tillis had barely gone from their sight when two people appeared at the edge of the woods. They seemed to be talking but not at each other.

"That's Frankie and Creticia." Jazzi's hand pointed even as she spoke.

"It is."

"What are they doing?"

"Looks like they're talking."

"To who?

"Look at the girls. Specifically at the girl in the red top."

"She...she's listening. She must have an earbud."

"I'm afraid you're right. They've had this set up ahead of time in case something like this happened."

"They're moving. He's giving them instructions." Jazzi trembled—either from fear or excitement. "They're going to get away."

"No, they're not. At least, the girls won't. Frankie and Creticia may unless Tillis has men stationed farther away." Ryle could sense Jazzi's intense stare at him.

"We can't let them get away, Ryle."

"You heard Tillis. He won't be happy..."

"Who cares? Let's do it."

"Jazzi, we have no guns, and I'm sure, both of them have weapons. We can't go against that..."

"No, but if we move now, I know how we can do it."

Ryle stared at this woman who was both resourceful and fearless—in some things. "I don't want you hurt."

"Nor I, but listen. Here's how we can stop them." She whispered her plan to him.

He laughed. "It might work, but if we're going to do this, we'd better move. Once Tillis realizes what's happening, he'll be after them like a bird of prey."

"Which means, it will be too late for him to stop them. If Frankie or Creticia sees one cop, they'll desert the girls and be off."

"You're right. Let's go." Ryle motioned with a hand. "We'll head this way and circle back to our target point. We've got to hurry."

Jazzi didn't answer. She was off like a streak, and Ryle followed.

In minutes, they burst out into the small clearing along the bank of the river. Sure enough, a large boat sat in the water, moored to a tree on the bank.

Ryle ran straight to the boat while Jazzi untied it. "I've got this. You go try to get the other two things done. Be careful, Jazzi. Promise?"

She straightened. "I promise, Ryle."

"I'll be back as soon as I can. Don't take any chances."

"Got it. See you in a bit."

Ryle shoved the lever at full throttle and the boat leaped forward. His blood was racing, but his heart was sinking as he wondered if Jazzi would be okay. If she'd be alive when he saw her again.

~*~

Jazzi hoped her plan would work. Thankfully, Ryle hadn't realized she'd allowed him to choose the least dangerous task.

Of course, she'd steered boats more than

once. Frankie had almost always insisted she accompany him when he went to parties or cruises with all the flashy girls, with his business associates or friends. She never had any idea which were which, and she didn't care. She'd associated, but hated these times, and fortunately, Frankie had watched over her like she was his possession. Though most people had thought she was his main girlfriend, she hadn't been. It was an odd association, being his ear, his confidant, his person, so much so, he couldn't bear for her to be away from him for long.

In spite of all that, she knew what she was doing. More than once, she'd played this trick on Amy and her unsuspecting friends. That was way back when, but she hadn't forgotten.

She was pretty sure she'd find the grapevines she was depending on to use for the trick. It grew in a lot of places around here, and if so, her plan would succeed. As long as time allowed.

She pulled from her pocket the pocket knife Ryle had thrust at her and began pulling down the vines she needed, hacking and sawing through their toughness. Once she had enough, she spread it in large loops and swirls, enough that, unless someone was expecting them, their footing would be precarious.

Finished, she surveyed her work. Not too obvious, unless someone was on guard against tricks.

She heard voices in the distance and backed away until she was sure she wouldn't be seen, hidden behind a huge oak tree, its branches hanging low.

Less than two minutes later, two people came into her view. Frankie and Creticia. Alone and angry if their voices were anything to go on.

Crossing her fingers, she hoped her plan would work. It might just be they'd step right through it without tripping...

A shriek—not from Creticia—but from Frankie, caused Jazzi to snicker. Too loud, she guessed, when a hand slapped gently over her mouth. A voice whispered in her ear.

"Easy."

Ryle.

The air gushed from her in relief.

Creticia's head had turned, staring in her direction, the gun in her hand lifting a little. Her gaze swept around the area, but she must not have spotted them, because she looked back at Frankie and moved forward. "Hurry it up, Frankie. We don't have much time. Stop your histrionics. Those cops—" a scream exploded from her throat as the small vine tightened around her ankle.

Frankie was paying no attention to his pal. He was on the ground, trying to loosen the vine around his ankle. Creticia was dancing around, kicking her foot, screaming, "Snake. It's biting me."

Ryle, pressed up against her back, was shaking with laughter, but he strangled out a question. "What should we do with them?"

"Look." Jazzi nodded in their direction.

Down the barely-there path came Tillis and two other men who rushed forward and slapped handcuffs on both of them. Only then did, Tillis swivel and stare into the woods. Once his gaze seemed to be resting in their direction, and Jazzi shrank back against Ryle.

But when the three agents walked back toward the house, Jazzi relaxed.

"Whew! That was close. I was sure Lincoln

Tillis would catch us."

Ryle laughed. "You sure you don't want a job with the police?"

"No, thanks. I'm perfectly happy doing what I do."

Ryle said nothing, only clasped her hand in his.

No words were needed.

In the quiet of the woods, in the lull of their previous activity in helping capture two criminals, with the sun shining overhead and the wind whistling softly past them, Jazzi had all she needed right then.

She hoped Ryle felt the same way.

Chapter Eighteen

Jazzi gave Ryle a little wave as she headed to her rooms. She needed another shower and clean clothes to feel human again. But the warmth in her heart made her smile. Heading to her office, she realized her office door was open. She seldom locked but almost always shut her door.

She peeked inside and saw a handsome black older man sitting in a chair, eyes closed. He spoke before she could.

"It's Miss Jazzi Sanderson, isn't it?"

"That's right. Who are you?"

He opened his eyes and smiled at her. His eyes were clear and honest, his hands steady and quiet, his demeanor polite and poised with confidence. And he looked vaguely familiar.

But something—she couldn't pinpoint what—troubled him.

"Can I help you?"

"I hope so."

"Please sit, Mr.?"

"Miller. Samuel L. Miller."

Instead of sitting at her desk, Jazzi moved to one of the single chairs. Something—she had no idea what—urged her to keep things simple. She waited.

"You have a good face."

"I don't know about that..."

"You've seen troubles and done some things you wish you hadn't, but you've finally gotten your life straightened out. You're on a good path.

I can see it in you."

"Thank you, I guess." Embarrassment heated her cheeks, she knew it, but, surprisingly, she was more impressed at his intuition. "Are you interested in reserving a room?"

"I'm interested in finding what happened to my great aunt."

"Your great aunt? How can we do that?"

He crossed his legs. "Let me tell you a story. Do you mind?"

"Of course not. Please."

"Years ago, my ancestors were slaves down south, and they escaped. They'd gotten word that there was a special and safe haven where runaways could hide on their way to freedom. In their escape, they finally made it to this place."

"This place? You mean, this state? This town?" Jazzi frowned.

He ignored her question. "It was far from what they'd been told. Enticed here by men who'd promised their help to get them to freedom if they made it here."

"No!"

"I'm afraid so. From what was passed down—I have copies of what happened told by my great grandparents and written down by their son—my grandfather—who'd had some schooling. When they got ready to leave, they were told they had two choices. Head for the north and leave their daughter who was just ten years old."

"But—"

He shook his head. "They had no choice. It was either that or stay and watch her and my grandfather—who was just two years older—be shot. My great grandfather swore he'd be back to rescue her, but it didn't happen. I think they both died of heartache, but they did get the story

240

down for those who came after them. My grandfather promised he'd do his best to save his sister, but that didn't happen either." The man rested his forehead on his fist for a moment and a long sigh slid from between his teeth.

"Mr. Miller, how can *we* help you though? Even as much as we would like to, we have no idea how to start, what to do. It was such a long time ago."

Mr. Miller lifted his head. "Because, from all the research I've done, this is the place where that happened. This is that supposedly safe haven."

"This place?" Shock ran through her as if she'd been struck by lightning. "You don't mean our inn, do you?"

"Yes."

"Then...you're the man who called twice warning us about this place, aren't you?"

A small smile spread his lips. "I am. You're my last hope."

"What's going on, Jazzi?" Ryle's voice preceded him into her office.

"This is Samuel Miller, Ryle."

"I recognize you. You were at our Open Night."

"I was." Mr. Miller smiled.

Jazzi repeated the man's story while he sat staring out the window.

"That makes sense." Ryle's thoughtful comment had both Samuel Miller and Jazzi switching their gaze to him. "Did you happen to bring those writings from your ancestors?"

Samuel Miller pulled a small, worn notebook from an envelope he held and handed it to Ryle.

Ryle skimmed through it, nodded and asked,

"Do you have anything else?"

"Do I need more proof?"

"I don't know, but it wouldn't hurt to have as much information as you can provide."

"I do have one thing that might help."

"Tell us."

"I'd rather show you." Samuel pulled a small object from his pocket and held it out between two fingers.

The small red glass stone sparkled in the sunlight.

Jazzi leaned forward and took the stone from his hands. "Ryle...do you think?"

"Maybe. Let me get it."

Ryle left the room to his own office and in minutes returned. He held out his hand to Samuel, opening his fist as he did.

The man stared then slowly picked up the small tarnished band. He placed the red stone into the grips and it slid right in as if it was home.

Samuel didn't look at them, his gaze remained on the small, cheap ring, but the tears in his voice broke Jazzi's heart. "My great aunt's ring. My grandfather wrote that his father found it, hid it from his master and gave it to his daughter with instructions not to wear it in front of the master."

"But we have more, Mr. Miller. Let's show him the book and photos."

Jazzi's enthusiastic remark spurred Ryle to nod his head and retrieve the book and puzzle box. "Take a look at these, Mr. Miller."

"Now look at the book we found. Check out the pictures." Jazzi motioned to the book she'd found at the library.

Even though the Ryle held out the book to the

older gentleman, Mr. Miller reached for the puzzle box, and Ryle allowed him to take it.

Sliding a hand over the box, he murmured, "You found this box?"

"We did. Hidden in a hole that we uncovered in our basement."

"Check on page fifteen of my father's recordings. You'll find a detailed description of the box, how my great grandfather gave it to his daughter with instructions on keeping it hidden. Check and you will see."

Ryle flipped through the pages, skimmed through the hand writing then slowly closed the book. He looked at Jazzi. "It's all there, just as Mr. Miller describes it."

"Now look at the book we found at our library. Check out the pictures." Jazzi motioned to the book.

He did as she asked, then flipped back to the front of the book, stared at the picture of a man— the author of the book.

"And see this." Jazzi opened the journal she'd lifted from the puzzle box, filled with the drawings she was sure now had been done by a ten-year-old little girl. Pointing to the hand-drawn picture of the same man as appeared in the book, she asked, "Do you think this is the man who threatened your family then?"

Ryle drew from his pocket the button and held it up. "Look at the man's buttons in the picture."

Mr. Miller did so and nodded. "I believe it's...it's..."

He didn't finish, only bowed his head and wept.

~*~

"Ryle, can he come with us when Athan shows us his discovery?"

"Yes, but remember, it may be nothing, or worse, a disappointment."

"He's come this far. He's strong. It's only right."

"Then, if he wants, he's welcome."

Athan thrust his head into the room. "Ryle, I see Tillis pulling in. Are you two ready?"

~*~

Once again Ryle ran his GPRslice over the ground, and again, it didn't take long before the noise began, showing once again he'd found something. He looked at Ryle. "Want to look?"

Ryle moved next to Athan, with Tillis and Samuel Miller moving in behind him.

"Is that...?"

"I'm afraid it is." Athan's grim voice echoed Ryle's feelings.

"What is it, Ryle? Athan?"

Both men looked at Jazzi first then the others. "Bones."

"How many have you found?" Tillis' spoke over the others' exclamations.

"I can't be sure, but it looks like—what I've seen so far—multiple skulls. A rough estimate and needs a professional judgement." Athan looked at Lincoln Tillis again. "I figured you'll need your people out here to recover everything."

Samuel Miller had said nothing, and now he walked a ways off.

"Ryle, should I go to him?" Jazzi touched his arm, her brows drawn together in concern.

"Give him a minute till he's ready. He's smart. He'll realize this..." Ryle waved his hand at the area. "...doesn't mean his relative will be in this spot."

"You're right. Not only that but there could be more than one burial spot."

He gave her a sharp glance. "I hope not. If his GPR is telling the truth, that's a pile of bones buried here."

"Do you suppose it's all from the 1800s?"

"I have no idea. I don't suppose we'll know till they exhume them and run tests on them."

Samuel Miller was walking back to the group. "Agent Tillis, how long before these can be recovered and examined? I'd like to know if my ancestor is buried here."

"I'm getting ready to call it in now, Mr. Miller." His gaze move to Athan. "Could you do a cursory sweep around this area, say, approximately a hundred feet circumference?"

"Sure. It'll take me some time, but I should have quite a bit done by the time your people are here." Athan gripped his machine again, turned it on, and walked off.

"How long, Tillis, will this take? Am I still good to go? I have people scheduled beginning this weekend." Ryle spoke in a low voice. "Not that I'm pushing you."

"Depends. If this is all Meadows finds, then we should be able to wrap it up in a few days." He shook his head. "But if there's more, then, I can't give you an answer."

"Any way I can book a room tonight and throughout the week? I'd like to be close by. Just in case." Samuel's voice was filled with anxiousness, but the resignation in his brown eyes drowned it out.

"Our first booked guests are this weekend, but we'll make sure you have a room. We'd love to have you stay with us." Jazzi smiled at the man, and Ryle nodded in agreement.

"Thanks. I appreciate it." Samuel turned to watch Athan moving his machine back and forth, back and forth, methodically covering each foot of the specified ground.

"I'm going to head back to the inn, Jazzi. Are you coming or do you want to stay and watch?"

"I think I'll head back. It'll take him at least an hour to finish. I've got a couple of items I want to get done today."

When they parted minutes later, Ryle headed straight to Emilia's rooms. He knocked on her door, wishing he didn't have to talk with anyone else the rest of the day.

~*~

An hour and half later, both Jazzi and Ryle were with Athan, Samuel, Chief Eddie and Agent Tillis.

"I found no more signs of bones anywhere. I think it's safe to say whoever buried these kept to this specific area." Athan spoke after turning off his equipment.

"We have a team on the way from Morgantown, including the local forensic anthropologist who should be here later tonight. I told them, Ryle, you'd have rooms to house them, saving them from driving back and forth from town. I hope I was correct in assuring them of that." Agent Tillis stared at his watch. "Meadows, if you'll give me a bill, I'll see that you get reimbursed."

"No problem."

"Do you need anything from me?" Ryle leaned against a nearby tree trunk. "What kind of problems will be in store for me?"

"I don't foresee any for you. You didn't know about these, obviously."

"Good. Then I'll inform Emilia."

"Emilia? Your lawyer? She's still here?"

Ryle smiled at the sudden interest in Agent Tillis' voice. "But not too much longer. She's a busy woman."

Agent Tillis didn't speak again, but he cast a quick glance at the inn then walked off a pace and answered his phone when it rang again.

Athan and Samuel Miller walked back with Ryle and Jazzi.

"Paddy and I thought it might be better to offer a simple supper tonight with the forensic people arriving shortly. "Will that work for you, Ryle?"

"That's a great idea. I'm bushed and want to make it an early night. Emilia's leaving tomorrow. I want to be clear headed when the excavating begins. Everything's in order for our opening, right? Why don't you take the night off and do something really special, Jazzi?

She laughed. "Like read a book? Take a walk? Relax in the luxurious Jacuzzi in my room?"

"If that's what you want to do."

"Are you sure, Ryle?"

"Positive."

"Then that's what I'll do."

"No buts. Stop worrying. I won't let anything or anyone harm you." He winked, opened his door and walked in, grinning as he shut it. He didn't move away from the closed door, but stood near it, head bent, listening. And he could feel her presence on the other side, her hesitation, her worry.

~*~

There was no way Jazzi would be able to sleep tonight. Not with Ryle acting so strangely. She knew in her heart that he hadn't told her all the truth. Protecting her? Or thinking she was butting in his business? Thinking she was getting too bold, too bossy, too nosey? Maybe.

And with everything seemingly going so good between them.

She stood at the window, staring into the dimming light outside. She could see Agent Tillis and the forensic people huddling together while the excavation was going on, the bright spotlight outlining each one of them.

Her mind flew back to the evening when she thought she'd seen Maxy at the edge of the woods, staring at her. It'd been really creepy, and she sure didn't want a repeat of that night.

Edging away from the window, she half-swiveled and caught—from her peripheral vision—the sight of someone standing at her door. Open door, and she knew she'd shut it.

Whirling, she opened her mouth to scream, but the man leaped across the room, and a big hand slapped across her mouth. His gruff voice, low and threatening, growled. "You're coming with me. If you want me to get rough with you, that's good with me. I'd as soon put you out. Less trouble for me, but then more trouble for your boss. Cause I really don't want to kill him now. You don't want that, do you?"

She shook her head.

"Good answer. I'm making no promises, see, just doing as our boss asked." He loosened his hold.

"Our?" Jazzi's question was a mumble.

"Yeah, our."

"But why are you here? You know if Paddy finds out, he'll—"

"He'll what?" His lips were at her ear again, snarling his question.

"Let me go. I'll be good." The fear of him hurting Ryle was bigger than fear for herself. If only she had a way to get ahold of Paddy. She could scream, but that might encourage him to knock her out, and she didn't want that. She could...

The knock on the door interrupted her thoughts.

Maxy, still behind her, still holding her in his iron grip, clapped a hand over her mouth again and hissed. "Not a sound."

"Jazzi, are you in there? Paddy says it's almost time for supper. Are you coming?" Silence, then, "Jazzi?"

Another knock. And then the soft, soft sound of the locked doorknob twisting.

Footsteps leading away, and Maxy hustled her to her door, cracked it and peeked out. Jerking her by the arm, he spoke again, "Let's go."

"There are men outside. They'll see us."

She could almost see the smirk on his broad face. He might be strong, but he sure wasn't very smart.

"I hope Paddy doesn't see you."

This time it was the flinch that clued her he wasn't as calm as he put on.

He didn't say another word as he checked then exited out her veranda door. He hustled her toward the opposite side away from where the excavations were happening. They hurried through the trees on that side and didn't pause until they reached a dirt road that led to a dilapidated truck.

Hoisting her into the truck, he pulled out a non-too-clean cloth and covered her eyes.

She fought him, but not too much then quieted

when he growled at her.

"Sit still or I'll guarantee to knock you out. Want that?"

"No."

He said nothing more, only finished the tying, including her hands, slammed the door and trotted to the driver's side.

When Jazzi felt the truck make a brief stop, and then a sharp right turn, she figured they might be heading into Appleton.

"Where are we going?"

"The boss wants you."

"What do you mean? He's in jail, isn't he?"

He didn't answer her question, but Jazzi could feel his body shake in spite of the truck's rough ride.

Was he laughing?

~*~

"Ryle. Mr. Ryle."

Outside, and headed to where the excavation was taking place, he turned at the frantic-sounding call from Jazzi's assistant, Barbara. "What's wrong?"

"Jazzi's missing. Paddy and I can't find her anywhere."

He stared at her, but in his peripheral vision he saw both Athan and Agent Tillis move toward him.

"What's wrong?" Agent Tillis snapped.

Ryle placed a hand over his forehead. Was he getting a headache? He never had headaches. "She goes where she pleases. She may have taken a walk. Did you check her room?"

"I did. Her hallway door is locked, but when Paddy checked her veranda door, it was open, her room is empty."

"Do you think something's wrong, Ryle?"

Agent Tillis' sharp tone indicated he was suddenly on the alert.

Ryle shook his head. "I don't think so, but, just to be safe, with all that's been going on, we'd better do a search. Rather her laugh at us for panicking then be sorry we didn't."

Agent Tillis nodded. "Right. I'll get a couple of my men to search the grounds. You check the house again and the tunnel, Ryle, and take Athan with you. Barbara, stay close to the phone and have Paddy prepare quick snacks in case they're needed."

Everyone turned to carry out their instructions, but Ryle hesitated.

There was nothing wrong, his mind insisted. She took lots of walks. Went into town occasionally. Did her runs every day.

But his heart refused to listen.

She didn't run at night. She didn't usually go into town without leaving word with someone. And, with all that had been happening, she would not have walked beyond the yard by herself.

What if there was something wrong? Something seriously wrong?

Chapter Nineteen

When the truck slowed, Jazzi could hear a slight rumbling sound. The truck moved again, slowly, and stopped.

"Where are we?"

"Never mind. Keep your mouth shut, and you may live to see another day." Maxy opened his door, climbed out and his seat groaned from relief.

Or, at least, she imagined it did.

She tried to find the door handle, but before she could find it, it jerked open.

"Get out."

She did as told, fumbling a little but steadied herself once on the—it was a cement floor. A garage?

In seconds, Maxy had her tied to a chair, mouth still gagged, eyes still covered.

A voice from the other side of the room spoke, but it was so far away, she couldn't make out whose it was—if she even knew the person.

She heard Maxy's clomping across the floor then...

"Any trouble?"

The person had lowered their voice even more, but she could hear the pitch. That pitch, the rapid speech—she was sure she'd heard it before, only where?

"Heard from Frankie?" This from Maxy.

"No, and I'd better not. He's got all the help he's going to get from me. The imbecile."

Whoever it was must have known Frankie. A friend? A co-worker?

"Any trouble from her?"

No answer from Maxy so he must have shaken his head.

"Good. You get back to NY as soon as you can and don't get caught. Check on the others and let them know all things are good here."

"Her?"

A sinister chuckle. "They'll soon learn you can't trifle with me."

This time Maxy did respond, and it was a protest. "Careful. That Sadler guy has been around a few city blocks. Smart, he is. Don't be fooled by his mild manners and thin build. And as for that federal guy, he's out to stop us, and he seems to be someone who doesn't take backsets well."

"Don't worry about me. I can take care of myself. No one suspects..."

They walked out of hearing range, and Jazzi could hear nothing more.

~*~

Two hours later, everyone met in the breakfast room, and no one had a good report. Ryle felt the edges of tension nibbling at his emotions. His head was throbbing.

It was not unusual for Jazzi to be gone that long, but she almost always did let someone know she'd be gone. Maybe she'd decided to leave, to shake the dust of the place off her feet— so to speak. That was nonsense. As far as he knew, she still loved her job. Unless she'd lied.

His thoughts were getting worse the more he thought.

"You have any ideas where she could be?"

Agent Tillis asked as he approached him.

"I'm not her keeper. She goes where she wants." Ryle knew he was being a little snappy, but why was Tillis asking? If Ryle knew, wouldn't he already have checked it out? He'd better take a deep breath. "Sorry. Didn't mean to snap at you."

"No problem. I understand. Let me ask you this though." Agent Tillis' eyes were sharp and probing. "Do you have serious doubts she could be in trouble?"

Ryle drew in a breath. Did he? "Yes. I do. I mean, we've had threats, rigged loud speakers that blared out noises at all times, a suddenly-found tunnel, a man claiming an ancestor died here from ill intentions, now bones discovered—what can I say? Is all this over or just beginning? Our chef, Paddy, sent that Maxy guy away after he attacked Jazzi. Those other two—Frankie and Creticia—were captured. Who else is trying to cause us trouble?"

"I understand. I don't really think Jazzi's disappearance has anything to do with all that."

"What do you think?"

"I think she's gone running and hurt herself, or had dinner with someone in town, or her family suddenly invited her to dinner..."

Really? Why hadn't she called then? Why had her inside door been locked, but the veranda door stood unlocked?

Ryle walked over to the window and stared into the darkening night. Where was she?

It was almost midnight before the phone in Jazzi's office rang. He barely heard it, because of the distance from the breakfast room, but when Ryle finally realized it was coming from her office, he ran and snatched up her phone.

"Hello."

"Is this Ryle Sadler?"

The disguised voice kept him from recognizing who it was. "Yes. Who is this?"

A dry, unfunny chuckle. "Get this. We have Jazzi. You want her back? Then cease your digging for those bones and any other snooping in these parts. Send that FBI agent home—"

"He won't listen to me—"

"You better make him do so, cause the next time, Jazzi will be coming back to you dead. Understand that? Dead."

Anger flooded his body. "Don't you dare hurt her."

Another chuckle. "Not this time. This time you get her back. But next time…"

"Where is she?"

"You'll find her out on Route Thirteen—well, that's if you're quick enough." And the person hung up.

Ryle whirled and almost ran into Agent Tillis. "She's out on Route Thirteen. That's all I know. Can you find her?"

Agent Tillis headed back to the breakfast room and yelled demands to his men and women. Two of them were on their computers in seconds, and thirty seconds later, a dark-haired woman lifted her gaze to Agent Tillis.

"There's an abandoned farm equipment place about three miles on Thirteen once you turn on it from our direction."

Ryle and Tillis, along with several of the others were running before she'd finished talking.

~*~

Jazzi had dozed off two times in spite of wishing she wouldn't. She hadn't heard any sounds—no footsteps, no talking, nothing, for quite a few minutes. Had everyone gone? Or were they—whoever they were—gone? Were they coming back? Or would she die here alone, forgotten, and abandoned?

In spite of her predicament, she chuckled.

She had tried to loosen her bonds, tried to wiggle, stretch them, and even thought about overturning her chair, but what good would that do, unless she had a reason for it? And nothing came to mind. After all, she wasn't exactly espionage material.

She wished she'd eaten lunch. Hungry wasn't even describing how she felt. Thinking about what might happen—or worse—what might not happen if someone didn't rescue her, sent waves of discouragement over her. She didn't want to do that so she allowed the drowsiness to creep up again.

The sound of a vehicle, no, more than one, came speeding down the county road and awakened her. A screech, two of them, doors slamming, and Jazzi woke up.

Furtive words, a bit of movement, and a door slammed open. Running footsteps headed toward her. What now?

Now someone was in back of her, removing the ropes tying her hands. The unknown person went to the front of her and gently untied the ropes around her ankles and unwrapped the band around her eyes. She looked up.

Ryle stood before her, and she read exactly what her heart had always wanted. He pulled her to her feet and swallowed her up with his strong arms, murmuring her name over and over. Neither one of them paid the least attention to the others' talking.

"Jazzi. Jazzi, I thought I'd lost you. I figured

you were sick of all the trouble that's happened. That my luck had run out. That I was too bossy, that you didn't—"

Jazzi pulled away from him just a little, laughing. "You silly guy, I would never do that to you. Never ever. Don't you know I came home when you hired me? That I'm happier than I've ever been in my life? I—"

"Jazzi, do you think you could talk to us now?"

It was Agent Tillis.

Ryle opened his arms, but his hand clasped hers and reluctantly let go as she moved away.

There wasn't much she could tell the agent, except Maxy had been the one who'd abducted her. "There was another man who seemed to be the boss, but I never got even a glimpse of who he was. He and Maxy talked in low voices away from me. He ordered Maxy back to New York. I heard that."

"Are you sure you're okay?"

Ryle's worried voice caused Jazzi to flick a glance at him. "I'm fine, Ryle."

"What bothers me is, why did they let you go, Jazzi? It makes no sense." Agent Tillis paced.

"Unless there's something more going on here than we know."

It was a reluctant statement coming from Ryle, but Jazzi understood his feeling. He wanted all this over and done. He had a business to run.

"As soon as I talk with our excavators in the morning, we'll let you know if we're finished. If so, that gives you two days to settle down before your opening day." Agent Tillis started to walk away but swung back. "If we find nothing here, we're headed back to New York. We may have a lead there."

He started to walk away then but turned back and motioned to one of the agents as he spoke to Ryle. "I'll have him take you home. We'll talk tomorrow."

Fifteen minutes later, both stepped out of the vehicle. Ryle spoke softly. "Want to take a short walk with me?"

"Sure. My emotions need to settle a little before I'll be able to sleep."

Ryle held out his hand, and Jazzi took it. They walked, not toward where the excavation was taking place and, hopefully, would be completed by mid-morning tomorrow, but around the yard.

He said little, and Jazzi didn't speak either, enjoying the starlit sky, the crescent moon hanging low in the sky, begging for them to grab hold and sit for a spell.

How different life was now. What had ever made her think life away from this perfect town, *this perfect man,* this perfect place could be better? She was done running, even if she had to talk with Agent Tillis, answering questions she would rather avoid. Even if her parents were at times a little too nosy about her affairs, even when life had its problems and she didn't feel strong enough to face them.

Ryle was strong. Ryle had his faith, and she realized that's exactly what she wanted too. Strength and faith. And one other thing too...

Her friend stopped walking at the front corner of the inn, close to their suites. Not speaking but savoring the darkness and the smell of the late blooming summer plants. Ryle reached toward the vine clinging to the sturdy trellis and plucked a blossom. He held it out to her.

She heard the smile in his voice when he spoke.

"Do you know one of the reasons I love this place so much?"

He must have seen the shake of her head. "Because of the smell of the white Jasmine vines, but the blue ones...they're my favorite..."

"You do know they're really Plumbagos? And they don't have any scent?"

"I prefer calling them Blue Jasmines, and I can pretend about the scent with all these other plants providing more than enough for us to enjoy, right? Let me finish." He smiled down at her.

She loved his rambling thoughts and nodded.

"From the first time I felt impressed to buy this place, the smell, above any other scent, was the smell of these vines, and all the old-fashion flowers and plants that had grown and held on in spite of neglect. They were strong and determined not to be crowded out by the wild and ugly brush that persisted in growing from the years of decline, persisted in allowing their beauty to be seen by anyone who ventured near."

"Ryle..."

"And they reminded me of you."

She heard her heart's rapid beat and had to swallow before she could answer him. "Me?"

"You. From the first time I saw you with that wild purple hair and that chip of uncertainty and dislike of anything normal, you interested me."

"You thought of me as another of your projects. I don't know what all you do, but I do know you help people."

"I do, but I certainly didn't think of you as a project. I saw the goodness in you hiding behind that tough layer you used as a shield from life. I saw a young woman who wanted to be free of that clinging load of rebellion, who wanted to truly do something wonderful, be something wonderful."

"Really, you thought all that? I still have a streak that wants to break away from normalness. You might have been mistaken."

"But I wasn't mistaken, was I, Jazzi? I've watched you conquer the fears and rebellion and hopelessness and become a strong, beautiful and smart woman. A woman I'm proud to say is..."

"Your manager? I love the job—"

"No, Jazzi. The woman I love. The woman I want to be by side forever."

"Me?" Her voice was faint. In fact, she was sure she was passing out from shock, the way her head swirled.

He leaned toward her, not to take her hand again as if they were the best of friends. Not to tuck her hand within his arm as if to protect her. He pulled her close and allowed his lips to touch hers, drew back and whispered. "My Jazmine, my beautiful, exotic flower, will you marry me?"

Chapter Twenty

"**J**azzi, I need your help. I'm prepared to overlook your, uh, previously associations with people we're searching for and those we've been watching, along with the few we've captured. Is there anything—anything at all you can tell us about Frankie, Maxy or who they've worked with?"

"I figured you'd be asking me questions again, so I wrote down everything I thought might help you. I did run errands and carried messages, made calls that could be considered threats, at the request of Frankie. And..." Jazzi swallowed her nervousness. But she'd vowed to do this, to confess all and hope for the best. "... I overheard that some of Frankie's flunkies took care of problematic people. I never interfered, never asked questions. Frankie had a vile temper when riled. I've seen him have Maxy beat a man within an inch of his life. It was less scary to turn a blind eye."

"This Maxy ever kill anyone?"

"Not in front of me, but he was—was odd. He made me uncomfortable, but I knew he'd never harm me. Not as long as Frankie was around. As for the others—the hit men—I figured but didn't know, they were the ones who did the hit jobs. I never saw any and I certainly never participated. Frankie pretty much kept me out of anything violent, but why I never knew. He was weird like that."

"Names of any of those hit men?"

"Only a couple. Big Red, 'cause of his red hair, of course, and Mighty Mart, which was funny, 'cause he was anything but mighty. Short and skinny, he had a habit of rocking on his feet when standing, but I heard he was vicious with a gun. Fearless."

"Did you ever get any feelings that someone above Frankie was calling the shots?"

"I never gave it a thought. I only wanted a fun time, but I did one time make a copy of names who I assumed were associates of Frankie's. I have no idea why I did it, unless I thought I might need it someday for leverage. I actually forgot about it until you came around." Jazzi handed it over.

Agent Tillis flipped through the pages then looked up. "This gives us some good leads here. Never heard anything that could help?"

Jazzi hesitated just a second. "One time Frankie gave specific orders to take out someone named Peretti. He didn't realize, or forgot, I was in the room, because as soon as Maxy nodded at me, Frankie sent me away. That's all I can remember."

"That's good." Agent Tillis nodded a little and shifted on his feet. "You do realize, both of you, that this isn't over. I hope neither of you have any more trouble here, but there's always the possibility. I wouldn't stress too much about it. You're safe from Frankie and Creticia, and though we have no idea where Maxy is or who the top guy is running this smuggling ring, I don't think they'll work around here again. Not with us on the alert. And you can always call us if you get the least suspicion."

He turned to stare at Jazzi. "You've given us

some good leads, Jazzi. Once we're back in New York, we'll be re-studying our evidence and, with help from God in heaven, we hope to get this finished before the kids and I move here.

"Right now, I think you're safe from any prosecution. Sounds like you've been on the outskirts mostly. You stay clean, and we'll leave it at that, for now."

For now. Kind of a scary, vague threat. Yet, he'd been generous in not hounding her further. She'd better show some appreciation. "Thanks, Agent Tillis. I haven't always been the best person, but I think I've finally found my way and want to keep it that way."

He pointed at her and a smile spread across his face. "You do that."

~*~

Four days later, Jazzi and Ryle sat on the veranda in the early evening. Four couples had just left, vowing to return as soon as they could. Ryle's hand clasped hers, but they were quiet. It was good to relax after the previous days and weeks of turmoil and uncertainty.

"Would you—"

"Am I interrupting?" The voice came from a man with whom they'd quickly formed a bond. Samuel L. Miller had become a friend, a close friend, one who'd traveled this journey with them although on different paths. "I wanted to share the news."

Jazzi sat up. "Have you heard?"

Ryle knew the man had hoped for a quick answer as to whether any of the bones belonged to his ancestor.

"I have. May I sit?"

"Of course. Please do." Ryle motioned to the third chair.

"Agent Tillis called just minutes ago. He said the DNA tests were conclusive. There were bones that came from my ancestor. Preliminary results indicate abuse, but they'll be in touch when the final results are conclusive."

"That's wonderful and sad news. But, at least, you know now. Your searching journey is over."

Mr. Miller didn't speak for a moment. "Yes, it is. It is. Now my next step is recording this journey on paper."

"You're writing a book?"

"I am. It will be written as fiction, but I want the details to be real. I will begin work on it soon as I return home. My family, I suppose, will be relieved, as I am."

"And the child's remains?" Ryle questioned.

"Agent Tillis promised to see they arrive safely home. At last, we, as a family, will have closure."

No one spoke as Ryle and Jazzi sat quietly hand in hand. And Ryle glimpsed Jazzi's movement when she reached across the short space and gripped Samuel's hand too.

Chapter Twenty-one

Two Weeks Later

Ryle and Jazzi's wedding turned into a bigger affair than either Jazzi nor Ryle had wanted. But when her parents, their friends and Emilia had found out about their intention of eloping, they'd all put their foot down, so to speak, and insisted on a real wedding.

They'd gotten their way in one thing, at least. If they had to have a wedding on the grounds, they wanted it small, with only a tight group of friends invited.

Emilia and Toby had stood with Ryle, while Jazzi's mother and sister had stood with her. Her father had walked her down the aisle, and as a last minute surprise, they'd discovered that Paddy was a bona fide minister.

Jazzi had giggled and Ryle had laughed out loud at the expressions crossing her parents' faces at their unusual wedding insistencies. But they'd given in without too much fuss, no doubt realizing they'd gained something by having their daughter marry such a wonderful man.

She'd teased Ryle, claiming they loved him the most. He'd just laughed and insisted he doubted that.

As she stood beside him underneath the same pavilion they'd used at the opening of the inn, he'd whispered, "I love you in deep blue and white."

She twinkled her eyes at him. That had been exactly why she'd worn the very same white dress she'd worn at the opening. Why she'd clipped the deep blue sparkly hair comb into her hair and why Amy had created the variegated and flowing bouquet of deep blue and white Jasmine flowers for Jazzi to carry.

Simple. Small. And stunning as the guests would proclaim later.

It was three hours later that Jazzi tossed her bouquet of flowers straight into Emilia Pavlo's arms. And it was twenty minutes later that they'd climbed into the inn's four-seated golf cart and snuggled into the back seats as Paddy drove them away from the house.

"Where are we going?"

"You'll see in a minute." Ryle tightened his grip on her shoulder, pulling her closer.

The sound of water flowing drew Jazzi's attention. "What is that?"

"Water. And your boat."

"Mine?"

"Ours then."

"What are we going to do with it?"

"We didn't want a big wedding, right?"

"Right."

"I wasn't about to skim on our wedding trip. You love the water. I bought the houseboat awhile back and had it brought here."

"We're taking a cruise by ourselves?"

"Yep. We'll make some stops, relax and be ready to tackle our next projects when we return. For now, it's just you and me, baby."

His laugh was like music to her heart.

When Paddy pulled up to the dock, Jazzi gave Paddy a hug. "Paddy, don't ever leave us. What would we do without you?"

The big man's face turned red, but he nodded his head. "You can rely on me, Jazzi. You go and have a wonderful time. Barbara and I will make sure all is well at home."

"Thanks." Ryle gripped the man's hand. It was all he said, but it was enough.

As Ryle and Jazzi stepped onto the dock, he paused and pulled her close. "Are you afraid, my sweet Jazzi?"

"Afraid? Of what?"

"Of the future. Of what may still be in store for us with Agent Tillis' investigation?"

"With you by my side?" Jazzi's blue-eyed gaze swept over his beloved face, and a hand lifted to stroke his cheek. "Never."

"Never?"

"Never."

With that, Ryle shifted his stance and lifted Jazzi into his arms, walked straight up the gangplank and settled her gently on her feet, singing softly to her in an untrained, off-key voice.

"You are so beautiful, my Jazmine, my love."

Jazzi loved every word, every note of his very unmusical voice and song. Her eyes filled with tears, but they weren't from sadness.

Not at all.

Still singing, Ryle used his thumb to wipe away her tears.

The End.

If you enjoyed reading *The Golden Touch*, let others know...and bless Carole Brown with an honest review.

Ne'er the Twain Shall Meet
Book Six of the
Appleton, WV Romantic Mystery series

The only good thing happening in Special Agent Lincoln Tillis' life was the entrance of a very successful, very beautiful lawyer named Emilia Pavlo. Of course, she ignored him most of the time, but like a moth to the light, he couldn't stay away from her. His heart was hopelessly in love.

But when his kids are kidnapped, and Emilia is the only person who has communication with the kidnapper, he wonders how much she can be trusted. Does she really want to help or is she weaving a web of lies to bring him down?

Is she as innocent as everyone else believes, or is his sixth sense that's never failed him before, right, and he needs to nab her before she hurts his kids? Is she the King—Queen Kidnapper after all?

Chapter One

The man stood silent and unseen beneath the huge pine on the opposite side of the road. Only a few windows in the mini-mansion across the street were lit, but it was enough. A man stood outside the door, flowers in his hand. He'd already rung a doorbell, and Lincoln Tillis knew the woman within had heard it. It wasn't the first time he'd watched this scenario playing.

The door opened, and the owner of the house stood there, spot lit by the warm light coming from behind her. How stunning she was. Way too good for the man, waiting there, no doubt wooing her again with expensive gifts he, himself, couldn't afford.

The man stepped forward, leaned down to peck her cheek, and the watching man cringed, as much as he wished he wouldn't do so. After all, he was tough, didn't allow his emotions or affections to get involved in his work.

But this woman...the first one who'd captured his attention since his first wife died...she was exquisite. From the first unplanned meeting, he'd been stunned at her beauty and brains. He'd thought wrongly, obviously, that she'd felt the same way.

Lincoln Tillis straightened as the door shut, and the couple disappeared inside. He drew in a long breath and turned his back on the mini-mansion. He had work to do, an important job to complete, and if the clues led to these two, then so be it.

Love had nothing to do with his job. His emotions were just that. Emotions. He would not be swayed by a pretty face.

He. Would. Not. Allow. Emilia. Pavlo. To. Influence. Him.

What a bunch of lies he was telling himself. For the first time ever, he wanted to flee from this job, quit this job he loved—if he was truthful, and flee away from this mountain state as far as he could.

A cackle slid from between his clenched jaw, because that was what it was. Not a smile. Not a grin. A heartbreaking, angry and hurting sound that felt like a heart attack.

Lincoln climbed into the SUV waiting for him and motioned to his driver to leave. He turned his head toward the passenger window, better to hide the moisture in his eyes. 'Cause FBI agents don't cry.

At least, he didn't.

Books by Carole Brown

Denton and Alex Davies Mysteries:
Hog Insane
Bat Crazy

Spies of World War II
With Music In Their Hearts
A Flute in the Willows
Sing Until You Die

The Appleton WV Mysteries
Sabotaged Christmas
Knight in Shining Apron
Undiscovered Treasures
Toby's Troubles
The Golden Touch

Troubles in the West
Caleb's Destiny

Women's Fiction:
The Redemption of Caralynne Haymen

Misc.
West Virginia Scrapbook
Christmas Angels (WW II short story in the Anthology *From the Lake to the River*)

Award winning author Carole Brown loves to weave suspense and tough topics into her books, along with a touch of romance and whimsy.

She is always on the lookout for outstanding titles and catchy ideas.

Carole and Dan, her pastor husband, reside in SE Ohio and have ministered and counseled across the country. Together, they enjoy their grandsons, traveling, gardening, good food, the simple life, and did she mention their grandsons?

Carole loves to connect with her readers. You can find her at any of these links:
Blog: https://bit.ly/3sIGfhC
FB Author Pg:
    http://www.facebook.com/CaroleBrown.author
FB Fan Pg: https://bit.ly/3vefQKC
BookBub: http://bit.ly/2PHT8cj
Instagram: amzn.to/2qZp15P